MURDER
in the
OVAL
OFFICE

Previous books by Elliott Roosevelt

Murder and the First Lady
Murder in Hyde Park
Murder at Hobcaw Barony
The White House Pantry Murder
Murder at the Palace

MURDER in the OVAL OFFICE

Elliott Roosevelt

St. Martin's Press • New York

Design by Holly Block

Library of Congress Cataloging-in-Publication Data

Roosevelt, Elliott.
    Murder in the Oval Office : an Eleanor Roosevelt
mystery   / Elliott Roosevelt
        p. cm.
    "A Thomas Dunne book."
    ISBN 0-312-02259-X
    1. Roosevelt, Eleanor, 1884–1962—Fiction. I. Title.
PS3535.0549M85 1988
813′.54—dc19   88-18848
                                                         CIP

First Edition

10 9 8 7 6 5 4 3 2 1

My thanks to my family, my friendly readers,
and of course, my wife Patti

MURDER
in the
OVAL
OFFICE

1

Swimming was important to the President. It was his only real exercise. Besides, in the water, where his buoyancy took the weight off his legs, he sometimes imagined he felt hints of strength returning to muscles he had been unable to use since 1921. The people of the United States had built a swimming pool in the White House for him—not from public funds but by private subscription. The pool was in the colonnade that connected the West Wing to the main house.

"Swimming time!" he boomed exuberantly as his valet Arthur Prettyman wheeled him toward the colonnade. "Harry! Louey! Jim! Front and center!"

He would hear no excuse from friends that they had no swimsuits. He kept a supply of them in various sizes in the changing room by the pool. He himself had already changed, in his study beside the Oval Office, and was wearing dark-blue wool trunks with a white web belt, a white swimming vest, and a white rubber bathing cap. Arthur took his pince-nez, helped him from the wheelchair into the water, and the President began to swim laps, stroking powerfully and sliding smoothly through the water.

Harry Hopkins knew there was no escaping a presidential swimming summons. If he did not come in swimming, the President would send Arthur to say he had to discuss something with him, and if he came and stood fully dressed by the pool, the President would splash him. He crushed a cigarette as he strode into the colonnade, dressed identically with the President. He jumped in, feet first.

"Harry the Hop," laughed the President. He slapped the water with the palm of his hand, splashing it toward Hopkins's face.

James Farley had known Franklin Roosevelt long enough to know that an invitation to swim was an order from the commander in chief. An order was what it took to get him into the pool. He sat down on the edge of the pool, and, anticipating a splashing, slipped into the water.

The President continued swimming laps. His arms and shoulders were muscular. He used them with practiced skill, swimming almost as well as he might have if he could have used his legs, too.

Missy LeHand came out of the West Wing, wearing a robe over her swimsuit, fastening the strap on her rubber cap. At the pool's edge she shed the robe and stood revealed in a black knit swimsuit. She alone dived into the pool, going to the bottom and coming up in the middle.

"Hey, you fellows! This isn't a bathtub. Let's see some swimming. A bit of exercise wouldn't hurt either one of you."

Hopkins smiled wanly and swam the length of the pool. Farley continued bobbing where he was. Missy arched her body and swam to the bottom, where she used a robust but jerky breast stroke to propel herself toward the end of the pool where the President had now stopped and was clinging to the edge.

Louis Howe walked in, dressed in a vested dark-blue suit streaked with cigarette ash. He sat down in a chair and drew deeply on the Sweet Caporal he was smoking. The smoke curled up his face, around his left eye, through his eyebrow, into his graying hair. Howe never came into the water, and the President never splashed him.

"Well, Louey," said the President, "what's the most important thing going on in America today?"

Howe dragged on his cigarette. "Dizzy Dean is pitching for the Cards this afternoon," he said. "Got a five-run lead on Brooklyn in the sixth."

The President laughed. He stroked for the opposite end of the pool.

Franklin D. Roosevelt was fifty-two years old. He had been President of the United States for sixteen months.

The chain-smoking, asthmatic Louis McHenry Howe, who was sixty-three, was his long-time political adviser, the strategist who, more than any other man, had made him President. Howe lived in the White House so he would be constantly available to the President.

James Farley, in his fifties, had been tactician to Howe as strategist. He, too, had worked for years to win the nomination, then the election, for Franklin Roosevelt, and, in accordance with longtime political tradition, had been rewarded with the office of Postmaster General.

Harry Hopkins, forty-four, was administrator of federal relief programs and an adviser to the President. He was known for a sharp tongue, particularly for his reply to a Senator who had resisted appropriating money for a relief program, observing that the economy would revive of itself "in the long run." Hopkins had replied, "People don't eat in the long run, Senator. They eat every day."

These four personified the New Deal; in them idealism and cynicism were mixed in recondite proportions.

Missy LeHand was the President's personal and confidential secretary—which she had been for many years before he became President. Knowing the President might call on her for work or just for companionship at any hour, she lived in a suite of rooms on the third floor of the White House. She was the President's friend as well as his secretary.

"Actually," said Howe to no one in particular, "I'm more interested in what kind of a season Babe Ruth has. I have a special interest in the older fellows."

"Me, too," Missy laughed.

The President reached the edge of the pool where Howe sat. He kept himself afloat with his arms. "Maybe we could get the Congress to pass a law requiring the baseball owners to shorten the outfields two or three feet a year. That might keep the Babe hitting home runs."

"You could do that by executive order, Mr. President," said Hopkins.

"You asked me," said Howe, tugging in smoke, "what's the most important thing that's happening in *America* today. You didn't ask what's the most important thing happening in the *world*."

"Consider yourself asked," said the President.

"With the death of old Von Hindenburg, that man Hitler is going to be the President of Germany," said Howe. "Then there'll be no restraint on him. None whatever."

The President grasped the edge of the pool with one hand. "Actually, his title doesn't make much difference. President . . . Chancellor . . . the title he really uses is *Der Führer*. The leader. And there's almost no restraint on him now."

"The Nazis murdered Dollfuss," said Hopkins. "They're going to try to take over Austria."

"Well, Mussolini stopped him this time," said Farley.

The President shook his head. "In two or three years Mussolini will be very small potatoes, compared with the armed forces Hitler will have at his command. Then who's going to stop him?"

"England, France, and Russia," said Hopkins. "We can hope."

"There's nothing *we* can do, anyway," said Farley. "We've got our own problems. We can . . . hope."

"I'd like to believe the peace of the world rests on something stronger than hope," said the President. "If it doesn't, the fellow who holds this office after me is going to have a terrible problem."

Mrs. Roosevelt was astonished at how much she enjoyed being First Lady. She had not been surprised at the enthusiasm Franklin had for the presidency; he had always undertaken new work with exuberance and gusto. She was more selective. She had come to Washington in the winter of 1932–33 with a sense that her new position would be burdensome and confining. Especially confining. She had feared, too, that her position would impose intolerable limitations of precedent and protocol.

She was pleased, therefore, to be driving her own car—a light-blue Buick roadster she had bought a year ago—back to the White House on this hot summer afternoon. She had the top down, but the breeze did not disturb her pinned-down white straw hat. She was wearing, too, a loose silk-print summer dress, blue and green and white, and comfortable white shoes.

This morning she had gone horseback riding in Rock Creek Park, with her dearest personal friend, Lorena Hickock. Back at the White House she had dictated her newspaper column, "My Day," then a dozen letters. After that she had bathed, dressed, and driven to a luncheon for Negro women, sponsored by the NAACP, where she had spoken about the Arthurdale homestead community that had been established in West Virginia, using low-interest government loans to enable families to buy their own small homes. She had been asked if such a community could be established for colored people, and she had replied that it was of course possible and had promised to call Harold Ickes, the Secretary of the Interior, and ask him to look for sites for such a community. After the luncheon she had in fact driven to the Department of the Interior to see Mr. Ickes. Then, as she was on her way back to the White House, she had stopped and chatted for a few minutes with the surprised workmen who were clearing debris from a vacant lot—a WPA project.

"It's *Mrs. Roosevelt!*" She had heard the whispers. One of the workmen, a big man with an unshaven, drawn-down face, looking something like a hound, told her, "We'uns wish you 'n your man all the best of luck, Ma'am. All the best."

She had established her White House office and study in a second-floor room traditionally called the Lincoln bedroom, though it had been President Lincoln's office and study, never his bedroom. When she arrived there a little after five, her secretary, Tommy Thompson, was still typing letters. Her friend Lorena Hickok was sitting on the settee, reading newspapers, waiting for her. The windows were open, and an oscillating fan stirred the air and loose papers.

"Oh, Eleanor!" said Lorena Hickok. "You've been out in this sun and heat! I swear, this city will *kill* us all. Sooner or later all of us are going to die of the Washington heat."

"Perhaps of the political heat, Hick," said Mrs. Roosevelt as she unpinned and removed her hat. "Never of the weather."

Hick rose and stepped close to Mrs. Roosevelt. She kissed her cheek. "Oh, my dear! You are so *warm!*" she protested. "We've had iced tea, Tommy and I. Perhaps—"

"Yes, order some more, Tommy," said Mrs. Roosevelt. "Or perhaps some iced white wine. Would you like that better?"

"I would," said Hick.

"Well, then."

Hick returned to the settee, and Mrs. Roosevelt joined her.

"Oh, I should mention," said Hick, "that the President sent word that he is serving cocktails in the west hall."

"With anyone in particular?" asked Mrs. Roosevelt.

"Mr. Howe, I believe. And Mr. Hopkins. Probably Missy."

"The usual group," said Mrs. Roosevelt. "I believe I'll stay here and have wine with you and Tommy. I should sign those letters, too."

Lorena Hickok was a short, fat woman, forty-one years old and so nine years younger than Mrs. Roosevelt. Her face was regular and pretty, softly round. She wore her dark hair in a very plain style, cut just below her ears. She wore a white dress, white stockings, white shoes—with a long, loosely knotted necktie that hung well below her waist.

She had been a wire-service correspondent assigned to Governor Roosevelt from 1928 on, then assigned to Mrs. Roosevelt during the 1932 presidential campaign. The two of them had become warm friends. Hick had been granted an exclusive first interview with the new First Lady, within an hour after the inauguration. For a year now she had been working for the government, investigating the conditions of the poor and writing reports for Harry Hopkins.

"I would like to see Arthurdales for Negro families," said Mrs. Roosevelt. "I promised the luncheon ladies I'd do what I can to see their race gets a share of the money appropriated for homesteads. Then I went to see Mr. Ickes."

"No wonder you're so hot," said Hick.

"Actually, Mr. Ickes was very nice," said Mrs. Roosevelt.

"Well, Negroes should get some of the advantages of the things we're doing," said Hick. "The conditions in which some of them live are unbelievable. Do you know what geophagists are, Eleanor?"

Mrs. Roosevelt, who had begun to scan some of the letters Tommy had typed, shook her head.

"People who eat mud," said Hick.

Mrs. Roosevelt looked up. *"Mud?"*

"Clay, actually. They eat a form of clay. Thousands of people in the rural south do it. They seem to have some instinct that clay contains nutrients they don't get from their meager and highly restricted diets."

"Are we doing anything about it?" asked Mrs. Roosevelt.

"One of the programs," said Hick with a little shrug. "To improve the diet of the rural poor."

"Mud . . ."

Tommy handed Mrs. Roosevelt two typewritten sheets. "The guest list for dinner."

Mrs. Roosevelt studied the list. Beneath each name Tommy had typed the name of the guest's spouse and in some cases the names of children, the city and state where the person originated, and some other information: college or university, if any, political affiliation, particular interests.

Hick looked over her shoulder. "What a wonderful evening you are going to have," she remarked dryly.

Dinner was served in the State Dining Room at seven-thirty.

The guest of honor was Alexis Saint-Léger Léger, Secretary-General at the Quai d'Orsay, the French Foreign Ministry. His visit to Washington was another effort in his constant quest for peace. He was seeking assurances from the United States that its government would continue to support the international security arrangements that had been made in the 1920s. He had met during the day with Secretary of State Cordell Hull. He would meet tomorrow with the President. His mission put them in a difficult position. Isolationists dominated Congress. It was all but impossible for the President to give Léger any sort of assurance or commitment. Still, he did not want to discourage him. Tomorrow he would have to choose his words with care.

Tonight he would enjoy lighthearted conversation with the suave Frenchman.

Seated at the dinner table were:

—The President and Mrs. Roosevelt;

—Alexis Saint-Léger Léger;

—Monsieur Lucien LeFebvre, French Ambassador to the United States, and Madame LeFebvre;

—Secretary of State Cordell Hull;

—Senator and Mrs. Carter Glass of Virginia;

—Senator Robert LaFollette of Wisconsin;

—Congressman Sam Rayburn of Texas;

—Congressman Winstead Colmer of Alabama;

—Author Upton Sinclair, candidate for Governor of California;

—Charles A. and Mary Beard, historians;

—Louis McHenry and Mrs. Howe.

The men wore white tie; the ladies wore gowns. The table was heaped with flowers, set with crystal and china and gleaming silver. Monsieur Léger had brought with him two cases of the finest vintage champagne, as well as cases of red and white wines— "Because he was afraid he couldn't get any in the States," muttered Howe behind his hand to Mrs. Roosevelt. A hundred candles lit the room. A string orchestra played softly.

"It is," said Secretary-General Léger, "my first visit in the United States, but I hope it will not be my last."

He spoke fluent English, but with an accent that made him difficult for Mrs. Roosevelt to understand, so she replied in French, hoping her French was more comprehensible to him than his English was to her.

Secretary of State Hull, formerly Senator from Tennessee, bore an unfortunate resemblance to the late President Harding—handsome, dignified, crowned with abundant, carefully combed white hair. He was chatting amiably with the bullet-headed Rayburn, bachelor congressman who had already served twenty-one years in the House of Representatives.

Howe smoked even between the courses of a sumptuous dinner. He let his ashes dribble over his white waistcoat, just as he let them fall over his blue and black vests. When he inhaled smoke from a cigarette, his cheeks drew in, until they were hollow. Mrs. Roosevelt knew it was pointless to remonstrate. Already suffering from asthma and emphysema, Louis smoked as heavily as ever. He would rather smoke than live.

The President, indeed, nibbled sparingly at his salad, then lit a cigarette, which he jammed into his famous black holder, leaned back, and essayed a small joke with Madame LeFebvre. Mrs. Roosevelt had no idea what he had said, but the ambassador's wife blushed and giggled.

LaFollette engaged the Beards in an earnest discussion. Mrs. Howe chatted with Upton Sinclair.

Representative Winstead Colmer talked with Mrs. Glass. An iron-jawed, strikingly good-looking, six-foot-three Alabamian, he was a five-term congressman and the chairman of the Auditing Standards Subcommittee of the House Banking and Currency Committee. Over the past three or four months, his name had appeared almost daily in every major newspaper, and films of his hearings had dominated newsreels in thousands of theaters. The evidence adduced by him had embarrassed bankers all across America, and his subcommittee was drafting legislation to tighten auditing standards on banks.

"I am looking forward," said Alexis Saint-Léger Léger, "to a performance by the famous American danseuse Sally Rand. You have seen her perform?"

Mrs. Roosevelt smiled weakly, at the same time frowning. "Uh—I'm afraid not, Monsieur Léger," she said. "Ah . . . Franklin." She leaned past Léger and caught the attention of the President. "Monsieur Léger is interested in a performance by the dancer Sally Rand. Do you know the name?"

The President grinned. "I've heard it," he said. He leaned past Mrs. Roosevelt. "I understand she's a fine dancer, but to have the word from a real authority, you should visit Justice Oliver Wendell Holmes, retired from our Supreme Court. He—"

"Franklin—"

"Mr. Justice Holmes is a connoisseur of that kind of dancing. He can tell you if—"

"Franklin. What kind of dancer is this young woman?"

"A *fan dancer,* Babs," the President laughed. "A fan dancer. She dances in the nude—concealing herself only with a couple of big feathered fans she—"

"Franklin!"

"I have heard of this," said Monsieur Léger. "A world-famous *artiste.* And where might she be performing now?"

"Louey!" the President called to Howe. "Monsieur Léger is interested in seeing Sally Rand. See if you can find out where she is dancing. Maybe a command performance . . ."

Howe lowered his head and stared at the President from beneath his great bushy brows. He nodded.

"You have sent to France the exquisite Josephine Baker," said Léger to Mrs. Roosevelt. "Another *artiste,* a true *artiste* and humanitarian."

"Ah . . . yes," said Mrs. Roosevelt.

The waiters began to serve. The dinner was roast pheasant, accompanied by potatoes, mushrooms, and artichoke hearts. The menu had been selected by the President himself, and the wines would be from those brought by Léger. From habit, Mrs. Roosevelt made a quick mental accounting of the cost of such a meal. Thank God this one came from the State Department budget, since the White House entertainment budget, appropriated by the Congress, would have been exhausted for the year by very few dinners like this. In fact, the President had been compelled to pay from his own funds several thousand dollars for food bills for the last fiscal year—money he had been compelled to borrow from his mother. He might complain—and he did, loudly—about tuna-fish sandwiches for White House luncheons, but that was what the appropriation paid for.

The guests murmured appreciatively over the food and wine. Mrs. Roosevelt subdued a thought that crossed her mind: If people in Alabama and Mississippi were eating mud, how could they sit here in the White House and eat pheasant?

"Will the death of Von Hindenburg unleash this fellow Hitler?" Senator Glass asked Léger.

Léger lifted his shoulders in a suave Gallic shrug and began a quiet exposition of his thoughts on that question.

Louis Howe lit another cigarette, to smoke even while he ate.

The President closed his eyes and savored a mouthful of the pheasant.

An usher stepped behind Representative Colmer and bent down to whisper in his ear. The congressman frowned, then pushed back his chair, and, with a soft word of apology to his dinner companions on both sides, hurried out of the room.

It was as Lorena Hickok had predicted: a not-very-interesting dinner, perhaps because of the way the guests were seated, perhaps because there were just too many of them. Mrs. Roosevelt would have liked to talk with Upton Sinclair or the Beards, but they were seated too far from her.

Léger went on talking about Hitler. It would have been interesting but for the fact that she *knew* what he thought; it had been reported at length in the newspapers before he arrived. Like every other

Frenchman, he was afraid of the resurgence of German power. Which well he might be.

Senator LaFollette was talking about Father Coughlin, whom he described as a menace. Upton Sinclair shrugged and observed that Coughlin was hardly more of a menace than Huey Long. The President, overhearing and joining their conversation, said the pair of them were hardly more of a threat to democracy than William Randolph Hearst.

"Ah," said Léger. "We must all suffer our Mussolinis, I suppose."

Mrs. Roosevelt marveled at so undiplomatic a statement from one of the world's supreme diplomats.

An usher brought a note to Howe. Mrs. Roosevelt watched him frown deeply over it. He sucked in his gray cheeks and shoved the note into a pocket. The toasts were about to be offered, and he could not gracefully leave the table. Still, she could see he wanted to, and she wondered what disturbing news had been brought to him.

Presently, she would find out.

"Louis," she said when they rose from the table and were mingling, shaking hands, saying good night, "is something wrong?"

Louis nodded. His face, normally sepulchral, was grim. "I don't want to tell Frank till I find out what's happened. Let's get these people on their way as quickly as we can. Then—"

He was interrupted by the French ambassador, who stopped to shake his hand, then bow deeply to Mrs. Roosevelt and express his gratitude for "a wondrous evening."

People stood aside as Arthur Prettyman wheeled the President out of the State Dining Room and to the elevator to the second floor and the private quarters. Mrs. Roosevelt put her hand on Howe's arm and asked him to accompany her to the portico, where she stood with Secretary of State Hull and bade the French guests their formal farewell. She shook hands one last time with the other guests. Finally she was able to walk back into the entrance hall of the White House and have a word alone with Louis Howe.

"Something tragic has happened," said Howe. "Congressman Colmer has committed suicide. Here in the White House."

"Where?"

"In the West Wing. In the Oval Office, of all places."

Mrs. Roosevelt was shocked, appalled. "Oh, *dear!*" was all she could think to say.

Howe sighed. "Why don't we leave it alone until morning? Frank doesn't need to lose sleep over it. I'm going over there now, to see what they're doing. By morning we'll know a lot more about it, and we can tell Frank then."

Mrs. Roosevelt nodded uncertainly. "Very well. What should we do about the reporters?"

"Give them the word in the morning, too," said Howe. "By then the body will have been removed, the mess will be cleaned up, and we can simply issue a statement. It hasn't anything to do with the President, anything to do with the White House."

"But why— Oh. Mrs. Colmer . . . has Mrs. Colmer been notified?"

"I think she is over there, in the West Wing."

"Well, I shall go over," said Mrs. Roosevelt firmly. "The poor woman will need—"

"Maybe she needs her privacy," said Howe.

"And maybe she needs help. I'll find out."

The West Wing, or Executive Wing, of the White House is reached through the west hall on the ground floor. Operating the elevator herself—which she did to the continuing consternation of the staff—Mrs. Roosevelt went down from the first floor and out through the colonnade. The silky satin of her long, straight iridescent-blue gown rustled audibly as she strode purposefully past the swimming pool and into the West Wing. Louis Howe strode beside her, dropping ashes on carpets and marble floor.

Police jurisdiction in the White House was a mixed bag. Primary responsibility for the safety of the President and his personal and official family was in the hands of the Secret Service. Responsibility for the grounds and buildings was with the White House Police, a small force of uniformed officers. Since neither of these maintained crime laboratories, detective assistance was often asked of the Federal Bureau of Investigation or of the District of Columbia Police.

When Howe and Mrs. Roosevelt hurried into the West Wing, it was brightly lit, and policemen guarded the halls. He and she were recognized, of course, and one of the policemen trotted ahead of them, to notify the agent in charge of the investigation that they were there.

"Mrs. Roosevelt. Mr. Howe. I am Gerald Baines, Secret Service. I'm the duty officer this evening, and—"

"Is the Congressman's wife here?" asked Mrs. Roosevelt.

"No," said Baines. "We haven't been able to reach her. We've located the family's pastor, and he's gone to the Colmers' home to wait for her. He'll break the word to her."

Gerald Baines, who was perhaps forty-one or -two years old, was a solid little man with a liver-spotted bald head, a ruddy face, and a solemn, bland expression. He wore a light-blue summer-weight suit and a broad red necktie. Mrs. Roosevelt had not heard his name before but had been aware of his presence in the White House—one of the more senior agents of the Secret Service.

They stood in the West Wing lobby, where guests were received and where they waited to meet with the President and the other officials who kept offices in the wing. It was modestly furnished, with worn and cracked green leather chairs, smoking stands, spittoons, and modernistic floor lamps that cast their light on the ceiling.

"How did poor Mr. Colmer die?" she asked Gerald Baines.

"Suicide, apparently," he said. "With a pistol. In the Oval Office."

"How'd he get in the Oval Office?" Howe demanded. "Wasn't it locked?"

Baines shook his head. "We don't know how he got in. The doors were not only locked but bolted. The windows were locked. That's what makes it suicide, of course—that the door and windows were all locked, and he was dead inside."

"Even so," said Howe. "How'd he get in? Did somebody let him in? What was he doing in the Oval Office?"

"That's one of several unanswered questions, Mr. Howe," said Baines.

"Has the body been removed?" asked Howe.

"No, sir. The D.C. medical examiner is looking at it now, and it will be removed as soon as he's finished."

Mrs. Roosevelt picked up a tattered magazine that lay on the cracked arm of one of the chairs. She did not want to read; it was a nervous gesture. "I . . . I think we must see the body, Louis," she said.

"Oh, that's not at all necessary, Ma'am," said Baines quickly. "You—"

"The incident has happened in the White House, in the office of the President," she interrupted. "It will be I who reports it to the President. I think—I think it would be well, Mr. Baines, if Mr. Howe and I looked at the office."

The Oval Office, official and ceremonial office of the President of the United States, could be entered from the West Wing through two doors only: one through the President's adjoining study, one through an anteroom used as an office by the President's secretarial staff. Ordinarily guests entered through the secretaries' office. Ordinarily that was how the President entered and left, though sometimes he left through his study. A set of French doors opened onto the grounds. Tall windows overlooked the rose garden and south lawn.

Walls had often been moved in the West Wing and would be again, but in the summer of 1934 the layout was as shown on the following page.

The sudden appearance of the First Lady in the secretaries' office brought half a dozen uniformed officers to attention and interrupted the work of three Secret Service agents. This was the room where Missy LeHand presided, assisted by Grace Tully and the other assistant secretaries. It was the room through which the President rolled every morning in his wheelchair, on his way to his desk. It was the room where every morning he exchanged cordial greetings with the women on duty behind the clacking typewriters.

Every bulb in every fixture glowed, casting yellowish light on battered old wooden desks, ranks of wooden filing cabinets, heavy office typewriters—Underwoods and Royals and Smiths—and straightbacked secretaries' chairs. The maroon carpet was threadbare. The dark-red plush draperies were faded from the sunlight. The Congress had never seen fit to appropriate large amounts of money for White House office furniture, and a succession of Presidents had never seen fit to press the point.

Mrs. Roosevelt turned to her right and walked to the open door that led into the Oval Office. Just inside that door, sprawled face down on the floor, lay the body of Representative Winstead Colmer.

WEST WING – 1934

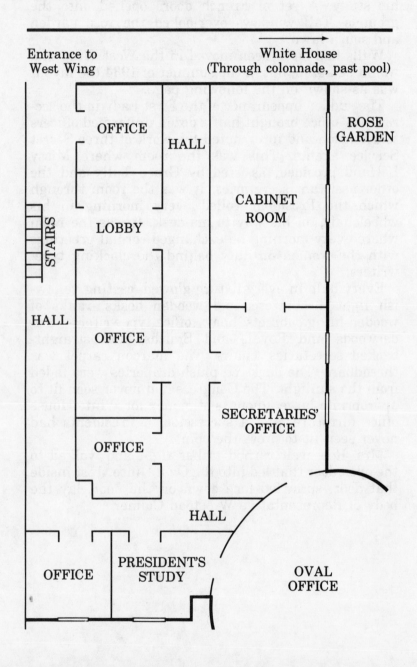

Entrance to
West Wing

White House
(Through colonnade, past pool)

ROSE
GARDEN

OFFICE

HALL

CABINET
ROOM

STAIRS

LOBBY

HALL

OFFICE

OFFICE

SECRETARIES'
OFFICE

HALL

OFFICE

PRESIDENT'S
STUDY

OVAL
OFFICE

2

The Oval Office was spacious. Its tall windows and glass French doors overlooked the rose garden and the south lawn. Now, at night, the city lights of Washington gleamed beyond the dark expanse of the lawn and the Ellipse. Anyone standing at one of the south windows could see the Washington Monument half a mile away.

The double doors between the Oval Office and the secretaries' office had been broken open. The cylinder of the bolt was torn from the wood.

The body lay with its feet nearest the door, the head toward the center of the room. The tails of the coat had flipped up, probably as the body fell, and the white waistcoat and shirt were exposed. The bullet wound to the head was visible; the bullet had entered the head from just behind the right ear and had not exited; it was still in the brain. Although the bullet hole was small, a large amount of blood had run out of it and was drying in a wide circle on the rug.

A man was on his knees beside the body, drawing

19

its outline in white chalk on the rug. Another man stood at the desk, focusing a huge Graflex camera on the body. As Mrs. Roosevelt and Howe stepped into the room, they were startled by a sudden explosion of light from the flashgun mounted on the camera. For a moment the Oval Office turned white in the intense glare of burning magnesium foil inside the fist-sized bulb, and then for a longer moment their eyes were filled with a dancing red-and-green glow as their startled retinas sent alarms to their brains.

"Epson! This is Mrs. Roosevelt!" Baines complained. "And Mr. Howe!"

The photographer was not distressed. "Sorry," he muttered as he grasped the burned flashbulb with a piece of flannel and tried to unscrew it without burning his hand.

Mrs. Roosevelt edged to the left and walked into the room. She looked once at the face of the dead man, then averted her eyes. It was enough to see him once. He did not have the look of a man asleep. He had the look of a man dead—dead by violence. His eyes stared at the floor. The wound on his forehead was no neat hole; it was a gaping rupture of flesh and bone. His right hand was extended beyond his head, as if reaching toward the chalked outline of a pistol just beyond his fingertips. His blood had splashed across his face and down across his white tie and collar.

Howe edged around the body, too, took a look as Mrs. Roosevelt had done, then moved toward the fireplace. He dropped into a chair, as if the horror of the corpse had staggered him.

"Please avoid touching things, Mr. Howe," said Baines. "We are still taking fingerprints."

"Why, if the man killed himself?" grunted Howe. He blew a cloud of tobacco smoke toward the ceiling. "Or is there some question about that?"

"He was found where you see him," said Baines. "All the doors were locked. The bolts were fastened.

The windows were locked. What could it be but suicide? Still . . . still, there are questions."

"Like how he got in here in the first place," said Howe. "He was at dinner with us, got up suddenly and left, and—"

"An usher brought him a message," said Mrs. Roosevelt. "Do we know what that message was?"

"I didn't know about the message," said Baines. "We'd better find out which usher carried it to him."

"It wasn't a written message," said Mrs. Roosevelt. "I saw the usher bend over and whisper to him. We can find out what the usher said to him."

"And how he got in here," said Howe. "I want to know who let him in."

"Uh . . ." muttered Baines. He pointed to the medical examiner, who was now wrapping the body in a heavy sheet. "Would you rather talk in another room?"

Mrs. Roosevelt moved to the leather-covered chesterfield couch before the fireplace and sat down with her back to the work being done just inside the door. The medical examiner and two policemen proceeded to wrap the body, then to lift it onto a stretcher. The officers carried it out, and the doctor spread another sheet over the bloodstains on the rug.

Baines shrugged lightly and sat down in a chair to Mrs. Roosevelt's left. "According to the officers whose duty it is to patrol the White House and grounds at night, the Oval Office is always locked after the President leaves for the day. They check the doors to see they are locked. Tonight the doors were not just locked; they were also bolted. And the windows were locked. The window locks and the bolts can only be fastened from the inside—"

"Which compels the conclusion that Mr. Colmer is a suicide," said Mrs. Roosevelt.

"Well . . . it's an odd case. It's a very odd case, but I don't know how else you could explain it. The officers had to break in. With the doors unlocked, they were still held by the bolts and had to be forced."

Mrs. Roosevelt glanced around the Oval Office. It was familiar and yet not familiar. She focused now on the ways entry could be made.

The interior doors to the Oval Office were both heavy oak double doors, painted white. They could be swung in from both sides, leaving wide doorways to the ceremonial office. Ordinarily, though, one of the double doors remained securely shut, fastened by vertical bolts at top and bottom, and only one of the double doors was opened.

Each door had a heavy deadlock, which was operated with a key from outside and with a knob from inside the Oval Office. The ornate brass handles on the doors controlled only a simple latch, not another lock.

The bolts were of heavy well-tarnished brass, not polished. The bolting devices were the old-fashioned kind: bolts and knobs running through heavy cylinders. The cylinders were attached to the oak doors with heavy brass screws. The sockets were fastened to the frames and opposing doors with identical screws—except at the bottoms, where the bolts shot through brass plates and into holes in the floor.

The French doors had the same hardware—somewhat futile, Mrs. Roosevelt thought, since anyone who broke the glass could reach in and shoot the bolt and turn the deadlock.

The windows were fastened shut by big old brass handles that turned blades into slots in brass plates and into holes in the oak window frames. These too could be easily opened by breaking the glass.

But, of course, the glass had not been broken. And it was obvious that the bolts and window fasteners could not be opened from outside. Mr. Colmer had died in a locked room.

Abruptly Mrs. Roosevelt rose from the couch. She walked to the door to the secretaries' office. This was the door the police officers had broken open. The brass socket had been torn from the left-hand door, which bore an ugly scar where the screws had given away, ripping out a hand-size hunk of wood.

Her eyes turned to the fireplace.

Baines read her thought. "Too narrow," he said. "A man could not have entered or left through the chimney."

"I want to know more, Mr. Baines," said Mrs. Roosevelt. "You say it is clearly a suicide, yet you also say you have doubts, and Mr. Howe certainly raises a pertinent question when he askes how Mr. Colmer gained entry to the Oval Office in the first place. Anyway, I'd like to know what message the usher brought Mr. Colmer at the dinner table this evening."

Baines glanced at Howe, as if to ask if Howe could not someway dissuade Mrs. Roosevelt from pursuing the investigation. Howe was phlegmatic. His cheeks collapsed as he sucked hard on the butt of his cigarette, and if he noticed Baines's appeal, he gave no sign of it.

"How did the officers learn that Mr. Colmer had been shot?" asked Mrs. Roosevelt.

"Well . . . would you like to talk to them?"

"If it doesn't interfere," she said with an ingenuous smile.

"Let's see. There's McIlwaine. Uh—"

"Let's sit down," said Mrs. Roosevelt. "We can make the Oval Office our headquarters for the moment. I'm certain the President won't mind."

The room was as the President had left it when he went for his late-afternoon swim. The cleaning staff would come in early in the morning, but now the ashtrays and wastebaskets were full. The room stank of stale cigarette butts.

The President's desk and chair. Although there were chairs and a couch before the fireplace, a visitor's eyes could not help but be drawn to the desk. It said something of the man. He obviously enjoyed his clutter of mementos and knickknacks—half a dozen Democratic donkeys of various sizes and materials, a clock set in the middle of a little brass ship's wheel, small family photographs in frames, a calendar torn off to the day's date, a tray filled with pens and pencils, a paper-clip holder, a green desk blotter, two black telephones, and of course the ashtray. Spread around and over all this were half a dozen documents—letters, memoranda, reports—that the President had been studying at the end of his day at the desk.

The President's chair did not swivel or recline. It was a four-legged armchair, upholstered in cut velvet. Out of sight in the kneehole of the desk was a wooden support on which he propped his legs during the day.

Mrs. Roosevelt sat down in a chair by the fireplace. She would not have considered sitting down at the President's desk. That would have seemed inappropriate to her; besides, she could imagine the kind of newspaper stories that would appear if a reporter should chance to look in and see her there. Howe sat on the couch.

"I'll bring in the men who heard the shot," said Baines.

Mrs. Roosevelt nodded at the departing Baines, then turned to Howe and asked, "Why in the White House, do you suppose? Why in the world would the man want to kill himself in the White House?"

"And in *the Oval Office*," muttered Howe.

"Poor Mrs. Colmer . . ."

Baines returned, bringing two uniformed White House policemen. He introduced them as officers Larry McIlwaine and Fred Weyrich. McIlwaine was a small, trim man with a shiny bald head and piercing brown eyes. Weyrich was larger, carrying an excess of weight, with a flat, coarse face that suggested he had perhaps been a boxer and taken hard punches on the jaw and nose.

"Just tell Mrs. Roosevelt and Mr. Howe what you heard and saw and did," said Baines.

"But sit down first," said Mrs. Roosevelt.

McIlwaine sat down on the couch with Howe and Baines. Weyrich took a chair.

"Well," Weyrich began, "we was making our rounds—"

"You have a regular beat in the White House, don't you?" asked Mrs. Roosevelt.

"Yes, Ma'am, a reg'lar set of rounds, through the house and around the premises. Through the halls, out around."

"Do you follow a schedule?" she asked. "I mean, would you ordinarily be about the same place at the same time, say each hour?"

"Well, we sorta follow the same beat, as you might say," said Weyrich. "We don't have to, exactly, but I guess we do, the same route, as you might say."

"Yes. Go on."

"Well, we was— Uh, just where was it we was at, Larry? Exactly—"

"We were in the colonnade," said McIlwaine. "We were on our way from the White House proper to the West Wing, to make our rounds in here. And we heard the shot. We couldn't tell where it was, but it had to be from somewhere in the West Wing. So we ran back into the West Wing and started looking. We ran through the halls first and didn't see anybody. We yelled. Nobody answered. Then—"

"I picked up the phone in the lobby and called the Secret Service office," said Weyrich.

"All the offices were locked," said McIlwaine. "We carry keys to most of them but not to the Oval Office and not to the President's study. The shot had sounded like it was in the cabinet room, so we unlocked the secretaries' office and then the door to the cabinet room."

"You didn't see or hear anybody during this time?" asked Mrs. Roosevelt.

Both men shook their heads. McIlwaine went on—
"We unlocked the door to the cabinet room. There was
nobody in there."

"So we had to figure it was maybe the Oval Office,"
said Weyrich. "We didn't have no key to it, so I run
out and tried the windows and the French doors. All
locked—which was odd, 'cause Mr. Roosevelt likes to
let the air in on summer days, and many times them
windows is left unlocked."

"So what did you do then?" asked Mrs. Roosevelt, a
bit impatient.

"We didn't figure we ought to bust down the door to
the Oval Office," said Weyrich. "So we waited for Mr.
Baines and Corporal Geiger."

"Corporal Geiger being—?"

"The chief man on our shift," said McIlwaine. "He
stays at the desk in the Secret Service office, and regular officers walk the beats. There are four men, plus
the corporal, on the night shift."

"And Mr. Baines and Corporal Geiger then arrived?"

"They come as fast as they could," said Weyrich.
"Mr. Baines had the key, and he unlocked the door."

"But it still wouldn't open," said Baines. "Obviously, it was bolted. I went around and tried the
door between the study and the Oval Office. Same
thing—I could unlock the door, but I couldn't push it
open. So I came back to the secretaries' office and told
McIlwaine and Weyrich to break the door open."

"Stout," said Weyrich. "She was stout. We thrown
all our weight ag'in her, three or four times, before
she busted."

"It was dark in the office, but there he was," said
Baines. "Mr. Colmer. On the floor."

"The lights were out?" asked Mrs. Roosevelt.

Baines nodded. "The office was dark," he said. "The
body was lying as you saw it. I stepped in and
switched on the lights."

Mrs. Roosevelt sighed. "And you concluded—indeed, how could you conclude otherwise?—that Mr. Colmer had killed himself."

Baines turned down the corners of his mouth. He lifted his shoulders, turned up the palms of his hands. "The door had been bolted. It could only be bolted from the inside. The other doors had been bolted the same way. The windows were locked. They can only be locked from the inside. The chimney is too narrow for a man to climb through it. There is no other way to get into or out of the Oval Office." He shrugged. "I don't like it, but there it is."

"Am I wrong in assuming," asked Mrs. Roosevelt, "that one cannot simply walk in off the street and enter the White House at night?"

"The gate is guarded," said Baines. "But with a dinner here tonight—someone could have hidden in one of the cars that came in. In a taxi, even. And it's not at all impossible to climb over the fence. The grounds are patrolled, but when it's dark . . . well . . . the White House is not impregnable. The Secret Service constantly asks for better security, but neither the Presidents nor the Congress have ever paid much attention."

"We live in a democracy, after all," said Mrs. Roosevelt. "The President's home should not be a castle."

"Who else was in the West Wing?" asked Howe.

"Mr. McKinney," said Weyrich.

"McKinney?"

"One of the happy hotdogs," said Howe. The term referred to the bright young men recruited for government service by Felix Frankfurter of the Harvard Law School. "Works day and night, I'm told."

"Where was he when the shot was fired?" asked Mrs. Roosevelt.

"In his office," said McIlwaine. "He didn't hear it. Or so he says."

"Where is his office?" asked Mrs. Roosevelt.

"Upstairs," said McIlwaine. "One of the offices

along the south wall. It's very possible he didn't hear the shot."

"Is he still here? I'd like to meet him."

"Yes," said Baines. "I told him to stay in his office, that we'd probably call him."

"Do call him, please, Mr. Baines," said Mrs. Roosevelt.

Baines stepped out of the Oval Office, but in a second he returned. A young black man, wearing the white jacket and black trousers of the White House ushers, accompanied him. "This is Washington Byrd, Mrs. Roosevelt," said Baines. "He's on duty in the ushers' office this evening. Washington is the one who got the call and took the message to Mr. Colmer."

"Please sit down, Mr. Byrd," said Mrs. Roosevelt. "You've been told, I suppose, that Mr. Colmer is dead."

"Yes, Ma'am," said Byrd. He was a man in his late twenties, quite dark, with his hair clipped very close to his skull. He sat down reluctantly. Obviously he had been told he should *never* sit in the presence of such people as the First Lady, but he recognized that the Head Usher who gave him that instruction had not anticipated the First Lady would *ask* him to sit. "I was told just now," he said apprehensively.

The young black man was apprehensive, but he was also enthralled to be in the Oval Office. He tried to keep his eyes on Mrs. Roosevelt and Baines and Howe, but he could not help glancing around the room, absorbing every detail.

Mrs. Roosevelt tried to put him at his ease. "All right. What we want to know is, what was the message you brought to the dinner table, to Congressman Colmer?"

"It was a telephone message," said Byrd. "It came on the phone in the ushers' office. The man said to take a message to Mr. Colmer, to tell him his wife was waiting for him in the President's Oval Office, that it was an emergency."

"A man's voice?"

Byrd nodded. "A man. He said take that message to Mr. Colmer. I had to ask the headwaiter which of the gentlemen was Mr. Colmer, and I went to him at the table and whispered the message to him."

"Yes, I saw you," said Mrs. Roosevelt. "But this voice on the telephone. I don't suppose you recognized it?"

Byrd shook his head regretfully. "No, Ma'am. I surely didn't."

"And Mr. Colmer got up and followed you out of the dining room."

"Yes, Ma'am. He asked me how to get to the Oval Office, and I took him down on the elevator and showed him the door out to the West Wing. He asked me how to get to the Oval Office, once he was inside the West Wing, and I said I didn't know."

"But the message was that Mrs. Colmer was in the Oval Office," mused Mrs. Roosevelt. "With an emergency."

"Yes, Ma'am. That's what the man said."

"He didn't say what kind of emergency?"

"No, Ma'am, only that there was an emergency."

"Is there anything else you can tell us, Mr. Byrd?"

"No, Ma'am. I'm 'fraid not."

"C'mon then, Washington," said Baines. "We won't need you anymore tonight."

"Actually," said Mrs. Roosevelt, "he might stop at the pantry on his way back and ask the man on duty to bring us a pot of coffee. Will you do that, Mr. Byrd?"

"I'll bring it myself, Ma'am," said Byrd.

"Has Mrs. Colmer returned home yet?" Mrs. Roosevelt asked Baines.

"I haven't checked. I can do that."

"I am deeply concerned for her. Perhaps—"

"I'll make a call," said Baines. "You remember, her

pastor is waiting for her. I'll have a D.C. car drive by and see if he has gone inside the house yet."

Mrs. Roosevelt nodded. Baines went out to telephone from the secretaries' office. Louis Howe added still another butt to the overflowing ashtray beside him and immediately lit another of the cigarettes that were killing him. He had fallen silent. He'd had little stamina of late years, she knew, and likely he was tired. Maybe she should suggest he retire. He—

"Eleanor! Am I intruding?" It was Missy LeHand. She was wearing a short-sleeved white blouse, an unstylish short black skirt kept over from the twenties, with a white patent-leather belt, no stockings, and low-heeled shoes. She wore no makeup, and her hair was not combed. "I heard—is something—"

"Missy . . ." said Mrs. Roosevelt, smiling. "Yes, something is wrong. They haven't told you?"

"My God, no! Eleanor, what *is* it? Is—" Her eyes fell to the white sheet that covered the blood on the rug. *"What—"*

"Congressman Winstead Colmer," said Mrs. Roosevelt. "He's dead. His body was found right there. Suicide apparently."

"Colmer! Oh, *God!"*

"Suicide *apparently,"* muttered Howe. "But there are some damned difficult questions to be answered."

"My God . . ." Missy whispered hoarsely. "You don't mean he could have been murdered? Do you?"

It was the first time the word had been spoken—though it had been on their minds: Mrs. Roosevelt's, Howe's, Baines's. It had dramatic impact. For a long moment they fell silent.

"It is essential," said Missy at last, breaking the silence, "that nothing of the kind be suggested until we *know.* It's the kind of thing the newspaper boys slaver over."

"We can't keep it secret, Missy," said Mrs. Roosevelt. "There will have to be an announcement, probably early in the morning."

"How and why could he have committed suicide
here in—"

"That's what we're all wondering," said Howe.

"Has anyone told F.D.?" asked Missy.

"I suppose he's gone to bed," said Mrs. Roosevelt.
"There's no reason to wake him. In the morning he
can have *all* the facts."

"I . . . probably right." Missy's eyes shifted around
the room. She was perhaps thinking she might make
her own judgment as to whether or not the President
should be wakened and told. "Okay."

"As long as you're here, Missy," said Mrs. Roosevelt, "you had better stay. You may have to help with
the announcement."

Missy sat down on the couch beside Howe, though
drawing to the opposite end to avoid the heaviest of
his smoke.

"There are people with motive to kill the man, you
know," said Missy.

"Indeed?"

"I need hardly tell you what impact his subcommittee hearings have had on the banking industry," said
Missy. "Apart from the acute embarrassment he's
caused individual bankers, the legislation his subcommittee is drafting is widely regarded as a threat
to the independence of the whole financial community. There are bankers who would like to see him
dead, Eleanor."

"More aptly said," grunted Howe, "they will be glad
to know he *is* dead."

"He's been nobody's quiet, cooperative little congressman," Missy went on. "Winstead Colmer has
been a tough, effective member of the House. A cru-
sader for good causes. I imagine he was looking for a
Senate seat and—who knows?—maybe even a presidential nomination in 1940."

"You ever hear any scandals about him, Missy?"
asked Howe.

Missy shook her head. "He came up here a bachelor: a handsome Alabama bachelor with a little money of his own and a promising future in politics. They supposed he'd marry some southern belle, likely from his home state; and he surprised everybody when he married Amelia Rowlandson. She's a Republican, you know—from Maryland."

"In spite of that the marriage was very popular in Alabama," said Howe. "Didn't hurt his name down there at all."

"Because she's a beautiful girl," said Missy. "Beautiful, personable, and smart."

"The poor thing," said Mrs. Roosevelt quietly.

"If you think he was murdered—"

Missy was interrupted. Baines returned, bringing Douglas McKinney. He introduced the young man, then stood back as McKinney accepted Mrs. Roosevelt's invitation to be seated. He took a chair and sat nervously with his hands tightly clasped on his lap.

Douglas McKinney was a handsome young man, Mrs. Roosevelt decided immediately. He was the sort of man the mothers of marriageable daughters described as "clean cut"—a term that referred to his appearance as well as his style. His blond hair was neatly trimmed and combed, but the features of his face looked as though they might have been neatly cut, too: sculptured to create a strong, masculine face. His clothes—a light-blue double-breasted suit—were expertly tailored, but they hung to advantage on a trim, athletic body.

"Except for the police officers, you may have been the only other person in the West Wing when poor Mr. Colmer was shot," said Mrs. Roosevelt gently to McKinney. "I understand you have told the officers you did not hear a shot."

McKinney shook his head. "I heard nothing at all," he said. Then he smiled faintly, gestured with his hand, and added, "That is, I didn't hear anything until I heard the officers running through the halls yelling. But as to the shot that must have been fired—"

He shook his head again. "I heard nothing at all. Of course, I did have a radio playing in my office."

"You were working late," said Mrs. Roosevelt. "I understand you work late every night."

McKinney nodded. "The opportunity to work in the White House . . . Well . . ."

"But doing what, Mr. McKinney?" asked Missy, unimpressed.

"Writing memoranda to be used on Capitol Hill, to get support for a social-security bill," said McKinney. "The President wants to—"

"Nobody else works so late," said Missy.

"I think you'll find Mr. Hopkins in his office over in the East Wing," said McKinney. "And Mr. Tugwell, and—"

"Okay, okay," said Missy.

"Did you know Representative Colmer?" asked Mrs. Roosevelt.

"Professionally and socially," said McKinney.

"Do you have any idea why he would want to kill himself?" asked Howe.

"No," said McKinney. "It's absolutely unbelievable."

"Can you think of any reason why anyone would want to murder him?" asked Mrs. Roosevelt. "I will ask you to hold this observation in confidence, but it does seem possible that his death was *not* suicide."

McKinney was conspicuously shocked by the suggestion. He frowned and pondered for a moment. "I suppose . . . well, I suppose an active, effective congressman, sponsor of some pretty controversial legislation, could have enemies. But—but for someone to want to *kill* him?" He shook his head. "I can't imagine."

"You say you knew him socially," said Mrs. Roosevelt. "Did you know Mrs. Colmer as well?"

"Yes."

"Do you have any idea where she might be? So far this evening, no one had been able to locate her."

"You mean she doesn't *know* . . ."

Mrs. Roosevelt shook her head. "Apparently not."

"My Lord . . ." breathed McKinney. "She'll be . . ." He sighed. "Devastated."

"I'd like to review some things with you, Mr. McKinney," interjected Baines. "In the first place, have you been in the West Wing all evening, without interruption?"

"No. I went out for dinner about six. I had a sandwich and coffee at the Blue Café on E Street. Got back well before seven. From then until I heard the commotion downstairs, I worked in my office. I left my office to go to the bathroom once or twice."

"Were others in the West Wing?"

"When I went out for dinner there were. When I came back, hardly anyone was here—maybe one or two people."

"No one stopped by your office? You saw no one when you went to the bathroom?"

He nodded. "That's right. It's usually that way in the West Wing. Almost everyone is gone by seven or seven-thirty."

"And you usually stay until—"

McKinney smiled. "Let's not exaggerate my industry, Mr. Baines," he said. "I work as late as nine o'clock maybe one night a week, until eight maybe one or two other nights." He glanced at his wristwatch. "I had planned to be home in bed by ten this evening."

"Did you ever see Mr. Colmer in the West Wing before tonight?"

"No. But then, he could well have come here often without my knowing it. He could have come to see the President . . . or anybody. I'd have been upstairs. I wouldn't have known."

Baines glanced around the group. "Any more questions for the young man?" he asked. "If not, you can go, Mr. McKinney."

McKinney rose. "It's an honor to have met you,

Mrs. Roosevelt," he said. "I wish it could have been in other circumstances."

"So do I, Mr. McKinney," she said. "So do I."

Byrd brought coffee: a heavy silver service, with china cups and saucers and thick linen napkins. When he had laid it out on the table before the fireplace and had left, Mrs. Roosevelt poured for all of them. All of them remained thoughtful, silent, watching intently as she poured the steaming black coffee and offered cream and sugar.

Missy looked like a woman who had been called abruptly from her bedroom after she had made ready to go to bed, like a woman who had thrown on the first clothes she could grab. Some rumor had come to her—Mrs. Roosevelt could not guess what—and she had rushed down to the West Wing to find out what was horribly wrong in the White House. She stared into her coffee with a distracted air. Maybe she was relieved to learn that the horrible news was not about the President. She had been his secretary since 1920, before he was stricken with polio, and the affection they shared was obvious and well known among his closest associates. Maybe she had been terrified when some vague rumor had been carried to her in her little suite on the third floor.

As they were drinking their coffee and saying nothing significant, word came that Amelia Colmer had arrived home and had been informed of the death of her husband. She was with her pastor and a doctor.

"I suspect," said Baines, "we are not going to learn anything more tonight. Tomorrow . . . well . . . we'll have a report on the pistol, a report on fingerprints, the autopsy, and so on."

Howe sighed and nodded. "I think I'll go on up," he said. He looked at Mrs. Roosevelt. "Will you tell Frank?"

"Missy will see him before I do, very likely," she said. "I'll be leaving by seven, for a breakfast meeting in Alexandria. Since you are here, Missy, and know—"

"I'll tell him," said Missy.

Louis Howe pushed his coffee cup aside, lit another cigarette, and stood. "An announcement, Missy," he said. "Tell Frank we'll have to issue an announcement."

Missy nodded. She looked at the sheet on the floor, watched Howe walk around it.

"Missy . . ." said Mrs. Roosevelt quietly. "To the best of your recollection, did Mr. Colmer ever come to the Oval Office?"

Missy turned down the corners of her mouth. "Not since *we've* been here," she said. "Maybe under Hoover or Coolidge."

"Not an habitué of the West Wing," said Mrs. Roosevelt.

"No."

Mrs. Roosevelt looked at Baines. "It wasn't suicide, Mr. Baines," she said quietly but firmly.

Baines scowled, his face turning rigid and red. "I'd agree. But—doors locked and bolted from the inside. Windows locked from the inside. If there is a murderer, how did he get out of here?"

"I don't know," said Mrs. Roosevelt, "but the other elements of the situation are illogical. In the first place, why would Winstead Colmer kill himself?"

"There may have been reasons," said Missy. "We don't know. But it certainly makes no sense that he would choose the Oval Office as the place to commit suicide."

"Or as the place to be murdered," said Mrs. Roosevelt. "But he didn't choose it. He came here because he was summoned. He was given a message saying his wife was waiting for him here, with an emergency he had to cope with. So he came here and met his death."

"He entered a locked room," said Baines. "Then he,

or someone else, shot the bolts on all the doors, and maybe locked the windows."

"And the pistol," said Mrs. Roosevelt. "Where did he get the pistol? What kind of pistol is it, Mr. Baines?"

"A .38 Colt revolver," said Baines.

"Could he have been carrying it while he was at dinner in the State Dining Room, or at the reception before? Wouldn't it have bulged out in his clothes?"

"I don't see how he could have concealed a .38 Colt in what he was wearing," said Baines.

"Someone called the ushers' office and left that message for him," said Mrs. Roosevelt. "One way or another, someone else is involved in this death."

"He came here . . ." said Missy slowly, sketching a scenario. "Someone let him in. He didn't get far into the office. Someone shot him just inside the door—"

"In the dark," said Mrs. Roosevelt. "If he came here to commit suicide, why didn't he walk farther into the room? Why didn't he turn on the lights?"

"So he entered the room and someone shot him," said Baines. "Then how did the murderer get out of the Oval Office?"

3

Mrs. Roosevelt left the White House early the next morning, as she had said she would. Her breakfast meeting was with the officers of several locals of the International Ladies Garment Workers Union, after which she would return to Washington for a conference at the Department of the Interior. Again driving her own car, but this time allowing a Secret Service man to accompany her, she drove west on Constitution Avenue in bright, hazy sun.

At the same hour the President was awake in his bedroom on the second floor. His breakfast tray was on his bed, together with the morning newspapers; and Missy LeHand sat beside him on his bed, sharing his coffee, nibbling on one slice of his toast. The President still wore his pajamas. Missy had come down from the third floor in her nightgown and a robe. An oscillating fan stood on a table before an open window and stirred the air, but it afforded little relief from the heat and humidity, and she had put the robe aside. The nightgown was modest enough—light-blue

38

cotton—but the scene was almost domestic. These casual morning conferences had been their habit of many years, since the President was Governor of New York and Missy lived in the mansion in Albany.

"I left orders that the rug was to be taken up early this morning," she said. "By the time you reach the office, there should be no sign."

"What should we say?" the President asked. "Suicide. . . ?"

"Eleanor expressed herself rather firmly on that last night, as we were walking back to the house," said Missy. "She thinks we should be reluctant to describe Mr. Colmer's death as suicide until we are sure that was what it was—out of respect for Mrs. Colmer's feelings."

"Would Mrs. Colmer feel any better if we announced it was murder?"

Missy shook her head. "Eleanor suggested we say the cause of death is under investigation."

"The cause of death was a bullet in the head," said the President. "Surely she doesn't think we can withhold that information?"

"No, of course not. What's more, the announcement is going to have to be made within the next hour. F.D., we're going to be overrun with reporters."

"Let the announcement be made by the Secret Service," said the President. "Or the D.C. police. Or the two of them jointly." He picked up a newspaper and seemed to have dismissed the subject, but then he smiled slyly and added, "Making sure we write the announcement. Let Marv McIntyre handle it. That's what a press secretary is for."

Missy consulted a note on the shorthand pad that lay on her lap. "You have two appointments this morning," she said. "Joe Kennedy at ten, Dean Acheson at ten-thirty. Sam Rayburn would like a few minutes sometime during the day to introduce you to the young man you've appointed National Youth Administration director for Texas—that fellow Johnson."

"I didn't appoint him," said the President testily. "Sam shoved him down my throat. And I still don't think he's qualified."

Missy frowned over her note. "Lyndon B. Johnson," she murmured. "Well— You want me to tell Sam you can't fit him in?"

"No. Tell Sam to bring him over here. I suppose I ought to take a look at this prodigy."

"Sam says he's an avid supporter of yours."

"That isn't all Sam says about him. Don't forget, I'm the one who had to listen to Sam's speech about him—complete with fist-banging and foot-stomping. The son Sam never had. Fit them in after Acheson."

The announcement of the death of Winstead Colmer was issued from the White House Press Office at nine-thirty:

> Representative Winstead Colmer (D., Ala.) was found dead in an office in the Executive Wing of the White House late last evening. His death was caused by a gunshot wound to the head. Whether or not the wound was self-inflicted has not yet been determined.
>
> Representative Colmer was a guest at last night's state dinner for M. Alexis Saint-Léger Léger. He was called away from the dinner to take a message and did not return to the dining room. His body was later discovered by White House policemen making their regular rounds.
>
> The investigation into the death of Representative Colmer is continuing.

The congressman's office issued its own announcement about the same time:

> Representative Winstead Ransom Colmer, Democrat, representing the Eleventh District of Alabama, was found dead last night in an office

in the West Wing at the White House. Although it is known his death was caused by a shot from a revolver, the circumstances remain unknown and are being investigated by the Secret Service and the District of Columbia police.

Representative Colmer was forty-three years old. He had represented the Eleventh District since 1924 and was in his fifth term. He was chairman of the Auditing Standards Subcommittee of the House Banking and Currency Committee. Before his election to Congress he was an attorney in Tuscaloosa, Alabama. He served as a captain of artillery in France in 1917 and 1918.

Representative Colmer is survived by his wife, the former Amelia Rowlandson of Bethesda, Maryland, to whom he was married in 1931. There are no children. He is survived also by his father, Alabama State Senator Winstead Colmer, Sr., and by his mother, Letitia Colmer; also by two brothers, Dr. Pickett Colmer of Tuscaloosa and Attorney Lee Bob Colmer of Birmingham.

Funeral arrangements are incomplete. It is expected that a service will be held simultaneously in Washington and Tuscaloosa, with interment in Arlington National Cemetery.

Mrs. Roosevelt left the Department of the Interior at about ten-thirty. She drove to the Colmers' small redbrick house in Georgetown. She parked at the curb and sent the Secret Service agent to the door to see if Mrs. Colmer would receive her. He returned saying Mrs. Colmer would be honored to receive Mrs. Roosevelt.

She entered the house with some trepidation. Although it was her duty to call, and she hoped she would be able to offer some small comfort to the young widow, the situation demanded poise she was not sure she had.

Amelia Colmer greeted Mrs. Roosevelt at the door

and led her into the living room where a man and woman stood waiting to meet her.

"This is my mother, Mrs. Rowlandson," said Amelia Colmer in a small, hoarse voice. Her voice suggested she had spent hours weeping. "And my pastor, the Reverend Mr. Gallop."

Mrs. Roosevelt smiled and greeted them, but her interest was fastened on Amelia Colmer. She was twenty-nine years old, Mrs. Roosevelt knew from inquiries this morning. She was a short, somewhat pudgy young woman, wearing a gray dress in the flapper style of some years ago. Her face was round, as wide as it was long. She had short dark hair, beautiful dark eyes, and a wide mouth dramatized with red lipstick.

"It is so very nice of you to come," she said.

"My dear," said Mrs. Roosevelt softly, "is there *anything* I can do for you? I mean, just *anything*."

Amelia Colmer sighed. "You've done a great deal by coming. I'm afraid there is not much anyone can do now. I am, of course, most concerned that . . . that all *questions* about Win's death be answered. You understand."

"I do indeed."

"Well, please sit down. We're having coffee. Won't you have a cup?"

Mrs. Roosevelt would have rather not, but it seemed the proper thing to do, to accept a cup of coffee with these people. "Thank you," she said.

Mrs. Rowlandson left the room to get the coffee.

"When will some of Mr. Colmer's family arrive?" Mrs. Roosevelt asked conversationally.

"None will," said Amelia blandly. "That's why there will be simultaneous funeral services in Alabama and Washington. Frankly, Winstead and his family were not on good terms."

"Oh. I'm sorry."

"They didn't like his marriage," said Amelia.

"Amelia . . ." cautioned the Reverend Mr. Gallop. "Perhaps it is better not to—"

"I will say it," said Amelia firmly. "They wanted him to marry some fatuous Alabama belle. To his family in Alabama, I am a Yankee—more correctly said, a Damnyankee. I have never been to Alabama, Mrs. Roosevelt. Even when he went back to campaign, I never went with him. How could he have explained to his district that his wife was not welcome in his family home?"

Mrs. Roosevelt nodded and remained silent.

"It wasn't our marriage, actually, that alienated the Colmers," Amelia continued. "I think he married me as an act of defiance. They were already alienated. His seat in Congress, you see, was the one his father wanted. What's more, his father wanted Win's elder brother to have it. They considered Win pushy. He ran against the old incumbent in 1926—and beat him—which the other two Colmers had been afraid to try."

"I see."

"Now one of them will run for his seat," Amelia said bitterly. "And get it. On the basis of *his* reputation."

"And what will you do, my dear?" asked Mrs. Roosevelt. "I understand you once worked at the White House. If you—"

"Mrs. Colmer will not be looking for employment," said the Reverend Mr. Gallop. "She will be staying at home, either here or in Maryland. You see, Mrs. Roosevelt, Mrs. Colmer is going to have a baby."

Amelia closed her eyes and sighed heavily. "Reverend . . ." she breathed. "That is supposed to be a secret."

"It remains one," said Mrs. Roosevelt. "You need not worry that *I* will disclose it."

"I would be grateful," said Amelia quietly.

*   *   *

When she returned to the White House, Mrs. Roosevelt decided to go to the West Wing. She wanted to talk to Louis Howe, maybe to Missy. In the colonnade she encountered Sam Rayburn, accompanied by a tall, lanky, dark-haired young man. They stepped into the rose garden for a moment, where Sam introduced him.

"Eleanor, I'd like you to meet Lyndon Johnson. I just had him in to see Frank. He's the new N.Y.A. director for Texas, you know."

The gawky, ill-dressed young man smiled broadly and said it was a great honor to meet Mrs. Roosevelt. "You have a broad and appreciative following in my part of the country, Ma'am," he said.

"Why, thank you, Mr. Johnson," she replied.

So this was the Lyndon Johnson over which Sam had made such a fuss. The President had appointed an experienced, deserving union leader to be N.Y.A. director in Texas, and not only Sam Rayburn but Senator Tom Connally had bluntly demanded the appointment be withdrawn and Johnson appointed. Twenty-six years old, he had no administrative experience. His only qualification was that Sam Rayburn wanted him.

Mrs. Roosevelt shrugged, inwardly. This awkward fellow, too conspicuously anxious to please, would never amount to much. She nodded to him and Sam and said they would have to forgive her, she had an appointment.

She sat down in a seat in front of Louis Howe's desk. Howe picked up his telephone and called for Baines.

"Oh, yes. A great deal more information," Baines said when he came in and took a chair. "More information which all but destroys the hypothesis that Mr. Colmer took his own life—in spite of the locked and bolted doors."

"Such as?" asked Howe dryly.

"The .38-caliber Colt revolver found in Mr. Colmer's hand quite naturally bore his fingerprints," said Baines. "But only on the grips and trigger. On the barrel and chamber and—what's more significant—on the cartridges in the chamber, there were no fingerprints at all. How could a man load a revolver without getting his fingerprints on the cartridges?"

"By wearing gloves, of course," said Howe.

"Precisely," Baines agreed. "But are we then to believe that Colmer wore gloves to load the pistol and put fingerprints on it only when he shot himself with it? That strains credulity, doesn't it?"

"It does," said Mrs. Roosevelt.

"Continuing," said Baines, "we found no Colmer fingerprints anywhere inside or outside the Oval Office—not on the door handles, not on the knobs that turn the deadlock, not on the bolts, not on the handles of the window locks. To lock himself inside and bolt the door, he had to touch at least one deadlock knob and at least one bolt, probably two. Although we didn't search the President's desk, we didn't find gloves anywhere around the body. So why no fingerprints where they would have to be if he locked himself in?"

"So he was murdered," said Howe. "But locked in? How did the murderer get out?"

Baines sighed and shook his head. "I wish I knew. I wish I even had a plausible theory."

"Assuming it was murder," said Mrs. Roosevelt, "then we shall learn how the murderer got in and out when we learn who he is."

"No one on Colmer's staff," Baines went on, "remembers his ever having come to the West Wing. He was an outspoken Democrat during the presidencies of Coolidge and Hoover—critical of both of them. It is doubtful either of them ever invited him to the Oval Office. We have records of callers during the present administration. Representative Winstead Colmer once met with the President in his study on the second floor. The appointment books show no visit to the West Wing."

"Remember, too, what the usher said last night," said Mrs. Roosevelt. "Mr. Colmer asked him how to find his way to the West Wing and also how to find the Oval Office once he was in the West Wing."

"And of course," Baines continued, "we don't know who telephoned the ushers' office and asked that an urgent message be taken to Colmer. But it was someone. Even if we were reluctant to believe Washington Byrd, another usher confirms there was a telephone call and that Washington went to the dining room immediately after that call."

"We must suppose, then," said Mrs. Roosevelt, "that someone placed that call to lure Mr. Colmer into the West Wing in the middle of the evening, when it would be all but abandoned, met him somewhere between the dining room and the West Wing, led him to the Oval Office, and there murdered him."

"After which he bolted the doors, dissolved, and went up the chimney like a wisp of smoke," said Howe, skeptical and annoyed. "Or walked through a wall. Really—"

"Have you a better theory, Louis?" asked Mrs. Roosevelt.

"Maybe not better," said Howe, "but an equally valid one. Colmer knew he would be at dinner in the White House. He arranged for someone to telephone the ushers' office. With that excuse, he left the table and went to the West Wing, which he knew better than you suppose. (The layout of the West Wing is, after all, no secret.) He or a confederate had keys. They went into the President's office looking for something—something to steal or a paper to read. They found it or didn't find it. They quarreled. The confederate shot Colmer. Then—then I have no more idea than you do how he got out, bolting the doors behind him."

"One problem, Louis," said Mrs. Roosevelt. "Why

would he have had his confederate give a message that Mrs. Colmer was in the Oval Office? If a question arose, it could be easily established that she was not, that she was at home all evening or wherever."

Howe shrugged.

"You've raised another point," said Baines. "Just where *was* Mrs. Colmer all evening? She didn't return home until after eleven. When she was asked this morning where she had been from seven-thirty to eleven, she refused to answer. In the circumstances, no one pressed her for an answer. Still . . ."

"Surely," said Mrs. Roosevelt, "you are not suggesting that poor young woman—"

"I will respectfully suggest, Ma'am, that you do not bestow your sympathy until we have more facts. It's curious, isn't it, that she *refused* to account for more than three hours of her time last evening—hours during which her husband either killed himself or was killed by someone else?"

"Could *she* have been in the Oval Office?" asked Howe. He was lighting a Sweet Caporal, and his mouth was distorted from sucking on the cigarette. "After all, she worked here once. She knows her way around."

"Louis," said Mrs. Roosevelt sternly, "that unfortunate young woman is *pregnant*." She put her hand to her mouth. "Gentlemen, I have broken a confidence. I think—" She spoke to Baines. "I think you must know, as an element of the investigation, but let us all, for heaven's sake, keep the matter secret. The young woman is entitled to announce her pregnancy when she sees fit."

Howe shrugged and turned up his hands. "When is the baby due?"

"January, I believe," said Mrs. Roosevelt.

"Not much of an impediment as yet," grunted Howe. "I mean, not much of an impediment to getting around, maybe committing a crime."

"Obviously, Louis, you have never been pregnant."

"Well, I thought I might be, two or three times,"
Howe said, with a quick little smile at Baines.

"Have you any further information, Mr. Baines?"
asked Mrs. Roosevelt.

"Not at the moment, Ma'am. I expect the medical
examiner's report yet today."

"I shall be in my office. I would be grateful if you
would bring me any new information."

Douglas McKinney glanced around Mrs. Roosevelt's
informal office and study in the Lincoln Bedroom. He
was plainly self-conscious and apprehensive. "I wasn't
sure I should—"

"Sit down, Mr. McKinney," she said.

"Uh, thank you. I, uh . . . as I say, I wasn't sure I
should come up here. I mean, it may seem an intrusion. I may be sticking a nib into something that's
none of my business."

"I shall never know whether you are or not, Mr.
McKinney, if you don't tell me why you've come to see
me."

As McKinney sat down, he drew a deep breath,
then let out an audible sigh. He was wearing a gray-
and-white seersucker suit, of the kind that was almost a uniform on the hottest days of a Washington
summer. It was, of course, shapeless and wrinkled. He
ran a hand over his neatly combed light hair and ran
the same hand down the side of his head to wipe a
bead of perspiration off his cheek.

"I spent a lot of time last night thinking about Congressman Colmer," he said. "The investigation raises
a difficult problem of jurisdiction. Anyway, Mr.
Baines isn't entirely cordial to me. It's as if he thinks
I must have had something to do with Mr. Colmer's
death, because I was in the West Wing last night. I
didn't know who to speak to, unless it was you."

"Do you know something about the death of Mr.
Colmer?"

"Not really. Not directly. But I know some things

that may not come to the attention of an ordinary police or Secret Service investigation. Those fellows are— Well, they have a rather limited perspective. There may be political implications in the death of Mr. Colmer. I'm not sure they'll see them."

"Tell me about them, Mr. McKinney. I'll try to understand."

Mrs. Roosevelt was sitting at her breakfront desk and had been reading Tommy's typescript of tomorrow's "My Day" column when McKinney arrived. Now she put the column entirely aside and gave him her full attention.

"In April I was assigned to go up to the Hill and listen to some of the testimony Mr. Colmer's subcommittee was taking. On bank auditing practices, you know. I heard some of it. I talked with Mr. Colmer a little, with some members of the subcommittee staff a lot more. I guess you know, Mrs. Roosevelt, that a lot of bankers think they had reason to hate Mr. Colmer."

"Because of the legislation his subcommittee is preparing?"

"Yes, but for another reason, too. The subcommittee is concerned with auditing standards, but to find out what standards are needed you have to find out what practices are now accepted. And to find out that, the subcommittee has been compelling bankers to testify—some of them about things they'd much rather not talk about."

"Sharp practices," said Mrs. Roosevelt quietly.

"Embezzlement," said McKinney.

"Actual embezzlement?"

"Misapplication of investors' funds," said McKinney with certainty.

"Specifically—"

McKinney leaned forward on his chair, clasping his hands on his knees, and speaking in a quiet, as though confidential, tone. "The National Rivermen's Bank in Pittsburgh lost half its deposits after its president, Bertram Crocker, was compelled to testify about how he invested the bank's funds in companies he and his friends own. Rivermen's may well go under. Crocker has been forced out. That's just one example. There are others."

"Are you suggesting some banker may have wanted to murder Mr. Colmer, for revenge?"

McKinney shook his head. "That's not impossible. I'd be more concerned with bankers who are still functioning in the old way but anticipate trouble from the subcommittee. I—maybe I shouldn't have done this, but I called a lawyer classmate of mine who works for the subcommittee and asked him who was about to be subpoenaed. Here's the list." He handed Mrs. Roosevelt a slip of paper.

She glanced over the names: four banks, six bankers. "But surely, Mr. McKinney, the death of Mr. Colmer won't mean the end of these hearings. What would anyone have to gain from—"

"Excuse me," said McKinney. "The subcommittee consists of five Democrats and two Republicans. The two Republicans oppose the inquiry entirely. One Democrat has severe doubts. The remaining four Democrats made the majority that kept the hearings going. Now it is three to three. The opposed Democrat is the senior Democrat left on the subcommittee, so he becomes chairman. The inquiry will be stopped. You can bet on it. Uh—Excuse me. I mean, you can be reasonably sure of it."

"Another Democrat will be appointed to replace Mr. Colmer."

"Yes. The lobbyists are already working on that one. I mean, already—this morning. The new chairman—Representative Kraft—will ask for the man he wants, and he'll ask for a conservative Democrat who'll oppose the inquiry."

Mrs. Roosevelt smiled gently. "Are you sure you're not being a bit too conspiratorial, Mr. McKinney? Do you really believe the death of Mr. Colmer is going to stop an important congressional investigation?"

McKinney frowned and lowered his eyes. "I *have* meddled," he said. "I'm sorry."

"Not at all," she said quickly. "But—" She looked at the names on the paper he had given her. "It is your thought that *these men* could countenance murder?"

"What is holy about bank presidents, if you don't mind?" asked McKinney. "Do you remember what Senator Burton Wheeler said after the president of National City Bank finished his testimony? He said if it was right to send Al Capone to the penitentiary for tax evasion, some of the crooked bank presidents ought to go, too."

Mrs. Roosevelt studied the names again. "Peavy . . ." she mused. "Ross . . . surely—"

"Obviously I'm not accusing them," said McKinney. "I have no evidence whatever. All I'm saying is, the death of Mr. Colmer comes as a tremendous piece of good luck for some of these men. I only wonder if it comes as a surprise to them, too."

"I will bring all this to the attention of Mr. Baines," said Mrs. Roosevelt. "Would you rather I kept your name out of it?"

"I'll leave that to your judgment," said McKinney. "I don't want to get a reputation as an officious intermeddler."

"I appreciate your coming to see me," she said. "You have been here since the beginning, I believe."

McKinney grinned. "I'm a happy hotdog," he said. "I came a little more than a year ago. It's been a rewarding experience."

"You're a Harvard man," she said.

"Yes. Mr. Frankfurter called me in and told me I had a duty to come to Washington and serve my country. Otherwise, I might be a very junior lawyer for one of those banks we've been talking about."

"Not married?"

"No, Ma'am. Curse the luck."

He had obviously relaxed. He was showing her a warm smile now, and his self-confidence had returned so easily that she wondered if its failure had been real.

"I should think you would find many opportunities, Mr. McKinney. Washington is crowded with eligible girls."

"But not with social opportunities," he said. "It is difficult to meet the . . . the *right kind* of girls."

"I do understand," she said. "I'm afraid our White House staff women are mostly rather older."

McKinney smiled. "So I've observed," he said with a playful grin. "But—but I'm taking too much of your time."

"I shall put your name on the list for an invitation to the first likely party," she said. "We do see some attractive girls around here once in a while. Congressmen's daughters . . ."

He rose. "Thank you, Mrs. Roosevelt," he said.

Gerald Baines telephoned just before Mrs. Roosevelt set out from the White House at five for a reception and dinner for the wives of the Tennessee congressional delegation. She asked him to come to her office, and she waited for him, though she was dressed to go out.

"The report of the medical examiner," he said. "I can give you a copy, but it's pretty gruesome stuff."

"Summarize it please, Mr. Baines."

Baines nodded and paused for a moment to choose his words. "The cause of death is no surprise. Mr. Colmer died of a single gunshot to the head. He died instantly—or nearly so—which of course negatives any fastening bolts after he received the wound. What's interesting is that the medical examiner says he never saw a suicide where the bullet entered the head at exactly the angle this one did. It is not impossible for Mr. Colmer to have shot himself this way, but the medical examiner says it's highly unlikely."

"Murder, Mr. Baines," said Mrs. Roosevelt.

Baines nodded. "I have almost no doubt of it."

"Harry the Hop, Louey the How . . ." sighed the President. "Marv, Pa. . . . Where *is* everybody?"

"I'm afraid it's just you and I," said Missy.

"Afraid it is," said the President. "Not that I don't appreciate *you,* Missy."

President Roosevelt was the most sociable of men. He enjoyed trading words over a couple of drinks, enjoyed little jokes shared with a few friends; and his early-evening cocktails were an important ritual to him. He had long understood that Mrs. Roosevelt did not share his taste for jests and banter, did not appreciate many of his friends, did not care for cocktails, and was, in any event, very busy. Tonight, for example, she was off to some meeting or dinner—probably something important and worthwhile, yet something that would occupy her time and attention until the middle of the evening, by which time likely he would be propped up in bed with his dinner tray. For Missy only, then, he began to mix his special martinis—gin and vermouth, five to one, a powerful combination.

Missy sat with him in the west sitting hall on the second floor of the White House, in the private quarters of the President. Arthur Prettyman had set out the shaker and bottles, the glasses and ice, and was on his way to the elevator now. Missy relaxed on the sofa, wearing summer white and looking cool. She had kicked off her shoes, which lay in the middle of the floor, and drawn her legs up under her.

"Hand me the telephone," said the President. "I'm calling out and having some dinner delivered. Let Mrs. Nesbitt eat whatever abomination she plans to send up here for my dinner. What would you like, Missy? Chinese?"

"I haven't had a decent Chinese dinner since we moved down from New York," said Missy. "This town favors southern-fried hog jowls to anything eaten by humans. We can try."

She checked through the telephone book and discovered a Chinese restaurant that offered delivery. The proprietor was at first dubious, then dumbfounded to find himself speaking with the President of the United States, and he promised to send a dinner "first-class, boss, first-class for sure," within the hour.

The President poured numbing-cold martinis into stem glasses. "To you, Missy," he said, raising the glass. "And to the United States of America."

"To you, F.D.," she said. "America thanks God for you."

The smooth, clear martinis went down soothingly.

"Colmer didn't kill himself," said the President. "Someone gave him a little boost out of this world."

"I'm afraid so," said Missy.

"Problem," said the President. "We have to set up an appointment with Speaker Rainey. The wrong appointment to that subcommittee will kill the auditing-standards investigation and the bill. Sam Rayburn went into it with me this morning. He thinks it's possible some banker arranged the demise of Colmer."

"I refuse to believe we do government business that way in the United States," said Missy. "By murder? Sounds like Europe or Asia, not America."

"I don't want to believe it," said the President. "And I don't want it to happen, either."

"Do you think the Secret Service and the D.C. police can handle a difficult investigation?" she asked. "Maybe you should order an F.B.I. inquiry."

The President shook his head. "Let John Edgar Hoover loose in the White House? That grandstanding egomaniac . . . never. But we may have to arrange some support for the boys who *are* responsible. I'm going to have to give some attention to this thing. Tomorrow."

"My name is Lee Bob Colmer."

Gerald Baines took the man's extended hand, shook it, then gestured toward a chair. "Sit down, Mr. Colmer. And please accept my sympathy on the tragic loss of your brother."

"Thank ya." The man lowered himself gingerly into a chair. He put his Panama hat aside on the floor.

This Colmer was so unlike his brother it was difficult to believe they were of the same family. Winstead had been a long, handsome man, carrying his years comfortably. Lee Bob was perhaps ten years older but looked twenty years older. He was fat, balding, flushed, sweaty. He wore thick lenses in gold-rimmed spectacle frames; and as he sat down in Baines's office, he removed these glasses and began to clean them nervously, breathing on the lenses, wiping with a damp handkerchief, holding them up to the light to stare at them, repeating the process as he talked.

"I left home soon's I heard 'bout Winstead. Rode the train most all day yesterday."

"You must be tired," said Baines.

"I'd follow this matter to exhaustion," said Colmer. He spoke with an Alabama drawl, laying an exaggerated emphasis on some words and syllables, as if to add gravity to his statements. (What he actually said was—"Ah'd *folla* this *mattah* t' ex-*hau*-stion!") "There's somethin' very wrong with Winstead's manner of death."

"We're conducting a thorough investigation," said Baines.

Colmer ran his hand down the lapel of his light-blue seersucker suit, apparently wiping the sweat from his palm. "Yes," he said. "You realize, I trust, that it is impossible to believe Winstead Colmer took his own life." (. . . tuk his *own* . . . *laf.*")

"It is difficult to believe, isn't it?" said Baines noncommittally. "Still . . . his body was found inside a locked room."

"Tush and nonsense," said Colmer. "They's always ways of gettin' in an' out of locked rooms."

"Not just locked, Mr. Colmer. Bolted. The bolts can be worked only from inside."

Colmer shook his head. He took a packet of paper and a cotton bag of tobacco from his bulging jacket pocket and began to roll himself a cigarette. "They's ways," he insisted. "If you jus' keep lookin'."

"I intend to."

"You in charge th' investigation?"

"Yes."

Colmer remained silent for a moment while he shook tobacco into his paper, licked and rolled it, and lit the ragged cigarette he had made. Then he said, "I can give you some facts you may not know."

"I'd appreciate having them," said Baines in the significant silence that followed.

"To begin with, Mr. Baines, you must understand that Winstead married very badly. Came up here to

Washin'ton, I s'pose was lonesome, and married a . . . a chippy. You know what I mean? An *acquisitive* young woman, who was after his money and position. He left a considerable estate, Mr. Baines. Our gran'daddy left each of us boys a share in some very val'able land in Alabama. After Winstead got married, he sold his share to me. I borried the money, Mr. Baines, and paid Winstead fifty thousand dollars. He tol' me he bought stocks when they wuz at their lowest, and I'd guess he's worth maybe a hundred thousand. Now, what do you want to bet there's a will, leavin' all that to his wife?"

Baines sighed. "Nothing terribly unusual in a man leaving his money to his wife."

"Maybe and maybe not," said Colmer. "Let me show you a letta he wrote our mama 'bout a month ago."

Colmer reached into one of the copious pockets of his jacket and took out a folded envelope. He handed it to Baines—a handwritten letter on the stationery of Winstead R. Colmer, Representative, Eleventh District of Alabama. It read:

Dear Mama,

People here in Washington think it's hot. They always think it's hot. And damp. The British embassy staff here gets tropical hardship pay for living in Washington! Anyway, I am well and not suffering from the heat, and I'm hoping the Congress will recess soon and I'll be home for a nice visit.

Amelia complains of the heat. She complains she is bored. I guess, Mama, I've got to admit after all this time that maybe it was a mistake to marry her. The marriage has not turned out like I expected. I do though ask once more that you and the family make the best of it, as I am doing.

Tell Mr. Ames that I do oppose that bill he asked you to mention. It's stuck in committee and is unlikely ever to come out, so he doesn't need to worry about it. My best to his family. My love to you and Papa. Will see you soon.

Win

"Y' see? He realized somethin' was wrong with the marriage. Never gave him a child, was one thing." Colmer refolded the letter Baines handed back to him, folded the envelope, too, and put it in his pocket. "I came up here, Mr. Baines, to try to talk her into sendin' Winstead's body back to Alabama, to bury it in the soil of his ancestors, 'stead of in Arlington. She *refused*."

"You asked her to *send* it back, Mr. Colmer? Not to *bring* it back?"

Colmer nodded.

"Maybe that's the reason."

"Be that as it may," said Colmer. "Y' got an answer to this question, Mr. Baines? The question—where was Amelia Wednesday night when Winstead was killed? She wasn't home. I asked. She wouldn't say where she was. Do *you* know?"

Baines shook his head. "We haven't questioned her much," he said. "It seemed we ought to let her get her husband buried before we asked too many questions."

"Well . . . That's *your* sense of values. I'm goin' to make two guesses where she was. Maybe you ought to check into my guesses. Guess one is that she was here in the White House and had somethin' to do with Winstead's death. She worked here a long time and knows her way around the place. She coulda been here. Guess two is that she was layin' around some-place with her lover."

"Oh, this is *cruel!*" complained Mrs. Roosevelt. She tossed the newspaper angrily on the floor at the feet of Lorena Hickok. "Look at that, Hick. Just look what they've done!"

They were in Mrs. Roosevelt's office. Hick had stopped by at the end of her workday for a cup of tea or a sip of wine with her friend.

Hick picked up the Friday-afternoon edition of the *Washington Record* and focused on the news story that disturbed Mrs. Roosevelt:

WHERE WAS MRS. COLMER?
Beautiful Wife's Whereabouts
When Colmer Died—Remains Mystery

By Jim Patchen

The whereabouts of Mrs. Amelia Colmer, beautiful young Maryland-born wife of Representative Winstead Colmer, at the hour of his death remains one of the intriguing unsolved mysteries of the case. Colmer died about nine o'clock on Wednesday evening. Mrs. Colmer's whereabouts from seven-thirty to eleven that evening cannot be determined.

What's more, she's not saying. This reporter and others have attempted to find out, by calling the Colmer home. Most calls are answered by Mrs. Rowlandson, Mrs. Colmer's mother. I was lucky. I got Mrs. Colmer on the telephone. She refused, however, to answer my question as to where she was that night. She told me it was none of my business.

Lee Bob Colmer, brother of the deceased congressman, told reporters at the White House this morning that Mrs. Colmer also refused to discuss the matter with him. She also refused, he said, to consider his request that the family be allowed to take the body back to Alabama for burial. Mrs. Colmer has decided the congressman will be buried in Arlington National Cemetery.

Mystery

Many aspects of the death of Representative Colmer remain mysterious. His body was found

in the President's Oval Office, with all doors and
windows locked and bolted. The obvious conclusion is that he took his own life. Still, no one
can think of any reason why he would. Reporters
are poking into every aspect of the deceased congressman's political and personal life, looking for
a clue. Mrs. Colmer's refusal to disclose her
whereabouts on Wednesday evening deepens the
mystery.

"Oh, that *awful* man!" exclaimed Mrs. Roosevelt.

"Actually," said Hick, "the story is not much worse
than what we're seeing in other papers. Mrs. Colmer
is making a mistake by trying to conceal her—"

"It's no one's business," Mrs. Roosevelt interrupted.

"I'm afraid it is, Eleanor. The young woman's husband was almost certainly murdered. Sooner or later
she's going to have to account for her whereabouts at
the time of his death."

Mrs. Roosevelt sighed. "I suppose so," she conceded.

"I have to tell you also that the couple were not on
the best of terms, apparently. I had to go up to the
Hill this morning, and I heard some stories. It seems
the Colmers had a reputation for squabbling in public. They were overheard saying some pretty bitter
words to each other."

"What are you telling me, Hick? Are rumor and
speculation building some kind of case against Mrs.
Colmer?"

"If she persists in being secretive about where she
was Wednesday evening, she is going to be suspected,
Eleanor. That's simply inevitable."

"You should meet her, Hick," said Mrs. Roosevelt.
"The poor little thing . . ."

"There are some other stories around on the Hill,"
said Hick. "Quite a number of people had reason to
want Winstead Colmer dead."

"Bankers, yes," said Mrs. Roosevelt. "I had something of a disquisition on that yesterday afternoon, from Mr. McKinney."

"Bankers, for sure," said Hick. "But others, too. Colmer seems to have been the man holding up the appropriation for the dam on Sipsey Fork. Do you know about that?"

"The name is unforgettable," said Mrs. Roosevelt, "but I'm not sure I could define the problem."

"A group of Alabama businessmen want a dam built on that little river. They talk about flood control and irrigation. They say the dam construction will put hundreds of unemployed men to work—it would be a W.P.A. project, of course. Actually, what they have in mind is to develop lots around the shore of the lake the dam would make. They've bought the land. They've been up here to lobby for it. I think they've got Harold Ickes sold. But Colmer has had the project hung up in the Appropriations Committee."

"Why? Did he see it for what it is?"

"That, plus the fact that the dam would flood out several score of Negro farmers."

"Are you suggesting that the businessmen who want this project would go so far as to *murder* Mr. Colmer to eliminate him as a block?"

Lorena Hickok shrugged. "Doesn't seem reasonable, does it? On the other hand . . . well, we *are* talking about Alabama."

"Hick! Really."

"Sure," said Hick. "They could've killed him when he went home to campaign this fall. Why bother to come all the way up to Washington to do it? And in the White House? But let's don't forget we're talking about the part of the country where lynching is still a quaint tradition. Our standards and values don't much impress a lot of those people."

"If you're about to call them rednecks, I will change the subject," said Mrs. Roosevelt with a faint smile.

"Anyone who calls a Negro 'nigger' is going to be called 'redneck' by me," said Hick.

Mrs. Roosevelt drew a deep breath. "The funeral is tomorrow," she said. "I would appreciate it if you would go with me."

Hick nodded. "Of course."

From time to time Felix Frankfurter journeyed down from Cambridge to Washington. He was always welcome. The brain trusters and the happy hotdogs held him in special regard and affection. On this Friday night he had suffered a minor disappointment. He had expected to have dinner with Acheson or maybe with Moley, but both of them had been compelled to cancel. He'd made a few phone calls. Now he sat at a table in the Mayflower dining room with the only hotdog who had proved available—Douglas McKinney.

"It's an honor, Professor," the young man said. "I regret that Mr. Acheson couldn't make it, but I guess your misfortune is my good fortune."

Frankfurter never put much stock in fulsome compliments—or any other kind of compliments. He knew how to pay them better than how to receive them, and he knew how much sincerity usually backed them. He was a short man, with a cherubic squat face and a rather dark complexion. His pincenez glittered beneath his bushy black eyebrows. His hair was white, thick, and combed flatly across his flat head. He was wearing a dark-gray double-breasted suit. He adjusted his pince-nez and regarded the menu without much satisfaction.

"There's talk around Washington," said McKinney, "that the President will appoint you to the first vacancy on the Supreme Court. 'Tis a consummation devoutly to be desired."

"I hope not, actually," said Frankfurter without looking up from his menu.

"You hope not?"

"The only seat on the Court that is conceivably available to me is the Brandeis seat. Face reality,

Douglas; no President is going to appoint a *second* Jew to the Supreme Court. So long as Louis Brandeis is a justice, there is no chance for me—and I certainly don't want to lose Brandeis."

"President Roosevelt—"

"Not this President, not *any* President," said Frankfurter. "Anyway, I enjoy being at Harvard Law. Actually, I probably have more influence on events from that office than I would from a seat on the Court."

"Well, I'd like to see you have the honor, Sir."

Frankfurter put down his menu. "Thank you, Douglas," he said. "Tell me what you know about Representative Colmer."

McKinney smiled faintly. "A tragedy, hmm?" he said cynically. "And a mystery. The Alabama Democratic Party will find some other redneck to replace him."

"It was my impression that Winstead Colmer was a rather progressive and rather effective congressman," said Frankfurter. "I understand he supported the President consistently and was of some help in achieving passage of the chief legislative elements of the New Deal."

"I don't like the type," said McKinney.

"Expand on that idea, Mr. McKinney."

"Rednecks are rednecks. What is there to say? He had no education—unless you want to call six years at the University of Alabama an education. He spoke a travesty of the English language. His political philosophy fell somewhere between Caligula and Attila the Hun. In sum, he wished he wuz where he wuz begotten, whuppin' niggers and choppin' cotton."

Frankfurter shook his head. "I recalled you had a facility for turning a phrase, Douglas."

"Well, I'm sorry, Sir. The man's mysterious death is a tragedy. To put him in his best light, he was some sort of populist, I suppose, and his death may impede the passage of an auditing-standards bill; but that whole Dixie crowd is disgusting to me."

"What about the Jews of the Lower East Side, Douglas? Do they disgust you?" asked Frankfurter.

"Well, *hardly*," McKinney protested. "There is a world of difference."

"Precisely. And difference is what makes this country good."

McKinney leaned across the table and spoke quietly to Frankfurter. "As much difference as is represented by Senator Thornberry? I notice he ostentatiously avoided speaking to you when he came in."

"Billy Thornberry is anti-Semitic," said Frankfurter. "You are anti-redneck." He shrugged. "Can you support your prejudice with any better rationalization than he can?"

"I believe so," said McKinney. "I sincerely believe so. I mean, there *are* standards."

Frankfurter glanced around the room. He plainly meant to terminate this discussion.

"Isn't that what a Harvard man hopes he can do?" pressed McKinney. "Separate valid ideas from invalid? Distinguish attitudes with rational underpinning from attitudes without them?"

Frankfurter lowered his chin and regarded McKinney from over his pince-nez. "And you couldn't have learned such faculties at the University of Alabama? Or Mississippi?"

"Could you?" asked McKinney.

"Oh, yes. Abraham Lincoln learned them without the assistance of any university."

"Well, I take pride in being a Harvard man," said McKinney.

"So long as it doesn't make you a Harvard prick, Douglas," said Frankfurter, and by his tone and expression emphatically ended the discussion.

McKinney flushed, but he grinned and nodded manfully. "That's always a possibility, isn't it?"

"Anyway," said Frankfurter, "if a Harvard education is something superior, then it is our obligation to share it with those who don't have it, not to scorn them because they don't."

"Mr. Colmer," said McKinney cautiously, "probably committed suicide. After all, his body was found in a locked room. He—"

"Did you ever read *The Big Bow Mystery*, Douglas?" asked Frankfurter. "By Israel Zangwill? If you haven't, you should. The body is found in a locked room. A locked-room mystery. Arthur Conan Doyle did something of the like. And Poe. They are challenges to one's powers of observation. The fact that Mr. Colmer's body was found in a locked room suggests suicide, but it doesn't prove it."

"I . . . I'm afraid I'm not much of a fan of mystery novels," said McKinney.

"Interesting intellectual challenges, Douglas. Don't scorn 'em."

"Well, I—"

"If you'll excuse me for a minute or two, I'm going to step over there and say hello to Senator LaFollette."

Frankfurter pushed back his chair. He and the senator had already exchanged smiles, and he walked across the dining room to where the Wisconsin progressive was dining with another man and two women. McKinney noticed how Senator Thornberry turned his head away and refused to look at Frankfurter as he passed by that table.

McKinney frowned over the menu. Left alone, his attention wandered—until after a moment it was captured by the conversation between Senator Thornberry and the two other men at his table. McKinney had no scruples about listening to other people's conversation. If they didn't want to be overheard, let them speak more quietly. But the three southerners had been drinking, from the sound of them, and it was not impossible they *meant* their talk to be overheard—to impose their thoughts on others nearby. Anyway, he heard:

THORNBERRY: "Well, I tell ya, Sam, I'm sure not mournin' the son of a bitch."

SAM: "Who is?"

THORNBERRY: "Far as I'm concerned, if he took a pistol and blew his goddam head off, it's good riddance. Right, Sam? Right, Woody?"

WOODY: (*raising his glass*): "Don't quite understand ya, Billy. Now, I was never one that what ya call *favored* the man—he was too stick-uppity for me—but I can't say it's good riddance that he's killed himself or maybe has been murdered."

THORNBERRY: "Well, maybe you don't know 'bout him what I know."

SAM: "Like what?"

THORNBERRY (*lowering his voice*): "Well . . . I guess y'all know Lester Stebbins's daughter's pregnant and all."

WOODY: "*No!*"

SAM: "Oh, hell yes. Didn't you know that, Woody?"

WOODY: "I never—"

THORNBERRY (*slamming down his glass after having tossed back the last of his whiskey*): "Pregnant, by God. Les'd like to kill the man that got her that way. An' . . . *maybe he did!*"

SAM (*glancing cautiously around the room*): "Careful, Billy. Y' don't know who's listenin'."

THORNBERRY: "And I don't give a damn."

McKinney stared hard at his menu. It was none of his business. Or was it?

"You know Clyde Tolson, I believe?"

Gerald Baines looked up at the dapper-clad pair who had missed him at his office but had pursued him to his car—J. Edgar Hoover and his fawning assistant, both of them wearing snappy cream-colored, summer-weight, double-breasted suits, black-and-white shoes, and crisp straw hats. They looked like

what a few people in Washington dared say they
were.

"Yeah, John," said Baines. He knew Hoover did not
like to be called John—which was why he called him
that. "What can I do for you?"

Hoover pursed his lips. "Murder of a member of
Congress, if that's what happened, is a violation of
federal law and comes within the jurisdiction of the
Federal Bureau of Investigation. We—"

"Murder within the precincts of the White House, if
that's what happened," Baines interrupted, "comes
within the jurisdiction of the Secret Service."

"It comes, Jerry," insisted Hoover, "directly within
our jurisdiction."

"No, John," said Baines. "It's within *ours*. If we
can't agree on that, I'll ask the President to decide
who he wants conducting the investigation. In the
meanwhile, if any of your snap-brims venture into
the White House, they'll be tossed out by the seat of
the pants. Now you'll have to excuse me. I'm busy."

Baines slammed the door of his car and started the
engine. In his judgment, J. Edgar Hoover was a half-
competent publicity hound who would have taken no
interest at all in anything happening in the White
House if it did not promise to make headlines. So far
as Tolson was concerned . . . well, the self-effacing little fellow was probably the better man of the two,
probably the source of what professionalism did in-
trude into the Bureau. As he drove away, Baines
looked at the pair in his rearview mirror. As a couple
they were disgusting.

He was on his way to D.C. police headquarters. He
would have rather gone home to dinner with his wife
and daughter, but the call from Lieutenant Kennelly
had suggested he should sacrifice an hour.

The Secret Service had asked the D.C. police to do
the fingerprint work, the autopsy, and the ballistics
examination—to keep everything away from the self-
promoting Hoover, as the President would surely

want. The pistol had been turned over. It was the subject of Lieutenant Kennelly's call.

"A wee drop of the juice of the grape, eh?" Kennelly asked when Baines was seated across his desk. "Not on duty, mind you. Never on duty. But"—he glanced at his watch—"I've been off duty for precisely twenty-six minutes. Haven't you?"

Kennelly was a formidable, flush-faced Irishman. His yellow hair was turning gray. His blue eyes bulged. He reached into his desk drawer and extracted a fifth of Old Bushmill's Irish. He winked at Baines and poured two generous shots into little paper cups from the water cooler—which he had thoughtfully grabbed out of the cooler on their way into his office.

"The President!" he said as he raised his paper cup.

"Erin go bragh!" Baines replied. His own ancestry was Belgian, but he knew the Irish toast.

"Well, sir," said Kennelly, "I'm prepared to return your pistol."

"Good," said Baines. "I hope it's the source of some information."

"It is, it is," said Kennelly lightly, taking his second swallow from the cup. "Fingerprints. You know, they told us nothing. Somebody had carefully wiped that revolver clean of every fingerprint—except those of the unfortunate Winstead Colmer, whose prints were on the trigger and grips. An odd circumstance that, which absolutely negatives the notion he committed suicide. Why would a man wipe his fingerprints off the pistol he meant to use to kill himself?"

"I am well aware of that, Ed," said Baines. "What else?"

"We took the serial number off the Colt revolver and telephoned the Colt Repeating Firearms Company in New Haven, Connecticut," said Baines. "Guess where that particular Colt went when it left the factory?"

"Enlighten me."

"The .38 Colt that killed Winstead Colmer was sold to a sporting-goods store in Tuscaloosa, Alabama, named Vigerie Fishing and Hunting—which buys a dozen or more Colts like that every year. This afternoon I called Vigerie. They don't keep track of serial numbers. But did they ever sell a .38 Colt to Winstead Colmer? Yep, they sure did. In 1929, as best they can remember. Could have been 1930. No big deal. He bought a pistol. Doesn't everybody?"

Baines put his empty paper cup down on Kennelly's desk. "Suicide again," he muttered.

Kennelly shook his head. "No. Why would he wipe off the fingerprints? No. It points another way."

"Assuming this Colt revolver was the one sold to Winstead Colmer," said Baines. "Obviously—"

"Sure. But it was sold to *somebody* in Tuscaloosa. Colmer was killed with a revolver sold in Tuscaloosa, Alabama. If he wasn't killed with the revolver he himself owned, then he was killed with one owned by somebody else from Tuscaloosa."

"Assuming somebody in Tuscaloosa didn't sell his Colt to somebody from Massachusetts or California," said Baines.

"Assuming that," said Kennelly. "Then Colmer was killed with a gun owned by someone from Tuscaloosa or vicinity. Which makes two possibilities—"

"Right," interjected Baines. "His own gun or someone else's. Which—"

Kennelly interrupted. "The charming Mrs. Colmer, who refuses to say where she was Wednesday night. Or someone else, who came here from Alabama to kill Winstead Colmer." He shrugged. "Or he killed himself—a theory I'm not willing to accept."

"We can't interrogate Mrs. Colmer for the time being," said Baines. "Not at least until her husband is buried tomorrow."

Kennelly poured into their paper cups. "Tell me something, Jerry," he said. "How often are the locks changed on the offices in the White House?"

Baines turned up the palms of his hands. "I'm not sure," he said. "They haven't been changed to my knowledge since I've been there—and I came in under Coolidge."

"Are the locks complicated?"

"No. Good, strong locks, but not terribly sophisticated."

"How many people might have access to keys to the Oval Office?"

Baines pondered. "Today . . . the Secret Service. The White House police. The President, obviously. I believe Miss LeHand has keys. The cleaning staff. I—"

"A dozen people?" Kennelly asked.

"It could be that many."

"And would have been that many under Hoover, that many under Coolidge?"

"I suppose so."

"When was the West Wing built? When were the first locks installed?"

"During the presidency of Theodore Roosevelt," said Baines.

"And you can't be sure they've been changed since."

Baines shook his head. "I can't be sure."

"Scores of people have had access to those keys."

Baines nodded.

"Hell!" grunted Kennelly. "My own home is better locked than the West Wing of the White House."

"From time to time," said Baines, "it is suggested to Congress that various modifications be made to the White House—better locks, more guards, a new telephone system, better heating, a better way to cool the offices in summer. All this would cost money. Visitors to the Oval Office walk across threadbare carpet on their way in. They look at tattered drapery. Some presidents have spent personal money on the place. President Hoover did. We—"

"All right," Kennelly interrupted. "Putting aside the question of the bolts, the doors to the Oval Office could have been unlocked, then locked again, by anyone who has worked in the West Wing since Theodore Roosevelt."

"You're not exaggerating much," said Baines. "That's the Secret Service nightmare."

"And," said Kennelly, "among the people who may have had access to keys is Mrs. Winstead Colmer, who worked in the White House for five years. Right?"

Baines nodded.

"Whose husband may have been killed with his own pistol, wiped clean of fingerprints. And was that pistol maybe in his house in Georgetown, maybe in his desk drawer or nightstand? Mrs. Colmer, who refuses to say where she was at the hour when her husband died. I'll wait until the funeral is over, as you suggest. But day after tomorrow, Jerry, I'm going to ask Mrs. Amelia Colmer a few questions."

5

On Saturday morning Winstead Colmer's funeral took place in the Thirty-third Street Baptist Church, in Georgetown. The small brick building and sturdy oak pews could not contain all the personal and official mourners, plus the curious.

Mrs. Roosevelt and Lorena Hickok were seated in a front pew to the left of the aisle and were joined there by Postmaster General James Farley; Henry Wallace, Secretary of Agriculture; Joseph Kennedy, head of the Securities and Exchange Commission; and General Hugh Johnson, Chief of the National Recovery Administration. Secret Service agents, including Baines, sat behind Mrs. Roosevelt.

From Capitol Hill came the entire Alabama delegation, plus four other senators and four other representatives—the official mourners from Congress. They were ushered to pews just behind Mrs. Colmer and her mother and sister. Other members of Congress, maybe twenty of them, who came unofficially and only because they genuinely respected the memory of Winstead Colmer, found seats where they could.

Newspaper, wire-service, and radio reporters crowded into a section reserved for them at the rear, leaving many standing around the walls behind. Somehow Douglas McKinney had obtained press credentials, and he stood on the wall to the right, grimly observant, apparently deeply moved.

The rest of the places in the church were taken by its regular members, many of whom knew the Colmers and insisted they would be seated in *their* church for "Brother" Winstead's funeral. This left no room for the merely curious, several hundred of whom milled on the sidewalk outside, peering into the hearse, wandering among the gravestones in the little burying ground beside the church. A few tried to climb trees to look in the windows, until they were ordered down by policemen.

The family arrived. They were led to the other front pew by the Reverend Mr. Gallop, and the little church filled with a rippling murmur of conversation. Amelia Colmer, dressed in black, her face covered with a black veil, was supported on the arms of her mother and father, who took seats to either side of her. Her sister Deborah followed her, on the arm of a young man who would be identified by reporters later as just a friend.

No Colmers. Lee Bob was still in town, as was well known to the reporters, but he did not come to the funeral. Neither did any other member of the Colmer family of Alabama.

The Reverend Mr. Gallop preached a long but adroit sermon, referring to "a tragic, untimely death" but avoiding any suggestion that the deceased might be a suicide or, worse, the victim of murder.

Afterward the family, the official delegation from the Congress, and all the reporters followed the hearse to Arlington. Mrs. Roosevelt returned to the White House.

"How petty of those people!" she exclaimed to Lorena Hickok in the car on the way back. They were seated in the rear seat of a black Packard driven by a Secret Service agent. "How very small! I mean, for the Colmers not to have come to the funeral."

"The story is that a simultaneous service was held in Alabama," said Hick.

"Indeed? And which service was attended by the brother who came to Washington? What's his name?"

"Lee Bob Colmer," said Hick. She sighed. "I'm afraid we have to accept the fact, Eleanor, that the family probably suspects Mrs. Colmer had something to do with Winstead's death."

Mrs. Roosevelt shook her head. "Such a pretty little thing," she said sadly. "I felt such *sympathy* for her."

"Eleanor . . ." Hick cautioned.

"I know— Don't let your sympathy run away with you, Eleanor. My husband says the same thing."

It was with great reluctance that Baines knocked on the door of the house in Georgetown in the middle of Saturday afternoon. "I'm terribly sorry," he said to Amelia Colmer's father, who answered the door. "I'm Baines of the Secret Service. I know I could not have come at a worse time, but—"

"Ask the gentleman in, Dad," said Amelia. From her small living room she could hear Baines at the door.

Her father stood aside, scowling at Baines.

"I *am* sorry, Mrs. Colmer," said Baines. "I wouldn't disturb you on a day like this, except that I hear you are leaving Washington, maybe as early as tomorrow, and I—"

"I am going out to Bethesda, Mr. Baines," she said. "To my family's home. Not very far away."

"Oh, well, then," said Baines, "I needn't trouble you

today. I do have a couple of questions, but they can wait."

"Sit down, Mr. Baines," said Amelia. "As long as you're here, we may as well find out what your questions are."

Baines put his straw hat aside on the table by the door, and he sat where she suggested, on the couch, facing her as she sat in an overstuffed chair. Amelia had removed the hat and veil she had worn at the funeral, but she still wore the black dress. She *was* pretty; there was no overlooking it.

"I am not an ogre, Mr. Rowlandson," Baines said to the scowling father. "I would defer these questions to a more appropriate time. I am sure, though, that all of you are as interested as anyone else in resolving the questions that still surround Mr. Colmer's death."

Rowlandson nodded. "I suppose," he conceded.

"In the first place, Mrs. Colmer," said Baines, "there's a question about the pistol. According to the serial number on it, it was sold by the manufacturer to a sporting-goods store in Tuscaloosa, Alabama. Vigerie Fishing & Hunting Supplies, it's called. Mr. Vigerie recalls he sold a pistol of that model to Mr. Colmer. Though it's not certain, it does appear he was killed with his own gun. He—"

"If he committed suicide, it *would be* with his own gun," Amelia observed quietly. "Wouldn't it?"

"Do you believe he committed suicide?"

She tipped her head to one side and turned down the corners of her mouth. "Don't I understand he was found locked inside the Oval Office, with the doors bolted and the windows latched?"

"Was he despondent?" Baines asked. "Can you think of any reason why he would take his own life?"

"Do you know what a saturnine personality is, Mr. Baines? That's what Win was. He was saturnine. In public he was all joy and gladness, but in private he sometimes sank into gloomy moods and was in them for days. He wouldn't talk. I could never find out what was troubling him."

"You think it's possible, then, that—"

She nodded and interrupted. "I think it's very possible." She shrugged. "Unlikely . . . but the alternative is unlikely, too, don't you think?"

Baines rubbed his hands together—a nervous gesture. "Returning to the pistol, Mrs. Colmer—did your husband keep a pistol in the house?"

"Yes."

"Can you tell me what kind it was?"

"A revolver," she said. "I don't know what make or caliber."

"Where did he keep it?"

"In the bedroom. Among his personal things in the bureau drawer."

"Is it there now?"

"No, it's not. It's gone. When I heard how he died, I went upstairs and looked for it."

"Would you recognize it if you saw it?"

She shrugged. "A pistol is a pistol, to me. Does the one—does the one you found have any special marks on it or anything?"

"No. It's very clean. Apparently it was never fired before."

"He already had it when we were married," said Amelia. "I saw it among his things, but I never mentioned it to him, and he never spoke of it to me."

"Was it loaded?"

"Yes. I could see the bullets in the little holes in the—in whatever you call it."

"The chamber."

"Yes, the part that turns when you pull the trigger. I could see them in there."

"Did he have any extra ammunition? A box of cartridges?"

"Not that I ever saw," she said.

"All right. Now, Mrs. Colmer, I have to ask you the question you've already declined to answer."

"Where was I Wednesday evening?"

"Yes. We're going to have to know."

Amelia shook her head slowly. "I was doing something very personal and very private, Mr. Baines, and I'm not going to tell *anybody* what it was. I'm sorry. If that makes me a suspect or something, it's just going to have to be that way."

"I urge you to change your mind, Mrs. Colmer. We can keep the matter confidential."

"No. I can't tell you—and I won't."

Douglas McKinney paused before he left the locker room. The long mirror by the door was there for gentlemen to view themselves before they went out—not to see how handsome they looked but to be certain their swimming suits were properly adjusted and nothing was exposed that should not be exposed: a stray curl of pubic hair, for example, which it would be painfully embarrassing to have seen. He was satisfied with himself both ways; he would not humiliate himself, and he *was* handsome in his blue trunks and white vest. He stepped into the pan of evil-colored antiseptic set in the floor—a requirement that was supposed to kill athlete's foot—and stepped out onto the hot concrete.

Women and children. The men were out on the links. In the shallow end of the pool a hundred shrieking children splashed, attended by a dozen harried mothers. At the far end the women sat at tables under umbrellas, sipping iced tea and lemonade—or some hard drinks—and chatted and smoked and watched two teenaged boys diving.

Most of them were wearing swimsuits, which this summer were almost uniform—the tight blue wool trunks, white web belts, and white wool vests. A few bold girls were wearing backless vests this summer, held in place only by a strap across the back and one around the neck; but Pine Arbor Country Club was no place for the bold. These were the wives and daughters of congressmen and senators, bureaucrats and officers.

Doug studied them for a moment and then climbed to the ten-foot board and introduced himself to all of them at once by doing a graceful swan dive. When he reached the edge of the pool and thrust himself up, most of them were looking at him. He went to the umbrella-shaded bar and bought a glass of beer.

At a table in a corner formed by the chain-link fence a young woman sat alone, not in a swimsuit but in a loose summer-weight dress. She was a lovely blonde, wearing her hair unstylishly long—to her shoulders. She was tall and slender. She was also conspicuously pregnant.

Doug walked toward her fence corner, as if he meant to lean over the fence and peer at a foursome of golfers teeing up. Very carefully, in a measured way, he brushed her arm and shoulder with his hip as he passed her.

"Oh. I'm sorry. Terribly sorry."

She nodded at him and said nothing.

"Uh . . . I believe we've met. I'm Douglas McKinney. I work at the White House. And—please forgive me. You are. . . ?"

"Jane Stebbins."

"Oh, sure. It's nice to see you, Mrs. Stebbins. You're from, uh, Mississippi, right?"

"Mississippi, yes," she said.

"But a Yankee by transplantation," he said. "You went to Radcliffe, right?"

"You have a good memory, Mr. McKinney," she said. She had rid herself of every trace of her southern accent. "Better than mine."

He grinned again. "I'm a Harvard man, myself. We have much in common. Uh . . . are you alone, Mrs.

Stebbins? Would I be intruding if I sat down to chat for a few minutes?"

"Sit down, Mr. McKinney. And I am not Mrs. Stebbins, I am *Miss* Stebbins."

"Oh."

"And I am pregnant. And no one here wants to sit with me. My father is playing golf. He insists I come to places like this and be ignored. It's my penance. He'd really like for me to sew a red A on my clothes, but—"

"I'm sorry," said Doug. He sat down. "I mean, I don't think you should be treated shabbily. It's none of my business, but—"

"You're kind."

"Well . . . I'm afraid Washington is not a very open-minded place. It's really a very provincial city in many ways, don't you think?"

"It's a wretched place," she said. She nodded toward nearby tables. "Look at them," she said. "Wives of majors and colonels. They think they're *society*. There *is* no society in Washington."

"If there were, it would be redneck," said Doug.

"Yes," said Jane Stebbins bitterly. "That's exactly what it would be."

"Have you had lunch, Miss Stebbins?"

"Yes. Right here. My father did come in long enough to have a sandwich with me."

Doug frowned sympathetically. "Would you have dinner with me?" he asked. "We Yankees have a duty to help each other to relieve the Washington boredom."

She was nonplussed. "You want to have dinner with *me*?"

"Yes. Unless—unless there's someone who—I'm sorry. This is awkward; but, yes, I'd enjoy having dinner with you."

"My father won't like it."

Doug smiled. "Forgive me, but I understand your father doesn't like a great many things."

Jane Stebbins laughed. "He may say wretched things to you."

"I can be very thick-skinned," said Doug.

"You should not be working on Saturday afternoon, Mr. Baines," said Mrs. Roosevelt. "Not this late, anyway. Surely your family—"

"I'll be working late every day, Ma'am, until we find out who killed Mr. Colmer."

"Have you anything further to report?" she asked.

"Some new information, yes," he said.

They had met by accident just outside the elevator in the center hall on the second floor of the White House. Mrs. Roosevelt had come up on her way to her office. Baines was on his way to the third floor, where the Secret Service kept a small office in one of the spare rooms. It was about half past five, and she would be leaving the White House at seven for a dinner with her friends Elinor Morgenthau and Lorena Hickok. In the meantime she would review some correspondence in her office.

"If you can spare me a few minutes, Mr. Baines, we—"

"*Who's home?*" The President's voice boomed through the long hall. He sat in his wheelchair at the door between the center and west halls, smiling and raising a beckoning arm. "Babs! Jerry! Cocktail hour! C'mon up!"

"Oh, I—"

Baines was grinning, honored to be asked to join the President for a drink. He had already half broken away from Mrs. Roosevelt and was nodding at the President.

A minute later they were seated in the family quarters in the west hall—the President and Mrs. Roosevelt, Baines, and Missy LeHand.

"Well, Jerry," said the President. "What word of the murder?"

"It still may be a suicide, Mr. President," said Baines. "Representative Colmer was apparently shot with his own pistol."

"Huh," said the President. "Just when I was coming up with something I thought you should look into."

"There are still more unanswered questions than answered ones," said Baines. "And a new one that's come up this afternoon." He nodded toward Mrs. Roosevelt. "What I was about to tell you."

"Another question," said the President.

"Yes. As Mrs. Roosevelt knows, the pistol that killed Colmer was free of all fingerprints except the ones on the trigger and grips. Even the cartridges in the chamber were clean of fingerprints. Now, we've established that Colmer owned a revolver, kept it in his bureau drawer. Also, that pistol is missing—has been since the night he was killed."

"Really?" asked Mrs. Roosevelt.

"What's more, so far as Mrs. Colmer knows, there was no extra ammunition for the pistol. He owned it when they were married. They never talked about it. It was loaded, but she never saw a box of cartridges."

"But—" Missy interrupted.

Baines continued. "Cartridges that had been in a pistol for several years ought to show some corrosion. The brass casings turn dull. The ones in this pistol are shiny."

"Meaning?" asked Missy.

"Meaning the pistol—assuming it is the same pistol—was not only wiped clean of fingerprints and reloaded, it was reloaded with fresh ammunition. Why? Why would Colmer have done that if he meant to kill himself with that pistol? Why would he have done any part of it—wiped off fingerprints, bought new ammunition, reloaded?"

"Babs," said the President to Mrs. Roosevelt, "do

you really find such a problem intellectually stimulating?"

"I do. I really do," she said.

"Hmm," murmured the President. He lifted his gin
bottle, eyed it with a critical eye as if he thought
someone had been sampling his gin, then began to
pour measures into a silver shaker. "It looks to me as
if every time you solve a problem, another one pres-
ents itself."

Arthur Prettyman had leaned over Mrs. Roosevelt,
and she whispered to him that she would like a small
glass of sherry. He hurried away to get it.

"Let Missy and me complicate it a little more," said
the President as he shook his gin, vermouth, and ice.
"I suppose you know that among the next group of
banks to be called on the carpet by Colmer's subcommittee was the Enterprise National Bank of Chicago.
The president of that bank is Otto D. Peavy, who
prides himself as a man not to be toyed with. I need
hardly tell you, I guess, that Otto Peavy is a hard-
nosed, self-righteous man. What's good for Otto Peavy
is good for America and William Randolph Hearst,
and the New Deal is anything but."

Baines saw the President's smile but also saw the
earnest intent behind it. As the President took a moment to pour the clear, cold martinis from the shaker
into glasses, Baines focused on his meaning. Otto
Peavy . . .

"If I don't judge him wrong—and I'm sure I don't—
Peavy is sitting in that colossal mansion of his in Chicago tonight, drinking a toast to Winstead Colmer's
funeral." The President resumed the subject. "The
sudden death of Colmer may have staved off justice
another six months or a year."

"Justice?" asked Mrs. Roosevelt.

"Justice to Otto Peavy," said the President, "is any
arrangement that allows him to go on making money,
no matter what it costs others or the community at
large."

Missy smiled. "F.D. doesn't hold the man in high regard," she said.

"I should like to know what tangible connection you can make between the facts you've stated and the facts of Congressman Colmer's death," said Mrs. Roosevelt.

"Oh, I have omitted that point, haven't I?" said the President with a smile. He took a small sip of his martini. "Well, it seems there is a Peavy Junior. Otto D. Peavy the Third, to be more accurate. And where do you suppose *that* Otto Peavy works? Here in Washington. At the Mechanics' & Husbandmen's Bank—M & H, a substantial part of which is owned by his father. A chip off the old block, Otto the Third."

"The relevance, Franklin," Mrs. Roosevelt prompted him. "The relevance."

"Otto Peavy the Third is a nice-looking young man," said the President. "And guess where you can find him sometimes?"

"Don't ask us to guess. Just tell us."

"Over in the West Wing," said the President. "Does the name Darlene Palmer mean anything to you? Missy knows her. She's a career civil servant, a secretary, inherited by Rex Tugwell when we moved in here. Darlene's thirty-two years old. Otto the Third is thirty-six. They are a pair."

"They. . . ?"

"They date," said Missy. "Otto the Third comes in to pick her up after work. He takes her to dinner, out dancing, to movies, to concerts. It's a flaming romance. Darlene is so flattered by his attentions that she can hardly talk about anything else. Whenever I go up to Tugwell's office, which is upstairs, you know, she just *has* to tell me about the most recent wonderful evening she spent with Otto."

"I don't have to guess what you think is relevant about this," said Mrs. Roosevelt. "Still, I wish one of you would say it. Specifically."

The President had just inserted a Camel into his

black cigarette holder, and he was about to light it. Instead, he paused with match in one hand, cigarette in the other. "Otto D. Peavy," he said, "had valid reasons to fear what Winstead Colmer was about to do—that is, subpoena him and put him on oath to tell the truth about certain of the operations of Enterprise National Bank. Motive to kill him?" The President shrugged. "Who knows? As good as any other anyone's suggested. The point is, Peavy had *access* to things around here, through his son who frequents the premises. It may be that a lot of people had motive to kill Winstead Colmer, but the list will be abbreviated when you limit it to people who had access to the West Wing and knew their way around."

"But do you really think," asked Mrs. Roosevelt, "that this banker or his son is capable of *murdering* someone?"

The President shrugged. "Otto Peavy is a banker today," he said. "A dignified, respected banker. The story in Chicago is that he made his first money selling beer—during Prohibition. I don't have to tell you what kind of people were involved in that trade. You asked for a specific. There is a specific rumor that Al Capone has a fortune on deposit in the Enterprise National Bank—under a false name, of course. The tax boys would like to know. Colmer would have liked to know what kind of bookkeeping practices Peavy uses to hide deposits like that."

"Is this a fact, Sir?" Baines asked. "That the Peavy bank holds gang money?"

"If we were certain, Peavy would be in a federal penitentiary," said the President.

"But the investigation will go on, won't it, Mr. President?" said Baines. "The death of Mr. Colmer—"

"Not necessarily," said the President. "Not in the same way, at any rate. There's a political problem. I'm asking for a good appointment that will keep it going, but I'm not at all sure I'm going to get it. Seniority is a powerful force, Jerry."

"And whoever killed Colmer—assuming that wasn't Colmer himself," said Missy, "—would have taken the political situation fully into account."

"Mr. Baines," said Mrs. Roosevelt, "I suppose this Darlene Palmer has the key to Mr. Tugwell's office. But obviously she doesn't have a key to the President's office."

"True," said Baines. "But the old locks in the West Wing are not sophisticated. If someone had one of those big old keys, it is not impossible he could have filed it down and made a skeleton key of it—capable of opening *any* office."

"That assumes the person involved is an expert," said Mrs. Roosevelt. "A locksmith."

"No problem," said the President. "If Colmer was the victim of a murderous conspiracy to protect gang accounts in Peavy's bank, then locksmiths, safe-crackers—"

"Glaziers!" exclaimed Mrs. Roosevelt. "A glazier could have removed the glass from a window or the French door and—"

"Sorry, Ma'am," said Baines. "That would have left fresh putty. We looked for that Wednesday night."

"And found none?"

"And found none," said Baines. "Every pane of glass was firmly in place, secured by glazier's points and old, hard putty."

"Which leaves us nowhere," said Mrs. Roosevelt, "on the question of how a murderer escaped from the Oval Office and left the body of Mr. Colmer lying there."

"Suicide," said Missy.

Mrs. Roosevelt shook her head firmly. "When we identify the murderer, then we can address the question of how he—or she—escaped from the scene of the crime. I take this matter of the Messieurs Otto Peavy, *père et fils,* most seriously, Mr. Baines."

"I have a suggestion for you, Jerry," said the President.

"Yes, Sir?"

"Let John Edgar Hoover look into it. That's his specialty, isn't it? Gangsters? He wants a part in the investigation. Let him take the part of it he's qualified for."

"If that's how you want it, Mr. President."

"Let's try it, Jerry. He called me. I haven't returned his call. I will, and I'll let him have this part of it."

Senator Stebbins cleared his throat. He cleared it three or four times a minute, Doug noticed, as if he had swallowed something that had stuck halfway down and would not move. He was an ugly bullfrog of a man, heavy, lumpy, wearing a white suit, sitting deep in an overstuffed chair, smoking a long cigar, keeping a glass of bourbon at hand.

"Y' takin' my daughter t' *dinner,*" he muttered. "At the no'th they call takin' a girl to dinner a *date,* as I understand."

"Uh, well . . . just for some conversation. Because we went to college in the same town," said Doug.

"Umm-hmm. Her mother's idea. She went no'th, lived amongst the Yankees four years, and learnt their *ways.* I s'pose you know she's not just growin' a belly *accidental.*"

"No, Sir. I understand Miss Stebbins is carrying a child."

Stebbins nodded. "I known nigger gals get pregnant without no husband. Fact, I known white gals. But— daughter of a United States Senator!" He sighed loudly, blowing white drops of saliva across the room. "Nevah happened befo'. *Nevah.* What's more, she refuses to say who's responsible!"

Doug allowed himself a minimal smile. "Uh . . . Senator, as for me, I only met Miss Stebbins—"

"*Ah!* T'ain't you. I know that. Believe me, I know it, or you wouldn't be standin' there. Never mind. *I know who it wuz.*" He nodded. "I know." And he nodded again. He sighed again. "Cain't think much of a boy'd

take out a gal in her condition. It's how you do at the
no'th, I s'pose. Wouldn't do nothin' like it where I
come from."

Half an hour later Doug sat with Jane Stebbins at a
corner table in a little Alexandria restaurant called
Boodles. They were drinking Red Top beer and
munching on chips.

"Your father is a caricature," he said to her.

"A caricature of what, Doug?" she asked.

Doug grinned. "Of a southern senator," he said.
"That's what a Mississippi senator is supposed to be."

"My father's uncle was killed at Gettysburg," she
said. "His father was wounded there the same day,
and for a long time the women at home didn't know if
either of them had survived. My mother's father lost a
leg at Chickasaw Mountain. Her family owned a hundred and fifty Negroes. My father's family owned
four—household servants. All that— Well, you can
imagine what my father heard all the years he was
growing up. He lived in Washington during most of
the Wilson administration—worked in the White
House, in fact, very much like what you're doing—
but it didn't change him. When I went to Radcliffe, I
was determined to wash Mississippi out of my soul,
but my father can't think of any finer heritage."

Doug nodded. "It made him what he is. Well . . .
when the Civil War was being fought, my grandfather
was in Japan. He was a Yankee ship captain, and the
whole war was fought during his voyage to Japan and
return. My mother's father was a private in a Massachusetts regiment. They made him a company clerk,
and he never fired a shot at the enemy."

"I'm glad my father didn't know all this," said Jane.
"I don't think he'd have let you in the house."

Doug smiled and glanced around the room. "I . . . I
assured him I had known you only a short time."

She nodded solemnly. "I understand. You needn't
have worried. He wouldn't have accused you. He
thinks he knows."

"It's someone you care for, isn't it?"

"Yes."

"And to protect him—"

"To protect him," she said, "I have refused to tell my father who he is."

"But—"

She, too, glanced around, as if to be certain no one was listening. "It's a matter of a divorce, Doug," she said. "He's a wonderful man. Really wonderful. His wife has abused everything in the marriage vows. The divorce is pending. But if that woman found out about me— Well. You can understand."

"And if your father found out?"

She shook her head. "He'd *kill him*," she whispered. "I swear to God he would!"

"But he has no idea who it is?"

"No. No idea."

"He says he knows, Jane," said Doug soberly. "He told me he did."

"He thinks he knows," she said, shaking her head. "He's told me he knows. But he doesn't. He doesn't have the remotest idea. When the divorce is over, I'll marry my baby's father, and we'll go where my father can't hurt us. It's all planned. We know what we're doing."

"Well, who does he think it is?" Doug asked.

"I don't know who he has in mind. God help the man if Dad gets to feeling certain about it!"

6

Mrs. Roosevelt would not allow Tommy Thompson to work on Sundays, but she herself worked seven days a week. It was known that she did, and in fact she received an occasional letter of complaint.

> We hear you spend mornings on The Lord's Day doing chores! Shameful! Another example of the way this present generation mocks The Lord! You bring a curse on our nation by profaning the Word and Works of The Almighty!

A month ago a Tennessee editorial, in a weekly newspaper published in a country town, had deplored her making a speech at a Sunday-afternoon picnic of Auto Workers, saying, "God has His ways of dealing with Sabbath-breakers, and we won't be surprised if something awful happens to that woman."

The President laughed at such letters and editorials. Mrs. Roosevelt didn't, but she continued to use part of each Sunday to scan the mail that accumulated all week, that she couldn't find time to read any other day. Some letters she tossed in the trash basket. Some she put aside to be filed. On others she wrote notes for Tommy, telling her how to answer them. A few she put aside for full answers on Monday.

This Sunday morning a small package wrapped in brown paper caught her attention. She opened the package and found a letter, plus two small magazines printed in garish colors on cheap newsprint. They were comic books, one called *Famous Funnies,* one called *Ace Comics.* She had heard of these. They were a new publishing phenomenon—little magazines given solely to comics, selling for ten cents. She flipped through the pages and was amused by the cartoon figures, most of them familiar—Mutt and Jeff, Hairbreadth Harry, Toonerville Folks, Popeye, the Katzenjammers, Dagwood and Blondie, Maggie and Jiggs, the Little King, Krazy Kat. . . . She was interested in these samples of a new kind of magazine.

But the letter—

> I send you the enclosed samples so you may see the vicious new threat to the morals of America's children. In the pages of these two magazines are to be found examples of every imaginable form of vice and corruption. Children who never open their Bibles may be seen everywhere, staring into the pages of these depraved comic magazines. I hope decent Americans will have your support in establishing laws to stop this horrible new hazard to traditional American morality.

Mrs. Roosevelt put the two comic books aside. They would make nice little gifts for someone's child. She tossed the letter in the trash.

Sometimes the mail was distressing. Usually it was encouraging. Altogether too often it included personal appeals for help. People sent small items—crocheted hats or doilies, embroidered handkerchiefs or pillowcases, carved dolls or napkin rings—and asked her to send them a little money for them. She was compelled—she simply could not do otherwise—to reply to these letters by returning the items with a form letter typed by Tommy, explaining that she just couldn't buy everything people sent her. More often, similar items came as gifts. Tommy sent the thank-you letters. The gifts were sorted and forwarded to places where they could be useful—hospitals, orphanages, homes for the aged. Gifts of food had to be put in the garbage, unfortunately—for fear of poison—but the thank-you letters went out just the same.

She turned toward the windows, her attention caught for a moment by the spatter of rain on the glass. A rainy Sunday morning. Maybe the heat wave would be broken. She returned to her correspondence.

Then the telephone rang. The White House operator told her a Mr. Douglas McKinney wondered if this was an inconvenient hour for her to speak with him. She told the operator to put Mr. McKinney through.

"I hope this isn't an imposition," he said.

"Not at all, Mr. McKinney."

"Would it be a *total* imposition for me to suggest I come to see you sometime today?"

"A Washington summer day . . . is nothing, I'm afraid. If you would not mind a tuna-salad sandwich and iced tea, Mr. McKinney, why don't you make a point of being here shortly after noon?"

She stopped by the west hall and suggested to the President that he might like to hear what Douglas McKinney had to say. The President said the heat had finally weakened him—rain or no rain—and he meant to spend as much time as possible that Sunday in the pool. She understood why swimming was so important to him. What was more, Missy would go swimming with him, and they would spend hours splashing and bantering, wasting time they could never replace. She would have been more than welcome to join him in the pool, but she understood that her presence would have diminished the rare enjoyment he found in these hours—because she could never abstain from earnestly raising some serious subject.

She met Douglas McKinney at a table set up in the rose garden between the House and the West Wing. The rain had stopped, but glistening drops still hung on the velvety petals of varicolored roses. She was casual in a white summer dress. He appeared in a blue-and-white seersucker suit.

"I can't tell you what an honor it is," he said, "to meet the wife of the President of the United States for lunch in the White House rose garden—particularly *this wife* of *this President*."

"We shall enjoy each other's company more, Mr. McKinney," she said, "if we eschew flowery speeches, no matter how sincerely spoken. It is *my* pleasure to meet with you."

McKinney sat down on a white-painted wrought-iron chair, wiped dry only a few minutes before by a White House usher. "I have this sense of intruding in what is not any of my business and imposing on your time, Mrs. Roosevelt," he said.

She fixed her attention for the moment on the black man who was placing a tray on the table. He bore a large pitcher of iced tea with slices of lemon floating among the ice cubes, plates of small sandwiches, sugar and pepper and salt, and a crystal vase of red roses.

"Your motive, Mr. McKinney?" she asked blandly.

He seemed stricken by the candid question. "I—uh—I was a friend of Mr. Colmer, in a minor way," he said. "I can't believe he killed himself. Such an idea is just . . . *unrealistic*. I have to believe he was a *victim*. You understand what I mean?"

"I do," she said as she lifted the pitcher and poured iced tea. "Sugar, Mr. McKinney?"

"Thank you," he said, nodding. "Besides, Ma'am, I believe you find the puzzle intellectually stimulating. Well . . . So do I. Am I presumptuous?"

Mrs. Roosevelt nodded. "Yes, Mr. McKinney, you are," she said. "In a way I find admirable, however."

"I've done something aggressive," he said. "I've meddled. I'm sorry. But my meddling—"

"Have you learned something?" she interrupted.

"Yes. I have found out who killed Mr. Colmer. It's a possibility, anyway."

A distant roll of thunder distracted them for a moment, and both looked up and judged the gray skies, wondering if they would be driven from their table before they could eat their simple lunch. Wind stirred their napkins. Roses nodded and dropped water.

"Another suspect?" she asked.

McKinney nodded. "Senator Lester Stebbins is the father of a very attractive daughter."

"Yes, I know Miss Stebbins. She is very attractive," said Mrs. Roosevelt.

McKinney ventured a wry little smile and a small quip. "As opposed to the senator, who surely must be one of the least attractive men alive." When Mrs. Roosevelt did not object to the comment but continued serving their plates, he essayed further. "The senator," he said, "is an ugly man in more ways than just his gross appearance. He is an illiberal, aggressive, violent man."

Mrs. Roosevelt looked up from their plates. "Indeed?" she asked. "So bad?"

"Miss Stebbins is pregnant," said McKinney solemnly. "She is unmarried . . . and pregnant. Senator Stebbins thinks Mr. Colmer was responsible."

"Oh. And— And how do you know this?"

"In the first place, the senator has publicly exulted over the death of Mr. Colmer. I was at dinner Friday night with Professor Frankfurter, and I overheard some southern congressmen talking about it. Yesterday I—well, I meddled. I made a point of encountering Miss Stebbins—apparently by accident—and asked her to have dinner with me last evening. I picked her up at their home. The senator spoke most bluntly, not to say obscenely, about her pregnancy. And he insisted he knew who was responsible."

"But surely, Mr. McKinney, that does not suggest he *murdered* Mr. Colmer."

"He lives by a violent code," said McKinney. "Miss Stebbins talked about it last night. She is afraid to tell her father the name of the man who is the father of her unborn child—for fear of what he might do to the man. The southern congressmen flatly speculated that Senator Stebbins may have killed Representative Colmer."

"It doesn't make a case, Mr. McKinney," said Mrs. Roosevelt. "For one reason, whoever killed Mr. Colmer had to have *access* to the White House and the West Wing, had to know his way around, too. Senator—"

"Lester Stebbins," said McKinney, "was an assistant to President Wilson from 1915 to 1921. He had an office in the West Wing. He would know his way around."

Thunder rolled again, and the wind freshened.

"It doesn't make a case," Mrs. Roosevelt insisted.

"Am I wrong to have meddled? Would you rather I not bother you anymore with my speculations?" McKinney asked deferentially.

She smiled at him. "No, you've done nothing wrong, and I shall always be glad to hear your ideas. Do beware, though. Others may not be so tolerant of your amateur sleuthing."

The storm broke after another quarter of an hour, and Mrs. Roosevelt hurried back to the second floor. Doug McKinney entered the colonnade and started for his office in the West Wing. He had left his umbrella there. In the colonnade he came on the President and Miss LeHand, swimming in the pool.

"I'm sorry," he said as he walked past. "On my way to my office."

"Ho, McKinney," said the President. "Come in. The water's fine. We have some extra swimsuits."

"Well, thank you, Sir, but I do have an appointment."

"Too bad. Everybody who works here has to prove himself in the pool, sooner or later. Ten laps, McKinney, sooner or later."

"I look forward to it, Sir," said Doug and hurried on.

His father, he reflected, as he walked into the West Wing, would be astounded to know his son Doug could have lunch with the First Lady and then turn down a swimming invitation from the President of the United States. He glanced back. The President was swimming laps. Miss LeHand swam beside him but could not keep up.

The President was a strong man, powerfully muscled except for his legs. His smoking didn't seem to have shortened his breath. Maybe he didn't inhale. His appreciation for the womanly qualities of his secretary was evident, too, and was something he didn't bother to conceal. Her black knit swimsuit fit her as tightly as her skin. Doug paused for a moment, staring back at her and the President, then hurried on to his office on the second floor.

His umbrella was there. He had puckishly used his wastebasket as an umbrella stand. For a moment he considered placing a telephone call to his parents. They always enjoyed hearing about his encounters with prominent people. His mother could not understand why he refused to ask for autographs so he could send them home to her. Maybe this year he would ask the President to sign a Christmas card for her.

He came down the stairs. The West Wing was oppressively quiet on a Sunday afternoon in summer. He did not hear so much as a typewriter clacking, a telephone ringing. Somewhere—at the Departments of War and Navy, anyway, and maybe at the F.B.I.— desks were manned even on Sunday. It wasn't necessary in the White House. The business of government could wait for Monday morning.

Or could it? He was struck by a vivid but indefinable sense that someone was in the Wing—not only that but was aware of his presence and didn't like it. He had an odd sense that he was intruding on something. Something in the air—

At the bottom of the stairs he stood, his ear cocked, alert for a sound. Nothing. Instead of turning toward the exit into the colonnade, he walked south in the hallway and turned left, into the cross hall that led to the Oval Office. Odd. Doors were ajar. The two Secret Service agents on duty that afternoon were in the colonnade, watching the President swim. The police clowns were strolling around somewhere probably; they came through here only at intervals.

The door to the President's study was ajar. Doug pushed it open and stepped inside. To his left was the door to the Oval Office. He tried it. It was unlocked and open when he pushed. He stepped into the Oval Office.

The room was oddly gray. Rain beat against the windows, and the gray skies offered little light. There were no shadows. He—

"It's a damned good thing you know how to scream, McKinney," said Baines.

That was the last thing he remembered—a roaring, guttural scream—and he had not guessed it came from his own throat.

"Minor concussion," the doctor said.

Doug looked around."Where . . . where are we?"

"This is the White House doctor's office," said

Baines. "You were lucky another way. There's no one on duty here on Sunday, but Dr. Hagen lives just a few blocks away—which the police knew."

Doug lay on a black-and-white examining table in an antiseptic room he had never seen before. His vision remained blurred, his head ached as if it had been struck with a blackjack. He pressed down on his elbows to lift himself and succeeded only in swimming away from Baines and the doctor and whoever else was staring at him.

"Back again. Here he comes. Don't force it, Mr. McKinney."

This time his vision cleared. Mrs. Roosevelt was there, and Miss LeHand, still in her black swimsuit, plus Baines and the doctor. The doctor was an old man with white hair and a white beard, wearing a shiny black suit and an old-fashioned wing collar and black bow tie.

"Who did it, Mr. McKinney?" asked Mrs. Roosevelt gently. "Do you have any idea?"

He fixed his attention on her face. "Am I—?"

"Not seriously injured," she said. "Really not. The doctor assures us."

"But who hit you, McKinney?" asked Baines gruffly. "And why?"

Doug tried to shake his head, but it was painful. "I don't know," he muttered.

"And what were you doing in the Oval Office?"

"The door was open. I went in to see why."

Baines nodded, but he was wholly unable to conceal his skepticism.

"We may feel sure, may we not, Mr. Baines," asked Mrs. Roosevelt, "that Mr. McKinney did not knock himself unconscious?"

"I promise you that," said Dr. Hagen. "Even a contortionist didn't strike that blow."

"One thing is perfectly clear," said Missy. "The White House is not adequately policed. Can people just wander through here, whenever they wish? *The Oval Office*—"

"Is not adequately protected," Baines interrupted. "I've been arguing that point for years."

"Though it wasn't bolted from inside this time," said Missy, "still someone had to use a key to get in."

"But why?" asked Mrs. Roosevelt. "Why was someone in the Oval Office?"

"Assuming it had something to do with the death of Representative Colmer," said Baines. "Assuming that—which is by no means an automatic assumption—then we have to wonder if some clue was not left in there. I mean something the killer felt compelled to return to get."

"Melodramatic," said Missy wryly. "What does the President have to do to protect his office against criminal intrusion?"

"Secure an appropriation, Miss LeHand," said Baines. "For a very long time it was an American tradition to regard the White House as a public building and let anyone off the streets wander in. That tradition has not altogether died."

"Still—keys to the Oval Office . . ."

"We are talking about changing all the locks in the West Wing, Miss LeHand. More than a few dollars."

"You're saying the keys are interchangeable?"

Baines nodded. "As we suspected. I spent some time filing one down this morning. Not every key used in the West Wing can be filed down and made a skeleton key, but many of them can."

"The President will insist on security for the Oval Office," said Missy firmly, "even if it means installing hasps and padlocks on the doors."

"Quite frankly," said Baines, "I would recommend it."

Doug tried again to sit up. The doctor helped him, and he managed it, though his head spun, and for a long moment he thought he would fall back. Mrs. Roosevelt frowned over him with motherly kindness.

The handsome Miss LeHand stood back, arms akimbo, regarding him with the cynical skepticism of a woman more nearly his age—though she was in her forties.

"Do you feel up to walking back to the Oval Office with me?" Baines asked.

"Oh, Mr. Baines, surely—"

"Thank you," Doug said to Mrs. Roosevelt, "but I really think I can. I suppose it's better to move around a bit and not give in."

"I would like to know just how he got in, where he was standing when he was struck, what he heard, what he saw," said Baines. "Tomorrow the office will be used again. Later today I suppose Mr. McKinney will want to get to bed."

"Oh, I can—" said Doug. "I'll—"

It was only when he swung his legs over the edge of the examination table and reached for the floor with his feet that he saw the brownish-red stains of his own blood on the trousers of his seersucker suit. It was only then, too, that he saw his jacket draped over a chair, similarly stained with blood. His head reeled, and he almost fell back. He touched his head and found it swathed in a thick bandage.

Dr. Hagen was licking the flap on a little pill envelope. "Here," he said. "When the head aches bad, take one of these. Not more than four a day."

Doug pressed his feet on the floor and found he could stand. "Ugh!" he said. "Like I had too much to drink. A whole lot too much to drink. Woo!"

"If that feeling continues, check in at a hospital," said the doctor. "But I think it will be much diminished by tomorrow, gone by Tuesday."

Doug started. He felt Miss LeHand's arm around his waist.

"We'll help you," she said. She nodded at Baines, and he stepped up on the other side and put a steadying arm around Doug's shoulder. "Ready, Doug?"

"Miss LeHand, I—"

"Missy," she said emphatically. "Missy, not Miss."
Mrs. Roosevelt hung back for a minute to thank Dr.
Hagen for interrupting his Sunday. He could send a
bill to her, she said. Then she followed as Missy and
Baines led the staggering Douglas McKinney out into
the colonnade and past the pool.

The West Wing was well guarded now. Uniformed
police officers watched the halls. Agents of the Secret
Service—wearing their badges on their lapels—scur-
ried from office to office, checking every room. The little party centered around McKinney made its way
slowly along the halls to the entry to the secretaries'
office. They went in and from there walked into the
Oval Office.

"Privilege," said Louis McHenry Howe from the
door to his office at the far end of the secretaries' office. "They wouldn't let *me* in there."

"Epson?"

"Your orders, Sir, were to let *no one* in the President's office."

Baines shrugged at Howe. "I'm lucky the President
didn't come. I will ask everyone, though, not to touch
anything, not to disturb anything. There may be
something to learn in here."

The Oval Office was as it had been when Doug was
there. Outside, the rain had diminished to a drizzle,
and the skies remained dark. Little light came
through the windows, and the room was gray and
without shadows.

They stood for a moment just inside the door, an
odd group—Mrs. Roosevelt in a white summer dress,
Douglas McKinney in the bloodied trousers of his
ruined suit, Missy LeHand in her black knit swimsuit, Gerald Baines in a beige suit with white but-
tons, and Louis Howe in dark blue with gray tobacco
ash—conscious of what place it was, conscious also
that within the past five days two acts of violence had
been committed there, by someone threatening and
not yet identified.

"Please," said Baines. By gesture he asked them not to proceed farther into the room until he had switched on lights. He did, and the yellowish light of floor lamps relieved the gloom. "Now," he said. "What's different? What's out of place?"

The five of them stood, intently staring at the room. Howe was first to shrug. Then Missy shook her head. Mrs. Roosevelt pursed her lips as she looked around. Baines frowned. Doug closed his eyes—his head ached, and his eyes rolled; he was not sure he could see anything smaller than an elephant.

"One thing . . ." said Missy. "You know, it *stinks* in here."

Doug nodded. "Yeah," he murmured. "It did— It did when I came in . . ."

"Stinks?" asked Howe.

Missy strode into the center of the room, an incongruous figure in her black swimsuit. "Stinks," she said. "Somebody's been smoking a cigar in here."

"Yes," said Mrs. Roosevelt. "Definitely."

"So," said Baines. "Are we supposed to believe somebody came in the Oval Office, sat down and leisurely smoked a cigar, was interrupted by McKinney here, and hit him on the head?"

"It stinks . . ." said Doug weakly.

The odor was distinctive. There could be no question. Someone had been smoking a cigar in the Oval Office—and not just any cigar, a cigar with a singular odor. It was not impossible, perhaps, that the odor had clung in the drapes and upholstery since yesterday, maybe even from Friday; but that seemed most unlikely; the odor was too sharp, too pervading.

"The smell was in the hall," said Doug weakly. "I *knew* there was something. . . . In the President's study. The door was ajar, and that's how I came in. And in here. *Strong.*"

"Well," said Baines. "What—"

"*Lord!*" exclaimed Missy. "Look here!"

She had moved to the front of the President's desk

and was pointing indignantly at the glass ashtray there. It had been cleaned. There were no cigarette butts or ashes in it. But lying in the middle, like something foul a dog had dropped, were two big round cigar ashes—and the cellophane wrapper off a cigar.

"Don't touch it!" Baines cried. "Fingerprints—"

Missy pulled back her hand. She leaned over the desk and squinted at the cellophane. "Who smokes Marsh Wheeling stogies?" she asked.

"I'll drive your car," said Missy. "Then I'll get a cab back."

It was apparent that Doug couldn't drive, and Missy was offering to take him home.

"You'll have to wait till I get dressed," she said.

"Really," said Doug, "I can't ask you to—"

"I wish you would accept the offer, Mr. McKinney," said Mrs. Roosevelt. "I won't feel right about you until I know you are safe at home, and neither Mr. Baines nor I can drive you right now. Missy is a very safe driver."

Doug smiled. "All right," he said. "It's kind of you, Missy."

Howe and Baines hurried back to what they had been doing when word came that Douglas McKinney had been attacked in the Oval Office. The President had been hurried upstairs to the family quarters by his Secret Service guard, and Mrs. Roosevelt thought she should go to him now and tell him what had happened.

"Can you stand up okay?" Missy asked when she and Doug were left alone in the Oval Office.

He rose painfully and fought off dizziness. "'Kay," he said.

She put an arm around him. He put his around her. Her swimsuit was still damp.

"Hey," she said playfully as they left the Oval Office and passed into the secretaries' anteroom. "Know what used to happen in that closet?" She pointed to a small coat closet in the corner of the room. "That's where Warren Harding used to make love to his sweetheart. On the floor."

Doug laughed. "I've heard that story."

"It's true. She wanted to do it in the Oval Office, but he said there were too many windows."

Doug laughed again. "On the floor. Among the overshoes and umbrellas."

Missy nodded. "Among the rubbers and umbrellas."

They made their way slowly through the colonnade and into the west hall of the ground floor, then to an elevator and up to the third floor of the White House, where Missy had a small apartment.

"Sit down," she said, offering him a place on the sofa in her small sitting room. "I'll change in the bedroom. There's a bottle of Scotch on the table by the radio, if you want a drink."

"I'd dearly love one," he said, "but I'm afraid of how it might mix with whatever the doctor gave me."

She left her bedroom door ajar as she changed, and the conversation continued.

"What do you plan to do after we leave the White House, Doug?" she asked.

"You mean . . . in 1941?"

"Assuming we're reelected in 1936," she said. "Otherwise, we have to pack our things and leave by January 21, 1937."

"That won't happen," said Doug.

He had never been on the third floor of the White House before. Miss LeHand's suite was comfortable, but it was small and certainly not luxurious. It did not include a kitchen. Apparently she had to have her meals brought up. The rooms seemed to have been laid out in the thought that they would serve not as living quarters but as temporary accommodation for guests who couldn't be accommodated in the single guest suite on the second floor. Missy's rooms were more like a hotel suite than an apartment.

"You can't make a career here, you know," she said

from the bedroom. "The only careers in the White House are for the ushers and so on. A young lawyer— You have to think about what happens when The Boss is no longer President."

"I have thought about it," he said. "Believe you me, I've thought about it."

"You couldn't be working in the White House for the money," said Missy. She appeared in the bedroom door, buttoning a white blouse. "The prestige is wonderful, but you can't deposit it in a bank."

"Actually, you can," he said. "Strictly between you and me. When Professor Frankfurter called me and asked me to come to Washington, I had already accepted an offer from a Wall Street law firm. When I finish my time here, my place in that firm will still be there, with seniority as if I'd been there all along; and the prestige of having worked in the White House is going to be worth many, many dollars."

Missy grinned. "You mean you're not a pure idealist?"

Doug shook his head. "Not I," he laughed. "I didn't sign on to get bopped on the head, either, I may tell you."

"By the man who smokes Marsh Wheeling stogies."

"Right. I'm going to be very anxious to identify that man. When we find him, we've found the man who killed Colmer."

"Not necessarily," she said.

"Ninety-nine percent," said Doug.

She shook her head. "There's something not right in that whole situation," she said. "Why would a man go in the Oval Office, knock you on the head when you came in, then leave such obvious clues as cigar ashes and a wrapper? Did he *want* to be identified?"

"I don't know," Doug sighed. "It's too mysterious for me."

"Okay, kiddo," said Missy. "Where're your car keys?"

He stood. His head protested, and he staggered for a

brief moment. Missy grabbed him by both shoulders and steadied him. Doug threw his arms around her, at first only to steady himself; then, moved by a different stimulus, he clung to her. He put his mouth to the side of her neck and kissed her.

Missy tipped her head to one side and regarded him with a quizzical smile. He kissed her mouth. She let him kiss her, but she shook her head. "Hmm-mm, Dougie," she said quietly. "I'm flattered, but—but no."

"I'm sorry," he said, stepping back from her.

"Don't apologize," she said. "I'm not offended. But the answer is no."

7

"I have a bit of information that may interest you," said Baines to Mrs. Roosevelt. "I'm afraid it is information you are not going to like. It has to do with Amelia Colmer."

He had caught up with Mrs. Roosevelt just as she was getting into her blue Buick roadster. She was on her way to a meeting at the Department of Commerce. Monday morning had dawned fine after the Sunday rain, and at ten it was already hot and humid. She'd had the top taken off the Buick.

"What information?" she asked gravely.

"She has been seen in the West Wing at night. Twice."

"How do you know?"

"As a matter of duty, Ma'am, I've been showing a picture of her to some of the night personnel. As it turns out, I didn't have to show the picture. Henry Taylor, the night butler, knows her from the days when she worked as a secretary in the West Wing. He was taking a tray of coffee to Mr. Howe one night when Mr. Howe was working late, and he encountered Amelia Colmer in the hall. She spoke to him."

"At what time of night?" asked Mrs. Roosevelt.

"Eight o'clock or thereabouts," said Baines.

"And there was another time?"

Baines nodded. "Weyrich, the uniformed officer, says he saw her one night. It could have been the same night, but he says it was ten o'clock when he saw her."

"Not, of course, the night when her husband was killed?"

"No. Several months before."

"It could have been a completely innocent visit," suggested Mrs. Roosevelt.

"It could have been," Baines agreed, "except that she denies ever having been there. I telephoned her this morning at her parents' home in Bethesda. They didn't want to let me talk to her, but when I was allowed to, I asked her to explain what she had been doing in the West Wing at night. She said she had not been in the White House since she quit her job to marry Colmer."

"Your witnesses could not be wrong?"

Baines sighed. "I don't see how. Henry Taylor is an old colored man who's worked in the White House many years. Weyrich is not the world's smartest man, but he's not stupid, either."

"Someone who looks like her . . ." Mrs. Roosevelt mused.

"But she spoke to Henry, called him by name."

"Oh dear, Mr. Baines," said Mrs. Roosevelt sadly. "It is distressing to think of having to subject that poor young woman to interrogation. Perhaps . . . perhaps *I* should do it. A woman can be gentler. Besides, she might respond more forthrightly to me."

"I can't object to your questioning her, Mrs. Roosevelt," said Baines. "I do think I have to be present when you do."

Mrs. Roosevelt glanced at her watch. "Perhaps we

should do it now," she said. "I'd like to have the matter cleared up. I—uh—can cancel my appointment. We can drive to Bethesda in my car."

People recognized the First Lady as she drove through the streets of Washington in her open car. This morning people who were accustomed to seeing her were surprised to see she was accompanied by a man who looked very much like a Secret Service agent. Ordinarily she would not allow the Secret Service to go with her, nor would she let agents follow her in another car.

Baines chuckled as someone waved and called her name.

"What's amusing, Mr. Baines?" she asked.

"I was thinking how very different this is," he said. "Mrs. Coolidge and Mrs. Hoover were fine ladies, but they would never have driven themselves in an open car."

Mrs. Roosevelt shrugged.

"It makes the Secret Service quite nervous, you know."

"So you've told me," she said.

So he had, and so had others; and every time the answer was the same, that she would not be restricted in her movements by having to take guards along wherever she went. "The world is not so dangerous a place, Mr. Baines," she said. "Anyway, who would want to harm *me*? I'm not so important."

They had to stop and ask for directions, and it was almost eleven before she pulled the Buick to the curb in front of the Rowlandson family home, a large white frame house shaded by oaks and elms. Mrs. Rowlandson was sitting in the porch swing.

"Good morning!" said Mrs. Roosevelt.

Mrs. Rowlandson remained silent for a moment, then nodded and murmured, "Good morning . . ."

Mrs. Roosevelt climbed the four concrete steps to the porch. "Is Amelia at home?" she asked.

Mrs. Rowlandson shook her head. "No, she isn't," she said.

"Ah. Will she be back soon?"

Mrs. Rowlandson shook her head again. "Not soon."

Mrs. Roosevelt hesitated.

Baines did not. "Where's she gone?" he asked.

"I don't know."

"Don't know or won't say?"

Mrs. Rowlandson stiffened. "Both," she said firmly. "I don't know, and I wouldn't say if I did."

"Really, Mrs. Rowlandson," said Mrs. Roosevelt gently, "you will have to answer the question sooner or later. I came with Mr. Baines so we could talk on a friendly, informal basis. I suggest your really should tell us."

"Why?"

"Mr. Colmer died in tragic, mysterious circumstances. Amelia is not suspected of . . . of killing him. She may, however, have some information that will be useful to the investigation, and the Secret Service *must* talk to her."

"Well . . . I don't know where she is."

"She was here two hours ago," said Baines.

"That's true, she was. But she isn't here now."

"Did she pack a bag?" asked Mrs. Roosevelt. "Is that why you say she won't be back soon?"

"Yes."

Rexford Tugwell was the President's general-purpose troubleshooter. His office was on the second floor of the West Wing, but most of the time he was away from the White House, traveling here and there. For a week he had been in California, and he was not expected back for another week.

This did not much relieve the work load on his secretary, Darlene Palmer. He sent back packages—scribbled letters and memos to be typed, instructions about people to be called, reservations to be made, meetings to be scheduled. When she was not entirely busy, Darlene helped the other secretaries.

Though she was satisfied with her job and recently was happy with the attention she was receiving from the young banker, Otto Peavy, people who didn't know Darlene might have assumed from her long, sad face that her life was a succession of tribulations and failures. She was a tall blonde. Though she wore glasses and had a long jaw and a pointed chin, she was generally an attractive young woman. She would have seemed more attractive if she had smiled more. Also, she spoke with an adenoidal voice.

This morning she was astounded and appalled to be confronted by an agent of the Federal Bureau of Investigation. At his suggestion they had gone inside Tugwell's office, where the agent now sat behind Tugwell's desk and she sat in the chair facing it.

"The Director has sent me to ask a few questions," he said. He was a young man with a shiny face, wearing a light-blue double-breasted suit. "This has to do with our investigation into the death of Representative Winstead Colmer."

"I don't know anything about it," said Darlene.

"Is this office kept locked when you are not here?" the agent asked.

"Yes."

"Do you have a key?"

"Yes."

"Do you carry that key with you when you leave the White House?"

She nodded. "In my pocketbook."

The agent had a little spiral-bound note pad, and he made notes of her answers—which she wished he wouldn't; it made her nervous.

"Now," he went on, "I believe you have a regular— How shall we say? Gentleman friend?"

"Yes."

"And his name is. . . ?"

"Mr. Otto D. Peavy the Third."

"The son of Otto D. Peavy, the Chicago banker, right? And you and Mr. Peavy are, uh— How shall we say? Intimate friends, right?"

"Yes . . ."

"In fact, you sometimes spend the night with him, don't you? At his home. Sometimes at yours. And sometimes you and he go to a hotel for a weekend. Right?"

Darlene closed her eyes. She nodded. "Yes," she said weakly, unhappily.

"During those times do you take your, uh, pocketbook with you?"

"Yes. Of course."

"And the key to Mr. Tugwell's office remains in it?"

"Yes, but— but what difference does it make? Why do you ask?"

The agent shook his head sternly. "The key could have been taken from your pocketbook, couldn't it?"

"I suppose it could have. But it never was. I've never lost that key."

"That you know about," he said. "But it could have been taken out and later put back in. It *could* have, right?"

"Sure," she said acidly. "And someone could have had a duplicate made and come here and gotten into Mr. Tugwell's office. But—" She shrugged and glanced around the room. "What would you steal out of here?"

"Have you ever tried the key in any other door?"

"Of course not!" she snapped.

"All right. Thank you, Miss Palmer. We would prefer you not tell anyone about this interview. Do you understand? Not . . . *anyone.*"

She nodded, but he was not out of the office a minute before she picked up the telephone and placed a call to the Mechanics' & Husbandmen's Bank.

"Peav," she said quietly and urgently, "I've got to see you. I've got to tell you something."

Gerald Baines sat down across the desk from Lieutenant Kennelly at D.C. police headquarters.

"I can give you a rundown," said Kennelly. "To start with, like you figured, Hoover's G-men are looking at it, too. I had a call this morning, not long after yours. You understand, I suppose, that if they have any information that amounts to anything, they won't give it to me, any more than they will to you."

"Not till they make some headlines," said Baines.

"Right. Anyway, your man Otto Peavy the Third is clean. He's clean in the District, clean in Chicago. On the other hand, what does a young banker need with a bodyguard? He's got one. In fact, he's got on his payroll a couple of guys with records. One works for the bank. And these guys are not clean. He's got an old Chicago hood working at the bank. This guy was a bookkeeper for Capone and Nitti. He did time in Illinois. Odd fellow to have working in a bank, wouldn't you say?"

"What's his name?"

"Walter Tebay. And the bodyguard is Izzy Mullin. His real name is—would you believe it?—Isambard, Isambard Mullin. Izzy's a good guy to have for a bodyguard. Did time for burglary, assault. Here in the District. A nasty little bastard. What's a banker want with him?"

"He rich? I mean Peavy. What kind of home does he have?"

"He gets a salary from the bank, which is not enough to live the way he does. Of course, his father is rich. Otto lives in Georgetown, in a pretty nice house. Drives a Packard. Actually, Izzy drives it for him."

"Did you discover the girlfriend?" asked Baines.

Kennelly shook his head. "No. Has he got a girlfriend?"

"Yeah. A secretary at the White House. Which is one reason why I'm interested."

"The other reason, I'd guess," said Kennelly, "is that you think the father might have wanted to make Colmer dead."

"Elementary stuff," said Baines. "You look at the people who might have had motive, then concentrate on those who had means—in this case, access. And if Otto the Third has hoodlums on his payroll, including a burglar— You see my point."

"What can I do for you?" asked Kennelly.

Baines shrugged. "I think we ought to lay off this element of it for a while—otherwise we and John Edgar Hoover will be stepping on each other's toes. However, I'll appreciate any help you can give me in locating Amelia Colmer."

"Don't s'prise me none," said Lee Bob Colmer. "Y' tell me she's disappeared, it don't surprise me at all."

Baines watched with idle fascination as Colmer rolled himself a cigarette—creasing the paper, pouring tobacco into the crease, rolling, licking the paper to make it stick, finally putting it between his lips and lighting it with a match.

"You wouldn't have any idea where she might be?" Baines asked.

Colmer shook his head. "I'm the last person she'd tell."

"Your brother didn't have a fishing cabin somewhere? Anything like that?"

Lee Bob Colmer shrugged. "Wouldn't've told me if he had."

"Well . . . So what can I do for you, Mr. Colmer?"

"Nothin'. I just stopped in 'cause I'm going home tomorra. Spent more time in Washin'ton than I wanted to. Got somethin' accomplished, I guess."

"What's that?"

"Bunch of us been tryin' to get a bill through the house, to have a dam built on Sipsey Fork, which is a river in our state. My brother wasn't doin' much to help. Fortunately, I was able to convince some congressmen, and the bill is goin' to be reported out of committee."

"So your trip wasn't entirely wasted," said Baines. He spoke innocently, but he was commenting on Lee Bob Colmer's failure to come to his brother's funeral. "Woulda been nice to be able to go back and tell folks you had Winstead's murderer in jail."

"Yes. I wish you could."

"Well . . . it'll be good to get home. I don't think Washin'ton likes me much," said Colmer. He ran the sleeve of his jacket across his forehead. "Rained on me. Twicet. I got caught out in the rain the day I got here and again yestiddy." He rose and turned toward the door. "Y' *will* let me know if y' find out anythin'."

Baines nodded, but his mind was fixed on something else. Rained on him the day he got here . . . rained on him. He said he had come to Washington on Thursday; rode the train all day, he'd said. But it hadn't rained on Thursday. Or Friday. It had rained on Tuesday. Maybe Wednesday, the day Winstead Colmer was killed.

He'd left Alabama as soon as he got word of his brother's death, Lee Bob Colmer had said. But if he got rained on the day he arrived, he was in Washington when his brother died.

"Epson!" he called out to his assistant. "Come in here a minute. I want you to do some checking with railroads, maybe with hotels."

He came to the office at five, as he often did. Otto Peavy was known to the gate guards. They let him enter the White House grounds at will. He could walk on the grounds, enter the West Wing, and climb the stairs to Tugwell's office. Sometimes one of the guards winked at him when he walked out again with Darlene on his arm. This afternoon he was a little earlier than usual. He knew Tugwell was out of town, and Darlene had sounded upset on the phone.

Otto Peavy the Third in early middle age was suffering the loss of his hair. Of a yellowish-sandy color, it was extraordinarily fine and thin, and he wore it very long, so he could comb strands over his pinkish pate. Because his hair was so fine, the wind stirred it as he walked toward the entrance to the West Wing. He was tall. He wore round, horn-rimmed glasses with lenses that were not thick and corrected only a minor tendency to near sightedness. His jaw was long. He had a habit of holding his upper lip slightly out over his lower, which gave them a sort of puckered look. His light-gray suit was single-breasted, expertly tailored to fit him perfectly.

A few minutes after he entered the White House grounds, he returned to the gate with Darlene Palmer on his arm. He exchanged smiles with the guards and walked out to his Packard. His driver was reading a racing paper and did not offer to get out and open the door. He opened it himself. Darlene entered the back-seat and scooted over, and Otto Peavy entered by the same door.

"Okay, so what's the trouble?" he asked her when the car was closed and the driver had pulled away from the White House and was headed out Pennsylvania Avenue toward Washington Circle.

Darlene nodded toward the driver. She knew Peav—as she called him—had few secrets from Izzy Mullin, but she was not sure he would want even Izzy to hear what she had to say. Peavy reached forward and cranked up the glass between them and Mullin.

"The F.B.I. was in this morning," she said quietly. "Asked me a lot of questions."

"About what?"

"About whether or not you could have taken the key to Mr. Tugwell's office from my purse and had a duplicate made. That's what it amounted to."

"What in the world would I want with a key to Tugwell's office?" asked Peavy.

"That's what I asked him. I didn't get an answer."

"Well, what was the idea? Could you figure it out?"

"He said it was part of their investigation into the death of Representative Colmer."

"Did he use my name?"

"Not only that. He knew all about us, that you and I spend nights together. Weekends. He knew that we check into hotels as husband and wife."

Otto Peavy glanced out the window of the Packard. For a moment he pondered, then he sighed and said, "I told you the cops keep an eye on me. It's the same old thing, because my father knew Al Capone and is supposed to have some of his money in the Enterprise Bank. They never give up, you know."

Darlene reached for his hand. "Oh, I know, Peav," she said.

"You didn't tell him anything?"

"No. What could I have told him? I don't *know* anything. Anyway . . . If I did, I wouldn't tell."

He leaned over and kissed her on the forehead. "Good girl," he said.

At the same hour Mrs. Roosevelt presided like a hostess serving tea in the White House rose garden— but over a pitcher of cold lemonade. Lorena Hickok was with her, and Gerald Baines, invited to join her when she stopped at his office to ask if the D.C. police had made any progress toward finding Amelia Colmer.

She raised the subject again. "It is possible something has happened to her," she said.

"It is possible," said Baines, "that her father has driven her somewhere. I found Duncan Rowlandson a bullheaded fellow."

"But what's she hiding from?" asked Hick.

"Me," said Baines.

Mrs. Roosevelt shook her head. "I'm afraid she is. It does look horribly suspicious."

"I'd like to change the subject for a moment," said Baines. "I spent some time going to all the offices in the West Wing, asking some questions. It seems that keys have disappeared with some regularity over the past six months. Half a dozen secretaries told me their keys had turned up missing over the past six months. Some of them showed up again. Some of them didn't."

"Could that bear any relationship to the death of Colmer?" asked Hick. "Could someone have been planning to kill him as far back as six months ago?"

"I'm beginning to think Colmer's death was a part of something bigger, something more complex and continuing," said Baines.

"But *six months* . . ."

"Mr. Howe's secretary told me something else that's interesting," said Baines. "A while back she got the impression that someone was entering his office and reading confidential papers at night. Without saying anything to anybody, she did a little test. For several weeks, before she left for the evening, she moved documents into stacks so they would be exactly two inches or four inches or whatever from the edge of his desk. Some mornings she would come in and find they'd been moved a little. It wasn't the cleaning staff; they were under strict instructions not to touch anything on his desk. She started locking everything up at night, in his office safe. He complains, but she does it anyway. She is convinced somebody was coming into his office and reading his papers—overnight."

"She didn't report this to the Secret Service?"

"She thought she'd solved the problem by putting everything confidential in the safe."

"In Louis's office . . ." sighed Mrs. Roosevelt. "There is utterly no limit to what could be found on his desk. The President confides in him about everything."

"After that conversation with Mr. Howe's secretary," said Baines, "I went back to some of the secretaries, to ask specifically if any of them had had the same experience. I found one more who suspected someone had been entering her boss's office. Darlene Palmer, Mr. Tugwell's secretary."

"Oh, and she's the one who dates Mr. Peavy," said Mrs. Roosevelt.

"Exactly. She told me she came into Tugwell's office one morning and found a paper on the floor that had been on his desk the night before. Once more it wasn't the cleaning staff; they hadn't been in that night. So how did the paper get from the desk to the floor, in a closed, locked office?"

"If it had been Mr. Peavy, she would hardly tell you, would she?" said Mrs. Roosevelt.

"No," said Baines with a thoughtful frown. "Of course—Peavy could be just *using* Darlene. I'm not impressed with her as being terribly bright, and she's no great beauty."

"Well, we—"

Their conversation was interrupted for a moment by the sound of the President's voice, summoning someone to join him in the pool—followed by a great splash as he threw himself from his wheelchair into the water. Louis Howe came walking along the colonnade.

"Louis!"

Howe paused, seemed for a moment indecisive, then decisive, and he walked into the rose garden. "Eleanor," he said. "Hick. Baines."

"Sit down and have a glass of lemonade," said Mrs. Roosevelt.

Howe blew streams of cigarette smoke from his nostrils, drew in more smoke, and sat down. "I spoke to your friend McKinney this afternoon," he said. "Damned if he didn't come to work today—head all wrapped in bandages. Wouldn't you think he'd take a day off? I like a go-getter, but . . ."

"He stopped by to see me," said Mrs. Roosevelt. "Just to assure me he was all right. I told him, incidentally, that Mrs. Colmer is missing and asked him if he had any ideas about that. He and the Colmers were friends, you know. Acquaintances, anyway. He supposed she had gone home to Bethesda. He had no other thought as to where she might be."

"We sent him up to Capitol Hill to observe the Colmer subcommittee hearings," said Howe. "That's probably when he met the Colmers."

"He seems to be an exceptionally intelligent young man," said Mrs. Roosevelt. "Am I correct in that impression?"

Howe nodded. "He's not just bright; he's perceptive; he catches on to things, anticipates what's coming up, and is always ready. Frank and I have talked about him. If he weren't so damn young, he could be the next attorney general. We'll have to give him something good one of these days."

Alexis Saint-Léger Léger had told Mrs. Roosevelt at the state dinner on Wednesday that he wanted to see a performance by the woman he called a world-renowned *artiste,* the fan dancer Sally Rand. This night, almost a week later, he had his wish. Louis Howe had learned that she was opening in a Washington nightclub, and he had telephoned the management and asked for a table close to the stage, yet out of the light, where he could bring a distinguished foreign diplomat to see the show. The manager had never heard of Louis McHenry Howe, but he had heard of the White House, and he consented to make places at his own table—he said—for what he called "the President's guest."

The club was called Coconut Grove—as half the nightclubs in America were—and it seated as many as five hundred people at tables and maybe two hundred more standing around the bar. Sally Rand had been the sensation of the 1933 Chicago World's Fair, called the Century of Progress Exposition; it was said she had drawn bigger crowds and made more money for the backers of the fair than any other show or exhibit, and the Coconut Grove filled to capacity that night.

Howe had thought it proper to bring a Secret Service agent along, and he had offered the duty to Baines, who had accepted. At Howe's insistence, he was carrying a pistol in a shoulder holster. ("Never know what kind of bozos you might run into in a place like this," Howe said.) The French embassy must have had the same idea—in different words—because Alexis Saint-Léger Léger was accompanied by an armed French security agent. The manager was distressed to find his guests of honor—whom he was strictly forbidden to introduce—were four men, not the two he had expected, but he led them to their table and sat down with them.

"My name is Tolstoy, gentlemen—you should believe it," said the short, swarthy manager of the Coconut Grove, speaking in a heavy accent. "Ivan Tolstoy. No relation to the great Russian writer, though he was my countryman. I'm one of those many Russians who fled the Bolsheviks and one of the few fortunate enough to find refuge in the United States. Welcome. Accept a bottle of champagne on the house, please."

"Honored," said Léger with a courtly nod at Tolstoy.

"We are fortunate to be able to book Sally Rand in our club," the Russian went on. "You know, she is not easy to get—and she is very expensive."

"She dances in the nude, I understand," said Léger.

"Absolutely naked," said Tolstoy.

"You won't be raided?" asked Howe apprehensively. Tonight a police raid at the Coconut Grove, with Alexis Saint-Léger Léger, could become an international incident.

"I can assure you they won't be raided," said Baines with a faint smile. "Not tonight, anyway."

"Ah, so," said Tolstoy. "Have I friends in high

places? Thank you. I will join you again later. The
waitress will be here in a moment."

Sally Rand was not the whole show. She was preceded by a pair of jugglers, a singer, a small troupe of
acrobats. Then, with a roll of drums, flashing lights,
and the breathless voice of Ivan Tolstoy roaring
through loudspeakers, she was presented: "The great
Sally Rand . . . and company!"

The "company" appeared first, six uniformly tall
dancers, uniformly blond, uniformly dressed—undressed, actually—in the absolute minimum of pink
feathers. They were a chorus line, and for ten minutes
they danced under the bright lights, kicking, whoop-
ing like can-can girls, and raising anticipation for the
appearance of the star.

The chorus girls pranced off. The stage was Sally
Rand's; she didn't share it. The lights dimmed and
turned a rosy color. She swept out from the wings, a
very tall blonde, a lithe graceful dancer, barefoot but
high on her toes as she took the center of the stage
and faced the crowd. She carried two large fans made
of fluffy white feathers. She held them to her body,
and they covered her. She moved them, and they un-
covered her a little.

The crowd cheered.

She turned and again rose on her toes. With her
back to the crowd, she spread her arms and held the
fans away from her. She let everyone see that she
was, in fact as promised, stark naked. Then she
turned again and began to dance. The band played
her music, and she danced.

Her performance was a most exquisite and erotic
tease. As she danced she moved the fans, always
gracefully. When she faced the crowd and moved
slowly, the fans covered her breasts and her most private part. When she exposed herself she pirouetted so
fast that the crowd had only a glimpse of her naked-

ness—enough of a glimpse to fire their imaginations and make them suppose they saw more.

Her act didn't amount to much, except that it was a display of talent; and she was able to keep her audience spellbound for almost half an hour. At the end she threw the fans apart as the lights went off, leaving the cheering crowd not quite certain if it had seen, or had not seen, the famous dancer absolutely naked and from the front.

"I bring her to your table," said Tolstoy.

A few minutes later she came down from the stage and sat down with the French diplomat, the President's closest adviser, and their two guards. Except that she wore stage makeup, she was a pretty young woman, with a fresh, innocent face. She wore a pink satin gown that hung over her figure like falling water. The lights in the club had been so dimmed that few people knew Sally Rand was seated at a front table, and no one approached.

"Miss Rand, meet Monsieur— Uh, *you* introduce him," Tolstoy said to Howe.

"Monsieur Alexis Saint-Léger Léger," said Howe. "I'm Louis Howe. Mr. Baines and . . ."

"Duclos," said the French security man crisply.

Sally Rand offered her hand to Léger. "I've seen your name in the newspapers, Monsieur," she said. "You are Secretary-General of the Quai d'Orsay, aren't you?"

"I am," said Léger, beaming. "And you are, Mademoiselle, a great *artiste*."

"Thank you," she said sweetly.

Ivan Tolstoy raised his hand and summoned a waitress. "More champagne for my guests," he said.

During her Washington appearance, Sally Rand was staying at the Langford Hotel. Her whole troupe was staying there—her musicians and the six tall girls of her chorus. Ellie, her makeup assistant and the girl in charge of her fans and clothes, could not stay there, since the hotel would not accept Negro guests. Ellie was staying in a Negro hotel, as she did in every city. This annoyed Sally Rand, who would have liked to have Ellie close to her, but she could do nothing about it.

She walked down the long hall of her eighth-floor suite. It was two in the morning, after her second show for the Russian, and she was tired. She had her key in her hand. She put it in the door, turned it, pushed the door, and— Dammit! The door was chained.

"*Amy!* Open the door!" Sally banged on the door. "Open the door, Amy!"

Nothing. Sally Rand stood for a moment in the hall, gritting her teeth, growing angry.

"*Amy!* Amy, goddammit! Open the goddam door! I'll *sue* you!"

"Sally. . . ?"

"Yes, Sally, you little bitch. Open up!"

Amy pulled the door shut, and Sally could hear her rattle the chain. She pushed the door back and stood there naked, eyes filled with sleep, her mouth open, yawning.

"Hey, kid! For Christ's sake! Hey, you're my friend; but, kiddo, you can't lock me out of my own goddam hotel room. C'mon, Amy! I'm tired! Stand to one side! What the hell is this?"

The dark-haired young woman stepped back and let Sally Rand into her own hotel room. Sally shook her head, grinned, and kissed her on the cheek. Satisfied, she laughed. The girl she called Amy tottered back toward the bed.

She was Amelia Colmer.

8

COLMER DEATH INVESTIGATION
FOCUSES ON—NOBODY IN PARTICULAR
F.B.I. Enters Case

By Jim Patchen

Six days after the mysterious death of Representative Winstead Colmer in the Executive Wing of the White House, the investigation into that death seems stuck on center. Investigators are not even prepared to say if the death was a murder or a suicide.

Gerald Baines, Special Agent for the Secret Service, has been placed in charge of the investigation, so far as the White House is concerned, while various detectives of the D.C. police seem to be taking an interest on behalf of the City of Washington. Lieutenant Edward Kennelly, speaking for the police, said his depart-

ment is "only helping the Secret Service." Agent
Baines acknowledged that the Secret Service is
without any positive clues as to exactly how Representative Colmer met his death.

Mr. Lee Bob Colmer, brother of the deceased
congressman, left on an afternoon train for Alabama yesterday, complaining sadly that "it
doesn't look as if they ever will figure it out."

The F.B.I. Enters

Yesterday the Federal Bureau of Investigation
officially entered the case. A statement released
by chief of G-Men, J. Edgar Hoover, says that
President Roosevelt asked him to take charge of
the investigation. "I have no doubt," says Director Hoover, "but that we will reach a conclusion
within a short time." He urged the Secret Service
and the District police to turn over to him all information they have gathered. "With their cooperation, we should clear up the case in a few
days."

The job of a Secret Service agent was to protect the
President. It ordinarily did not involve detective
work. In particular it did not involve entering other
people's houses without their consent. So when
Gerald Baines decided he should have a look inside
the Colmer home in Georgetown, he called Lieutenant Kennelly and asked him to come with him.

They arrived in mid-morning, driven to the house
in a marked District police car by a uniformed officer.
Kennelly told the officer to drive down the street and
turn around, to be available if they came out, but not
to be conspicuous. He used a skeleton key to admit
him and Baines to the modest red-brick house.

"I want to check something upstairs first," said
Baines, and he climbed the stairs. He entered the bedroom, then immediately turned and nodded at Ken-

nelly. "Somebody's been here. Somebody besides Amelia Colmer."

"I'd guess so," said Kennelly. Two drawers had been pulled from the dresser and emptied on the bed. A few pieces of woman's underwear and some handkerchiefs were scattered across the bed. A brassiere and a panty girdle had been tossed on the floor. "Somebody was in and out in a hell of a hurry," he said.

Baines glanced around. He looked in the closet. "Somebody knew just what he was looking for. Nothing else disturbed. Somebody was looking for something he expected to find in those drawers."

Kennelly opened the drawer of the nightstand by the bed. "Look at this. Checkbook. Look. One check missing, with no entry for it. Uh-oh! You thinking what I am?"

"Yeah, right," said Baines.

They hurried back downstairs to the telephone in the living room. Kennelly carried the checkbook with him. He dialed the telephone number of the bank and asked to speak to the chief cashier.

"Lieutenant Edward Kennelly, District of Columbia police. I'm going to give you an account number. I want to know if a check was cashed on it yesterday. You can call my headquarters if you want to, and I'll call you back in five minutes. . . . No? Okay. Here's the account number—one-one-three-four-eight. . . . Yes, it's an official investigation. . . . That's right, Colmer. All right, you got a check signed by Mrs. Colmer—four hundred seventy-five dollars. Leaving a balance of—? Eighteen dollars. Good enough. Thank you."

Baines nodded. "No surprise, huh? When she moved, she moved fast. And with that amount of money on her, she could be a long way from Washington by now."

Kennelly sighed. "Yeah. Well, we might as well look around."

They explored the kitchen, then the living room

and tiny dining room, then climbed the stairs to the second floor once more, neither of them able to diminish their sharp sense of intrusion. This was someone's home, and they were in it without permission. Neither of them felt easy about it.

Even so . . .

"Ed, this room almost tells a story," said Baines as they stood once again just inside the bedroom door. "She packed before she left. Summer clothes. See, her wool things are still in the closet. She took a suitcase to her parents' home in Bethesda. Then, I'd guess, when she got my call she rushed back here, grabbed a check, and hurried to the bank to withdraw money. Then after that somebody else entered the house and—" He nodded at the scattered underwear.

"What makes you think the somebody else came here *after* she did? Why not before?"

"Oh, I could be wrong," said Baines. "But— Well, if she had come in *after* this was done, wouldn't she at least have picked the things up off the floor? It couldn't have taken her two minutes to stuff all her things back in the drawers and push the drawers back into the dresser. Somehow I think she'd have done it. I— Am I wrong?"

Kennelly shook his head.

"And how'd he get in, do you suppose?"

"It's easy enough. *We're* in."

Baines smiled. "Cops and burglars have their ways. Regular citizens don't. Maybe the guy had a key."

"A friend of Amelia's, you think?"

Baines shrugged. "A possibility, isn't it? And possibly her husband's killer."

Mrs. Roosevelt had accepted an invitation to a picnic lunch on the grounds of Fort Humphreys. General Douglas MacArthur, chief of staff, had invited her somewhat casually during a visit to the White House. She had all but forgotten the invitation—though she had made no conflicting plans for that Tuesday's lunch hour—and was a little surprised when she received the call saying that a Major Eisenhower, aide to General MacArthur, was downstairs, ready to escort her to lunch at Fort Humphreys.

She knew why she had been invited to this little picnic. General MacArthur was constantly wheedling the President for more funds for the army. He went around Secretary of War Dern, used his personality and influence to gain entry to the West Wing, sometimes without even an appointment, and caught the President at odd moments to explain the urgent necessity for this and that. The President tolerated him. The President thought him a capable officer and was willing to allow him his idiosyncrasies—though he allowed himself to be little influenced by MacArthur's entreaties.

The President and Missy had a little joke about General MacArthur. It was in fact a serious matter, but to them it was a small joke on the sometimes-pompous general. The columnist Drew Pearson had come to the President several weeks ago and in private had told him that General MacArthur kept a beautiful girl in a suite in the Hotel Chastleton—this though he lived with his aged mother in the chief of staff's official quarters at Fort Myers. The serious part was that the girl was demanding money of the general, for her silence. He was being blackmailed, nothing less. The President, though, could not take it terribly seriously, because it was hardly a major scandal for a divorced middle-aged man to have a girlfriend. The joke was that the general was so afraid of his mother.

Major Eisenhower was a raw, dead-serious officer who seemed awed by his assignment to pick up the First Lady in a car and drive her to Fort Humphreys. Dressed in boots and breeches, with a Sam Browne belt over his jacket, he was elaborately deferential; and she wondered if he was able to smile.

Shortly she learned that he could. "I'm surprised

you're not taking me down to the fort on a streetcar," she said. "I've heard that's how officers go from the War Department to the Capitol when they testify before committees." Major Eisenhower proved to have a broad, merry grin.

What General MacArthur had described as a picnic was of course an elaborate luncheon on tables set with linen and silver. He provided champagne and courses of hors d'oeuvres, then cold meats and a salad, later coffee and a tray of desserts.

It *was,* though, on the lawn, and for a diversion the general had arranged for the officers stationed at the fort for the Army War College to play softball on an adjacent field. Actually, Major Eisenhower told her later, they played nearly every day.

"The War College, General," she said to Mac-Arthur. "It seems almost a contradiction in terms, doesn't it?"

MacArthur smiled. "'Ain' gonna study war no more,' hey? Unfortunately, we have to. I'm afraid we have no choice at all, Mrs. Roosevelt."

"World is full of enemies? Are you thinking of Herr Hitler?"

"Personally," said the general, "I'm thinking of Comrade Stalin. Also—and more immediately hazardous—the Japanese militarist clique. I find it entirely possible we will have to fight a war with Japan to protect our interests in the Pacific."

"Have we, in fact, any interests there that are so vital?" she asked. "I know, of course, that we have Hawaii, but that is farther from Tokyo than from San Francisco and could hardly be the subject of Japanese ambitions."

"The Philippines," said MacArthur. "We have promised the Filipino people liberty and democracy. I take that obligation very seriously. And China. What kind of world will we live in if we allow China to fall into the hands of a military dictatorship imposed by Japan?"

"I hope you are unduly pessimistic, General," she said. "We have such difficult problems to solve here at home, it is difficult to focus one's attention on such distant places."

MacArthur raised a glass of champagne in salute. "May God grant that my pessimism is exaggerated and my commitment to military preparedness an excess of caution," he said.

Mrs. Roosevelt sipped champagne. She looked at the younger officers playing softball. "What do these officers study?" she asked.

"Contingencies," said General MacArthur. "What our country would do if Stalin invaded Germany, Hitler invaded France, the Japanese attacked the Philippines, someone attacked the Panama Canal, and so on. Contingency plans. So our country would not be wholly unprepared, in terms of strategic planning."

"Who are they?" she asked.

"Ike," the general prompted his aide.

"They'll be our generals if there's a big war," said Eisenhower. "Except the shortstop. He's Bill Halsey, a navy captain. The umpire is Captain Jonathan Wainwright. They call him Skinny. The pitcher is Major Omar Bradley. He'll be leaving in a few days. His next assignment is teaching at West Point."

Later she was introduced to these officers and others. She found them unprepossessing. As always, she observed in professional military and naval officers a certain country-clubbishness, a sort of detachment from reality. Though what they were studying might be the ultimate reality, they lived their lives very much separated from the ordinary realities, and it marked them.

Major Eisenhower drove her back to the White House. "It's been an honor," he said to her. "We have met before, you know. At the reception you and the President held for officers."

"Yes, of course. Did I meet a Mrs. Eisenhower?"

"Yes. Mamie. She was honored."

"Oh, Major Eisenhower, you are not honored every time we meet. Let's say it's pleasant. That's good enough."

Once more he displayed his wide grin.

Mrs. Roosevelt chuckled. She had insisted on riding in the front seat with him, so she saw his grin.

"Military strategy is something of an intellectual puzzle, isn't it?" she asked. "That's why military leadership, along with law, medicine, teaching, and the ministry, are called the five learned professions. Right?"

"Yes—plus the fact that each of those professions is supposed to be devoted to the public benefit, rather than just earning a living."

"But you are devoted, to a great extent, to finding novel solutions to difficult problems, are you not?"

"Yes, Ma'am. I think you could say that."

"Well, tell me, Major— If you wanted to murder a man, why would you choose the Oval Office, of all places?"

He glanced away from the street ahead, into her face, perhaps to judge how seriously she asked. "You are talking about the death of Congressman Colmer?"

"Yes. Does it strike you—as a problem of strategy and tactics—that the Oval Office is a most unlikely place? Doesn't it present enormous difficulty, more than almost any other place? What's more, since a limited number of people have access to it, wouldn't you in some sense be pointing a finger at yourself if you killed a person there?"

"I can think of only one reason to do it there," said Major Eisenhower. "Maybe it was the only place where the killer could get the Congressman to meet him alone."

"He left on the floor a pistol bearing no fingerprints but Mr. Colmer's," she went on. "And he left, and somehow he managed to get out of a room where all the windows and doors were not only locked but bolted."

"Maybe by that he outsmarted himself," said Major Eisenhower.

"What do you mean?"

"There has to be some idiosyncrasy in the Oval Office," he said. "There has to be a way out of the room with all the doors and windows apparently fastened from the inside. *There has to be*—unless we believe in witchcraft. The point is, the murderer knows that idiosyncrasy. Apparently no one else does. But he does. So the killer is someone with special, intimate knowledge of the Oval Office."

"So we are looking for someone who—"

"We are looking for someone exceptionally observant," said Major Eisenhower. "We are looking for someone who stood in the Oval Office and saw something everyone else has overlooked. Or we are looking for someone with special, intimate knowledge of the room."

"I had supposed," she said, "that we would find our killer first, through his motives and so forth, and when we knew who it was we would discover how he did it. You are suggesting that maybe we are going about it backward."

"I wouldn't want to suggest that," said Major Eisenhower, "but if I were you, I'd give some additional attention to how the murderer got out of the room."

She did. Returning to the West Wing, she found that the President was meeting with some of the members of his cabinet, in the Cabinet Room. The Oval Office was open but vacant. She asked Missy to join her, and she stood in the center of the room, pondering, studying every feature of the windows and doors.

They examined the windows once more. When each

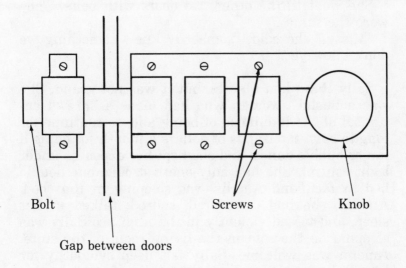

Bolt   Screws   Knob

Gap between doors

handle was turned, the blade filled the hole behind the brass plate. Every handle and blade was solid.

The bolt had been replaced on the double doors between the Oval Office and the President's study.

"Locks . . . *and bolts,*" said Mrs. Roosevelt to Missy.

"The trouble with the bolts is that they're so damned *simple,*" said Missy.

Mrs. Roosevelt bent close to each of the bolts on the three sets of double doors. They were all alike. "Yes," she said. "So childishly simple. Like this."

She seized the knob on the door to the study and slid the bolt back and forth. It did not slide easily; some pressure on the knob was required to move it. She shrugged and discarded the idea that a thin blade, thrust through the narrow gap between the doors could have been wobbled back and forth and moved the bolt by friction. No. The thickness of the doors and the narrowness of the gap, plus the stubbornness of the heavy old bolt, precluded that.

She went to the other two doors with bolts. They were the same.

"Missy," she said, "somebody knew something we don't know yet."

Sally Rand had a suite, but it was not grand. She was a businesswoman who had made a shrewd appraisal of the likelihood of being able to continue for long to earn thousands of dollars a month for doing a fan or bubble dance, and she kept her expenses under tight control. She had only one bedroom, one double bed in fact, and Amelia was sleeping in that bed. Amelia, she had discovered, snored, talked in her sleep, and tossed violently in the night, so Sally was sleeping on the sofa in the living room of the suite. Amelia was welcome. Sally felt deep sympathy for her. But somewhere there had to be an end to this arrangement.

Also, Amelia intruded on her privacy.

"I don't mind who sees any other part of me bare," she said to Amelia, "but, dammit, I do hate for *anybody* to see my face bare of makeup."

Sally was preparing to go to the Coconut Grove for her two evening performances. "Look," she said to Amelia. "Be sure you have something to eat brought up."

"I'd rather you'd bring me something," said Amelia.

"Okay, I'll have something sent up from downstairs," said Sally. "I'll tell 'em one of my girls is sick in bed in my room, so they should put the tray down and leave. 'Kay."

"'Kay. You understand, don't you? It's the reporters I—"

"Not the cops. Yeah. Sure. Listen, I do ask you one thing. Don't invite the guy here. I mean, *you* may not be suspected, but I betcha *he* is."

"He had nothing to do with . . . anything. Besides, nobody knows."

"Your husband didn't know?" Sally asked suspiciously.

Amelia shook her head. "He didn't even know I was pregnant."

Sally was dressing and now pulled her dress down over the elaborate underwear she had been tugging into place as they talked. "I still don't know what you're hiding from, kid," she said.

"Win didn't kill himself," said Amelia. "Somebody murdered him, and they think I did it."

"With you on the lam, of course they think that."

"They'll catch the guy," said Amelia. "Then they'll leave me alone."

"Maybe with you on the lam, they'll quit looking for anybody else," said Sally.

"Bingo!" exulted Bill Epson. To him "Bingo!" was an all-purpose expression, hardly related to the game they played in the parish hall at St. Catherine's. When he was a child and fell down, his mother would exclaim "Bingo!" When his father found a tool that had been lost, he would yell "Bingo!" instead of "Eureka!" And young Bill, when an idea came to him, or when something that had been mysterious suddenly clarified itself in his mind, "Bingo!" was invariably his thought.

The Exeter Hotel! "Bingo!" Thank God at least he had been able to sit in the office and contact hotel after hotel by telephone, rather than tramp the streets. He had called—how many? Twenty-five? Anyway, the Exeter responded affirmatively. Yes, a Mr. Lee Bob Colmer had been their guest. When had he checked in? Monday evening of last week.

Epson settled his straw hat on his head—a hard, flat boater with a sporty blue-and-gray band instead of the canonical black. He stopped at the office manager's desk on his way out and drew expense money— two nickels for trolley fare. The manager pushed the nickels across the desk as Bill signed the chit—with as much gravity as a man might affect if he had been disbursing a thousand dollars.

Shortly Bill was on the trolley, and shortly after that he walked into the lobby of the Exeter Hotel on Second Street, handy to the railroad station.

Lee Bob Colmer had stayed at a modest hotel, not a luxurious one, yet a hotel typical of Washington, typically filled with politicians from the city halls and state capitols, come to Washington on government business. The floor of the lobby was a mosaic of little octagonal white tiles, with some blue ones set in to make the letters of the name of the hotel, in a frame. Ceiling fans stirred the air and cigar smoke. The fans also stirred the skimpy green fronds of the potted palms. Heavy, sweating men sat on heavy oak-and-leather chairs and couches, smoking, talking, fanning themselves with their hats. Some held canes between their knees. Some read newspapers. In late afternoon their cigar and cigarette ashes filled the brass bowls of the smoking stands. Some of them sat near the big brass cuspidors and hawked tobacco juice more or less accurately into their wide funnels. It was a lobby that women did not enter, except on their husbands' arms. In fact, an unescorted woman venturing in—unless she was sixty years old or more—would be politely but firmly asked to leave.

Bill Epson went past the cigar-and-news stand, to the desk. "Epson," he said. "Secret Service." And he showed his badge to the clerk.

"You're too late," said the clerk. "John Wilkes Booth checked out of here on November 4, 1864, and never even came back for the valise he left in his room."

Bill had heard jokes like this before. The smile with which he acknowledged it was so brief and so wan that the clerk cleared his throat and asked what he could do for him.

"I want to see the registration of a Mr. Lee Bob Col-

mer," said Bill. "He checked in a week ago yesterday."

The clerk turned over the pages of the big registration ledger until he came to the right day. "Colmer . . . Okay. Checked in about nine that evening.
Took a three-dollar room. Checked out yesterday."

Bill took a folded piece of onionskin paper and a
pencil from his jacket pocket. "I'll trace that signature," he said.

The clerk watched, frowning curiously, as Bill laid
the sheet of translucent paper on the page and with
laborious care made a pencil tracing of the signature.
He also traced the guest's writing of his address in
. . . in Alabama.

"Anything else?" the clerk asked.

"Who's the night clerk?" Bill asked.

"I am. To midnight, anyway. Noon to midnight is
me."

"All right. Tell me about Colmer. Did he have visitors in his room?"

"You mean girls? No, Sir. We don't allow that in the
Exeter."

"I don't mean girls," said Bill.

"Ah . . ." The clerk frowned, looked around, then
leaned forward and said quietly, "Are you here because of what happened to Mr. Colmer's brother?"

"Yes."

"So. All right. Look. Mr. Colmer was an . . . ordinary sort of guest, nothin' unusual about him. He
came down here to the lobby mornings and met other
gentlemen. They talked. He usually had breakfast in
the coffee shop, usually with other gentlemen. But—
Well, there was one unusual incident. You slip back
in the office, around the corner there and the door to
your left, and I'll—"

Bill rounded the corner. The clerk unlocked the
door. He asked Bill to wait a minute while he went to
get someone who could tell something about the fat

gentleman from Alabama. In a minute the clerk returned.

"This here's Lincoln Randolph. He's the room-service waiter, nights. Let him tell ya what happened."

Bill Epson glanced toward a chair, but he suspected the Negro would not sit down in the office—which he didn't. He was a thin man, almost emaciated in fact, with a shaved head. He wore the white uniform of a room-service waiter.

"Tell the man about Mr. Colmer, Lincoln," the clerk prompted.

"Gent'min called fo' pitcher of ice water every night," drawled Lincoln Randolph. "He drink it with his whiskey. Every night. No tip. Never give me a nickel. Never say thanks, even. Jus' say, 'Put it on the nightstand, boy.'"

"This gentleman would be interested in the fight, Lincoln."

Lincoln Randolph nodded. "Second night he wuz here. That'd be . . . Tuesday, week ago tonight. He calls for ice water, same as always. I fetch it. But come to the door of the room, I kin hear terrible argument inside. Gent'mins yellin' at each other. I mean, *loud!* They's mad, plain enough. I don' think I should knock on door, that goin' on, so I carries the pitcher back downstairs. Pretty soon come a ring. 'Boy, where's that ice water?' I go back up. 'Put it on the nightstand, boy.' They stop they big fight jus' long enough for me to come in and get out. Then back at it. I could hear 'em as I go down the hall."

"What was it about, could you tell?"

"Naw, Sir. The one gent'min did yell somethin' about as how t' other gent'min was goin' make him go bust. I hear that."

"Anything else?"

"Naw, Sir. I didn't hang around. I wuz afraid, tell you the truth, they might go to shootin' at each other, they's that mad."

"All right," said Bill. "Now I'm going to show you a

picture." He reached into his pocket and took out an envelope, and from that a small print. "Is that one of the gentlemen?"

The black man stared solemnly at the photograph for a moment. He nodded. "That's him. Not Mr. Colmer. That's the other gent'min was in the room."

"Which one yelled he was going to go bust? Could you tell?"

"Yes, Sir. That was Mr. Colmer. He talk like southern gent'min. T' other man didn't."

"T' other man" was Winstead Colmer.

Doug McKinney couldn't settle a hat firmly on his head, over the thick bandage that wrapped it, so he went out without a hat, feeling a little strange, feeling indeed that he must look like a Hindoo. He still did not feel like driving his car, so he took a cab to the senator's house.

He knocked on the door. Senator Stebbins himself answered.

"Good evening, Senator. I wonder if I could speak with Miss Stebbins for just a moment?"

Senator Lester Stebbins stared at him for a moment. "Wha' happen t' you?" he asked. "Been in a fight in a barroom?"

"As a matter of fact I was slugged from behind in the President's Oval Office," said Doug loftily.

The senator grinned. "Frank Roosevelt does let funny folks in the White House. What y' wanta see my daughter 'bout?"

"I spilled some steak sauce on my shirt the night she and I had dinner, and she was kind enough to wipe it away with her handkerchief. I've had her handkerchief laundered, and I want to return it."

"Well . . . Y' *are* some kind of gent'min. Come in an' set. I'll tell her you're here."

Doug took a seat in the senator's living room. In a moment the senator returned.

"Excuse me, Senator. Do you mind if I light a cigar? Can I offer you one?"

Senator Stebbins pointed at a bottle of bourbon and some glasses on a table by the window. "Pour y'self a shot, boy," he said. "What kind cigars you smoke up Connecticut way?"

"I happen to have a couple of nice Havanas here," said Doug.

"Well, I do accept," said the senator.

Doug smiled and nodded and handed him one of the two Havana cigars he had bought on the way here. Neither of them had a cigar clipper. They bit off the tips, Doug spitting his in his hand and putting it in an ashtray, the senator blowing his across the floor. They lit the expensive, fragrant cigars, and the senator leaned back and savored his with conspicuous pleasure.

"I don't smoke cigars often," said Doug. "Frankly, I don't much enjoy any but these Havanas, and they are expensive."

"I won't offer you one of mine," said the senator. "Not right now, anyways. It would be offensive to this fine handful of tobacco to match it against one of my usual smokin' stogies."

"What kind are those, Senator?" Doug asked.

"A real man's smoke, I'll tell ya," said Senator Stebbins. "I do favor 'em. Yessir, I do favor my Marsh Wheeling stogies."

9

"I suppose," said the senior Otto D. Peavy coldly to J. Edgar Hoover, "that a man ought to have some emotional reaction to the fact that the Director of the Federal Bureau of Investigation traveled all the way from Washington to Chicago—*and by airplane at that!*—to confront him in his office and ask accusatory questions. In fact, you count on that, don't you, Mr. Hoover? You count on a man's becoming emotionally distraught by the news that the F.B.I. finds him so important a fellow. Well, allow me to tell you, Mr. Hoover, that I am *not* distraught, I am not impressed, and I am not in the least afraid of you. So state your business pretty damn quick, or I will have you *thrown* out of here."

Clyde Tolson rose from his chair. "The Director—"

"Sit down, Junior G-man," said Peavy. "I'm not talking to you."

Otto Peavy, Sr.—actually he was Otto Peavy, Jr.; his son was Otto Peavy the Third—was a great bull-frog of a man, with a great square head, wearing a

141

formidable white mustache. His white hair had departed from the top of his imposing head, but it was thick behind. He wore a pince-nez attached to a black ribbon, an old-fashioned wing collar, a big diamond tiepin, and a double-breasted fawn waistcoat under the black wool jacket of his suit. He faced J. Edgar Hoover with a stern, defiant, condemning stare.

"Do you have a warrant, a subpoena, or something?" he asked Hoover.

"Uh . . . We came for an exploratory talk," said Hoover.

"Are you soliciting a bribe?" asked Peavy.

Hoover shook his head. "Why, no, not at all!" he protested.

Peavy nodded. "Then what's an 'exploratory talk'?" asked Peavy.

Hoover glanced at Tolson, then around the room. The president's office in the Enterprise Bank was an oak-paneled sanctuary, and the bank president sat at a massive desk on which he had a battery of four candlestick telephones. Behind him two tall windows rose to a twenty-foot ceiling, guarded by dark-red velvet drapes. The walls at the two sides of the office were lined with glass-front bookcases, filled with leather-bound books. The couches and chairs in the office were upholstered in redolent black leather. The carpet was the same dark red as the drapes, and thick; it took footprints.

Hoover drew breath and made one more attempt to master the situation. "A member of the Congress has been murdered, Mr. Peavy," he said. "That member of Congress was the chairman of a subcommittee that was about to subpoena you—"

"You mean Colmer," said Peavy.

Hoover nodded. "Representative Colmer."

"Are you suggesting, Mr. Hoover, that I had anything to do with *murder*?"

"Mr. Peavy . . . I'm not suggesting anything. I am trying to get as much information as I can about—"

"You flew to Chicago on the off chance I might know something about the death of Winstead Colmer?"

"I—"

"I know nothing about it, Mr. Hoover. Does that make your trip worthwhile?"

Peavy settled back in his chair and clasped his hands on his vest front, in the attitude of a man who has just rid himself of a nuisance. Ostentatiously, he withdrew a large gold watch from his vest pocket and carefully studied the time.

Hoover opened his mouth to speak, but Peavy had something more to say.

"You do win my approbation for a part of your work, Mr. Hoover. I like the way you track down bank *robbers*. That's good. But I suggest that *bankers* are out of your league. So far as Mr. Colmer was concerned, I judged him to be a headline-seeker. He was damaging the financial community. I'm not going to say I am sorry he met misfortune. I am going to demand of you, though, that you disclose—*now*—any information you have that might tend to suggest I had anything to do with his death."

"I . . . uh, I have none at this time," said Hoover.

Peavy smiled. "Ah, I thought not. Such being the case, I invited some representatives of the newspapers to attend us at this hour. Let us issue a joint statement, Mr. Hoover—that you came to ask me for some information, that I cooperated fully and gave you all I had, and that you are fully satisfied that no one in my several organizations is in possession of any information that would suggest a solution to the unhappy mystery surrounding the death of Representative Colmer. Let us meet the press, Mr. Hoover. Or . . . Or we can meet my lawyers, who also await."

"Damn!" yelled Baines the next morning, Wednesday. "Damn!"

He pushed the newspaper across Kennelly's desk. The page-one story that angered him read:

F.B.I. PROGRESS IN COLMER MYSTERY
HEAD G-MAN IN CHICAGO
Special to the Washington Record
from the Chicago Press

J. Edgar Hoover, chief of the F.B.I., in Chicago as a part of the Bureau's continuing pursuit of surviving members of the Dillinger gang, took half a day off this morning to meet with Otto D. Peavy, president of the Enterprise National Bank. The purpose of the call was to solicit Mr. Peavy's cooperation in the nationwide investigation into the mysterious death of Congressman Winstead R. Colmer (D., Ala.). Mr. Hoover asked Mr. Peavy to give the F.B.I. access to the extensive investigative resources of the big Chicago bank.

"A banking organization like Enterprise," said Director Hoover, "comes into possession of vast amounts of valuable information in the course of its business. Mr. Peavy has agreed to set his staff to work to sift the bank's files, looking for clues that may help the F.B.I. to close this case rapidly."

Bank president Peavy said he was always happy to extend his cooperation to agencies of the federal, state, and local government which . . .

Kennelly grinned and pushed the paper back across his desk. Then he shook his head. "You can't fight him in headlines. That's his specialty."

"I'm tempted," growled Baines, "to back out of the investigation and let him flounder."

"*We* have, a couple of times," said Kennelly. "So

he'll fail to catch a bank robber, then he'll run off and grab headlines for catching another. You can't win. What he's chiefly captured is the public imagination."

When Baines returned to the White House—still early, before nine o'clock—he found a note on his desk, saying that Douglas McKinney would like to see him and would come to his office if Mr. Baines would call. Instead, Baines walked over to the West Wing and climbed the stairs to McKinney's office.

Except for the President's office and maybe that of Louis Howe, offices in the West Wing were modest. The whole wing had the character of a structure hastily thrown up for temporary use, in the anticipation it would shortly be torn down and replaced by something grander—which had in fact been the intention when it was built thirty years before. McKinney's office was spartan.

He sat behind a desk that bore marks put on it by three decades of predecessors—black burn scars from forgotten cigars, blue-black ink stains, scratches. His wooden chair reclined a bit, and swiveled, but it squeaked shrilly with every move. Stacks of papers were scattered over the desk, the window sills, even on the floors. McKinney was untidy.

He sat in his shirt sleeves and light-gray vest, the bandage still wrapped around his head. "I appreciate your coming, Mr. Baines," he said. "Believe it or not, I am still a little woozy."

"You're entitled," said Baines.

McKinney leaned back in his chair, which emitted a nerve-shattering shriek. Baines started and grimaced, and McKinney smiled. "I, uh . . ." he ventured. "I realize it would be intrusive of me to meddle into your investigation of the death of Representative Colmer."

"Why? Everyone else is doing it."

McKinney grinned. "Well—I do have a personal interest, now that I've been injured by—can we say, by the murderer? No, I suppose not. But by someone. Anyway, I have meddled just a bit. I want to tell you what I've found out."

Baines nodded. "Go ahead."

"Miss Jane Stebbins, the daughter of Senator Lester Stebbins of Mississippi, is pregnant. She is not married, but she is pregnant," McKinney said. "The senator thinks the man who caused her pregnancy was Winstead Colmer. I don't know what justification he had for thinking so, but that's what he thinks. Now—"

"Are you suggesting the senator killed Colmer?"

"No. I am only giving you information. You can draw your own conclusions. I took Miss Stebbins to dinner Saturday evening. Last evening I called on her again."

"*You're* not the one who—"

"No, Mr. Baines," McKinney laughed. "I never met her before last week—though I had seen her around town and knew who she was. Anyway, last night I dropped by their house, saying I was returning a handkerchief, which wasn't true. While I waited for Miss Stebbins to come downstairs, I chatted with Senator Stebbins for a few minutes, and I found out something. In fact, I found out something I had suspected might be true."

"And that is. . . ?"

McKinney smiled, with an unmistakable air of triumph. "The Senator smokes Marsh Wheeling stogies," he said.

Baines lifted his hands before his chin and rubbed the palms together. He frowned thoughtfully. "The makers of Marsh Wheeling stogies might be curious to know you suspect only one man in the city of Washington smokes their cigars."

"A small series of coincidences, then," said McKinney. "A man who smokes this somewhat unusual brand was in the Oval Office on Sunday afternoon. A man who smokes this unusual brand suspected Colmer of having violated his daughter. A man who smokes this brand prides himself on what he imagines is a southern gentleman's code of honor—which would include doing violence on a man who did that to his daughter. *And* a man who smokes this brand and had this motive to kill Colmer—who was killed in the Oval Office—is very familiar with the West Wing."

"How would he be familiar?" asked Baines.

McKinney put his finger on a long black scar in the wood of his desk. "Cigar burn, hmm? Maybe a Marsh Wheeling stogie. Lester Stebbins, then a young Mississippi lawyer, occupied *this* office from 1915 to 1921. He did for President Wilson much the same job I now do for President Roosevelt—though God knows how, considering the level of the man's intelligence. Politics makes strange bedfellows, as they say. Anyway, he was in the West Wing every working day for six years. He knows his way around here."

"And when he left, he kept his keys, you think?" asked Baines. "Kept them twenty-three years, against the day when—"

"Or remembered that the locks are primitive," said McKinney.

Baines sighed. "Yes. All right. Obviously you've given this much thought. If we suppose that Senator Stebbins killed Representative Colmer in the Oval Office last Wednesday evening—sneaking past all the guards, overcoming the locks, and somehow managing whatever trick was used to get out of a locked and bolted room—we still don't have an explanation of *why* he was in the Oval Office, happily smoking a stogie and leaving the ash and wrapper. That's a bigger mystery than how he got through a bolted door."

McKinney frowned darkly. "Is it absolutely clear that Congressman Colmer did not take his own life? Is that possibility entirely—"

"If for no other reason," said Baines, "I think the condition of the pistol settles that. Why would a man wipe every fingerprint off a pistol, then handle it with his bare hands when he used it to kill himself? Why would there be no fingerprints on the ammunition in the chambers? Whoever killed him did it very, very cleverly; but he outsmarted himself in the way he handled the pistol."

McKinney nodded. "Yes, I see that. But, returning to my experience in the Oval Office on Sunday—"

"*Why did he come back?*" Baines interrupted firmly.

"To pick up a clue he had left behind," McKinney suggested.

"And then leave his cigar wrapper in the ashtray?"

"Fingerprints on the cellophane?" asked McKinney.

"No. None."

"Like the pistol then," said McKinney.

"Well . . . Yes. Like the pistol," Baines admitted.

Amelia had ventured down to the hotel lobby as soon as the early crowd was gone. She wanted to use the telephone, and she was not sure if the hotel operator kept a record of calls made from the rooms. She did not want this call recorded on Sally's hotel bill.

She said her name was Jane Stebbins, and the call was put through immediately.

"Honey? It's me. I had to call you. I know you said don't, but . . . No. It's okay. . . . Yes, I've come down to the lobby, but there's no one here. Honey, I . . . I can't. I can't even think of that! They might put me in jail! You . . . I *know,* but I just . . . Well, how long's it gonna take? End of the week, I'm gonna get out of town. Promise me . . . Okay. Okay, it was stupid. But you know why I had to do it. Jesus, what a mess! I . . . Listen, don't forget how much I love you. Don't forget for a minute. Right. I'll take care of it some way. I haven't got much time. You might send some money. For you know what. . . . Okay. I love you, baby. Always."

Mrs. Roosevelt had just finished telling Gerald Baines about the suggestion made by Major Eisen-

hower when Bill Epson came to the door and diffi-
dently asked if he could have a word with Baines.

Baines gestured that he should step in. Mrs. Roosevelt had come to his office, and so far the conversation, turning as it did around the suggestion by the
army officer and McKinney's tale of the Marsh
Wheeling stogie, was—in Baines's judgment, anyway—leading nowhere in particular; and he was willing to interrupt the conversation to see if Epson had
learned anything new or useful.

"You've been a little difficult to reach this morning,
Mr. Baines," said the young agent. "And were last
evening. I have some information I think you want."

"About Lee Bob Colmer?"

"Yes, Sir."

"You can talk in front of Mrs. Roosevelt. Uh . . .
You *have* met Mrs. Roosevelt. You damn near blinded
her last Wednesday night with your flash camera."

Bill Epson blushed. "I'm sorry, Ma'am," he said.

"Quite all right, Mr. Epson," she said. "Please sit
down."

He sat rigidly erect on a straight wooden chair and
stiffly recited what he had learned at the Exeter
Hotel. "Then I went on to the railroad station," he
said. "It wasn't so easy. I had to go back this morning.
Anyway, I found out that Mr. Lee Bob Colmer did not
go home to Alabama when he left Washington Monday. He set off for Chicago, on the B & O Railroad.
Anyway, that's the ticket he bought—B & O and the
New York Central, to Chicago."

"Chicago . . ." Baines repeated.

"I should like to know what he's doing in Chicago,"
said Mrs. Roosevelt.

"There are a million people in Chicago," said
Baines, "but what would you like to bet I can name
the one he went to see?"

"Your theory, Mr. Baines?"

"Otto Peavy," said Baines grimly. "I'd bet anything
he went to see Otto Peavy."

When Bill Epson had left the office, Mrs. Roosevelt

got up and closed the door. "I have a suggestion, Mr. Baines," she said. "I suspect the files of Representative Colmer's subcommittee may contain information pertinent to the investigation. I suspect the subcommittee staff may have information that would be helpful. I shouldn't be surprised if they are not confused, unsure of just how they could be helpful."

"That could well be," said Baines.

"My suggestion is that Mr. McKinney be sent up to Capitol Hill to interview the subcommittee staff. He was sent there before, as a White House observer of the subcommittee hearings. The staff lawyers know him."

"Good idea," said Baines.

"I will ask my husband or Louis Howe to have Mr. McKinney particularly commissioned to make the inquiry. He can go up there with a bit of *status*."

Congress was in recess. It was not customary for it to remain in session through the soporific heat of Washington summers. Besides, 1934 was an election year; members had to get home and campaign. Even so, many members of both houses were still in Washington. Politicking kept them there. The New Deal had made the capitol city the nation's focus; and politicians who wanted to get things done—and wanted to get newspaper coverage and have people back home *know* they were getting things done—stayed on in Washington, worked days, and at nights enjoyed the hospitality of the lobbyists.

As Doug McKinney entered the House office building, he saw nearly as many congressmen and staffers as he would have seen on a day when the Congress was in session.

He had a vivid sense of being at the center of the most important things happening in the world right now. He had a sense also that he had made a place for himself in the seat of power and that he had a bright future. He had, anyway, if he did not make some asi-

nine mistake. Washington was a city of opportunity,
but it was also full of traps.

In spite of the inroads by the southerners and west-
erners, Washington was also still a town where background and connections counted. When he reached
the office of the Auditing Standards Subcommittee
and gave the secretary his name, a young lawyer he
had roomed with at Cambridge broke off whatever he
was doing and came out.

"H'lo, Bucky," he said. The lawyer's name was
David Buckingham, a fellow happy hotdog, recruited
for government work by Felix Frankfurter. He and
Bucky had been together at Harvard as undergradu-
ates, then as law students. "When we gonna get away
for a clambake?"

Buckingham shook his head. "Can *you*?" he asked.
"The death of the chairman has got us really screwed
up. Hey, what the hell happened to you? Somebody
bean you with a baseball?"

"Long story," said Doug. "And I'm here on official
business. Got an hour?"

"You kidding? Official business?"

"Mission for The Boss," said Doug.

"F.D.R.? Well, come in anyway. What's the story?"

Buckingham was a young man of chronically sober
demeanor, short, slight, anemic-looking. He wore
round, horn-rimmed glasses. Doug knew that Buckingham could drink strong men under the table,
which he had done, Prohibition or no Prohibition,
during their years at Harvard. He drove too fast. He
was known in every high-class bordello from Boston
to Washington. He spent his father's money and enjoyed life. People who didn't know him wouldn't have
guessed it from his appearance.

He shared an office with two other lawyers. Only
one was in, and when he told him Douglas McKinney
had come on official business from the White House,
that young man left, said he'd slip out for a drink.
Buckingham sat down before one of the battered old

rolltop desks, and Doug sat before another. An oscillating fan atop the third desk blew air across them alternately, also stirring papers and dust.

"Haven't seen you for a while, Doug," said Buckingham. "They keeping you busy?"

"Yeah. You wouldn't believe how I've been tied up."

Buckingham shrugged and sighed. "Same here. But we have a feeling it's all over. "The death of Colmer—"

"Say, I'm sorry about that," Doug interjected. "I know you liked the guy."

"Didn't *you*? I thought you did. He liked you. He used to ask about you when we were playing poker. Wanted to know why you didn't come for Friday-night poker anymore."

Doug grinned. "To be perfectly honest, Buck, I got bored with all the southern-fried claptrap. Every Friday night—" He shook his head. "No, thanks. Twice a year would have been plenty."

Buckingham frowned. "I learned to respect the man," he said. "Not all his friends, maybe. But Winstead Colmer . . . If you'd gotten to know him, Doug . . . There was *depth* to the man. If you'd played poker with him enough, you'd have found out how much, how very damned shrewd he was. Anyway, we think the investigation is all over. He was the driving force."

"Too bad."

"Yeah. Well. Official business, you said."

Doug nodded. "Official business. As you know, it's pretty well been concluded that Colmer didn't commit suicide. Somebody did him in. The Secret Service and the F.B.I. are working to find out who. The President—actually, Mrs. Roosevelt—thinks there may be clues in the subcommittee files."

"They think he was getting too close to somebody?" asked Buckingham.

Doug nodded.

"Like the Peavys," Buckingham suggested.

"Like the Peavys. Got any ideas, Bucky?"

"I can tell you—in confidence—what we were looking for," said Buckingham. "I can tell you what the rumor is and what we thought we might find out."

"Please."

Buckingham leaned back in his chair; it tipped and squealed, and Doug grimaced.

"The repeal of Prohibition ruined the illegal beer and liquor business," said Buckingham. "The mob tried to keep it, but the public deserted them for the lawful brewers and distillers—for the good, honest product. On the other hand, the gangsters still had a lot of money, plus organization, and they looked around for other businesses. I need hardly tell you some of the things they've gone into—gambling, prostitution, corruption of labor unions, waterfront rackets, construction, laundry services, and above all trucking."

"Why trucking?" Doug asked.

Buckingham grinned. "To haul beer, you needed a lot of trucks. Now you're out of the beer business, and you've still got a lot of trucks. And muscle boys. It fits. Anyway—"

"Banking," Doug prompted.

"Right. You're a mobster, you make a lot of money. What are you going to do with it? You can't just splash it around. Al Capone's doing time for tax evasion. The boys caught on. So they're putting their money in legitimate business, where it will be difficult to trace. Now . . . Loan-sharking is no good. That's a street racket, with violence. But suppose you could lend your money out, for a good rate of interest. You'd not only get the interest; you'd gain control of worthwhile businesses."

"So Enterprise Bank of Chicago," said Doug.

"Maybe," said Buckingham. "Mr. Colmer thought so. That was the next focus of our investigation."

"What would he have found out?" Doug asked. "Off the record."

Buckingham drew a deep breath. "He would have

found out that the Enterprise Bank holds some fifty
or sixty million dollars in funds that cannot be ac-
counted for by any proper standard of bank accounting. He would have found out— Well, you have to
understand, Doug, that Peavy and his lawyers would
have done anything they could to prevent having to
disclose any of this—so I'm *assuming* he could have
forced the testimony out. Anyway, he would have
found out that the bank pays interest on those funds
at a rate of about eight percent—"

"*Eight!*"

"Eight," Buckingham confirmed. "Which means the
bank is lending the money out at maybe eighteen.
Usurious rates. Totally illegal. And of course the
loans are going to all kinds of questionable enterprises."

"What about the bank here in Washington, where
Peavy the Third works?"

"Mechanics' & Husbandmen's? It's a funnel. Some
of the money comes to Washington, Baltimore, Phila-
delphia, Richmond . . . The loans are arranged here,
by Peavy the Third."

"None of which has been proved," said Doug.

"Anything in which racketeers are involved also involves violence—or potential violence at least," said
Buckingham. "If you are talking about murder, I am
talking about people who are capable of committing
it."

"Inside the Executive Wing of the White House?"

"Wherever. I understand Mr. Colmer was killed inside a locked room. These are the kind of people who
would know how to pull that off."

"Get in the *White House,* Buck? It's not the same
as—"

"Not the same as what? You think it would be more
difficult to get inside the White House than to get inside a bank? These bankers have bank *robbers* on
their payrolls."

Doug frowned. "Complicates everything . . ." he muttered.

"Complicates what?"

"I've begun to favor the theory that Colmer was killed by the angry father of a pregnant daughter. I know, he was your hero, but—"

"I know what you mean," said Buckingham. "I've heard the story."

"Did Colmer hear it?"

"It's pretty widely around on Capitol Hill," said Buckingham.

"Then why didn't he squelch it? Why didn't he go to the senator and tell him it wasn't true?"

Buckingham shrugged. "I don't know, Doug. I wish I did."

When Bucky suggested the two of them go to dinner, maybe afterward to a performance by Sally Rand at the Coconut Grove, Doug was elated. "If you don't mind going with a man who looks like a Hindoo," he said, touching the bandage around his head. "On the other hand, I doubt we can get tickets. I hear her performances are sold out."

"Oh, ye of little faith," laughed Bucky. "Did you ever know Buckingham the Magnificent to fail to scrounge up the necessary admission? I mean, who was it got you in backstage at the Old Howard in Boston? Who was it who got you appointed an escort at the debutante cotillion in—"

"Right," said Doug. "Who was it who got me a date with a debutante with the face of a horse and voice to match?"

"She was worth ten million bucks, Doug-o."

"Worth it is right," said Doug. "That's what I'd want as compensation for having to take her out again."

"Oh, ye of little taste," laughed Bucky.

He made some phone calls. Doug was used to his

phenomenal abilities as a manipulator, but even having witnessed them repeatedly he was astonished when they arrived at the Coconut Grove and were not only met in the lobby by the proprietor—a man with the improbable name of Ivan Tolstoy ("No relation to the great Russian writer")—but were escorted backstage to meet Sally Rand before she went on stage.

"I've heard your name so very often," Doug said to her.

"From the White House," she said. "I seem to have devotees there. When is the President coming?"

Doug was surprised at the scene backstage. Here sat Sally Rand, a star who was earning God knew how much for her week in this club, in a squalid little dressing room, ill-furnished, ill-lit, and not very clean. She had already undressed and was sitting in a short pink satin robe, applying some sort of coloring to her legs. The famous fans stood in a corner. Her other prop, the immense balloon she used for her tease in the second show, filled much of the room.

"Poke it," she said, pointing to the balloon. He did, with a finger, and found it a surprisingly tough, resilient balloon. "Can't pop it with a pin," she said. "Not even with a cigarette. If they could do that, they'd leave yours truly standing in mid-stage mother-naked, and likely that'd bring on the cops."

"Could you join us for a drink somewhere after the show?" Bucky asked her. "Or dinner?"

"Thanks," she said, "but I've got to get back to my hotel. One of my girls is sick and rooming with me. Can't leave her alone too long."

"Maybe if she feels better she could join us," Bucky suggested.

"Don't press Miss Rand, Buck," said Doug.

"Some other time, boys," she said. "So, pardon me from here to there, but I've got to let my hair down, get my clothes off, and get on stage. See you out front."

Ivan Tolstoy had given them a front-row table—

with the comment that someone else from the White House had sat at that table opening night. Bucky declined his offer of champagne and called for a bottle of Scotch. "Your good stuff, Ivan, not what they make in Chicago."

They watched the performance. Twice Sally Rand flicked her fans across their table, once leaving a tiny bit of feather floating on Doug's drink. She *was* fascinating. So much that they decided to stay for the second show.

"Ask you something," Doug said as they sat between shows, drinking their Scotch—the Cutty Sark was now gone halfway down the label. "Was Colmer by any chance getting ready to subpoena anyone from any little bank in Alabama?"

"You're thinking of brother Lee Bob," said Bucky. "No. There was no love lost between those two, but Lee Bob is not an officer or stockholder of a bank."

"He didn't go to the funeral."

"So we noticed. I'm not surprised. He was always after the congressman to do something—sponsor this legislation, oppose that—and he was a nuisance around the office. He'd come in sometimes and take over the congressman's office when the congressman was out. He'd sit in there and roll those damn home-made smokes of his and go through the desk. He was big brother, and he seemed to figure he had every right."

"They argue? I mean, so you could hear it?"

"Oh, yes. Bitterly."

"Tell me something," said Doug. He was well aware that Bucky's speech had become slurred; he was unaware that his had, too—and worse. "Can you think of anything *negative* about your hero congressman. There must have been a chink in his shining armor someplace."

Bucky shrugged. "I don't know. He drank a bit too much. I don't think his relationship with his wife was too good."

"Why do you say that?"

"She used to call him sometimes when he was playing poker, urge him to come home. He would be drinking, and he spoke pretty hard to her, I thought. Then she quit calling. I think he . . . I think he may have regretted marrying her. His family hate her. And they didn't have children."

"She's pregnant now, of course," said Doug.

"She *is*? I didn't know that. How do you know she is?"

"Uh . . . Well, Mrs. Roosevelt told me."

"And how would *she* know?"

Doug grinned. "Mrs. Roosevelt knows *everything*."

Sally Rand's second performance was with the balloon. Because she could not cover herself nearly as well behind the balloon as she did behind the fans, she wore brief, flesh-colored panties, which people at up-front tables could see but which the rest of the audience only suspected. Once again, she danced gracefully. With the lights very low, she held the balloon above her head and showed side and rear views of her long, smooth, slender body. There was something nearer art, and much less tease, in the balloon dance than in the fan dance. But it won her less applause.

The show was over. The crowd pushed for the door. Doug and Bucky were caught up and jostled. They were in good spirits, even so, happily on the verge of staggering drunk. Bucky carried the nearly empty bottle of Cutty Sark, his fist tightly squeezing the neck.

"Hey!" he said abruptly to Doug. "Looka there!"

Doug looked around. He shook his head. He wasn't sure what Bucky was talking about.

"There ya go," said Bucky. "And there's the key to a hell of a lot. Right there."

"What you talking about?"

Bucky gestured that Doug should lean close. "Look who's together over there. Look who brought whom to the show. You don't know them? The guy with the glasses like mine is Otto Peavy the Third. And the guy with him is Roland Kraft, the senior Democrat on the subcommittee, the one who's gonna succeed Winstead Colmer as chairman—and the one who's gonna kill the investigation into the Peavy banks."

10

Darlene Palmer had mixed feelings about the long absences of her boss, Rexford Tugwell. Although she had less work to do, she was always self-conscious about sitting in an office with little or nothing to do, hearing from up and down the halls the clacking typewriters of overburdened secretaries. She could never escape the nagging fear that she might be looked on as *unnecessary*, that someone walking past and seeing her at her desk reading a newspaper would decide to eliminate her job and leave her unemployed. Unemployment was a fearful thing, she knew; her father had lost his job in 1931; and she would never forget the impact of that dread notice. So, while she enjoyed being able to relax with a cup of coffee and scan the Thursday-morning *Washington Record;* her pleasure in it was mixed with guilt and apprehension.

This morning the newspaper carried a feature article on the mysterious death of Congressman Winstead Colmer. All the papers had been following that, some

160

more assiduously than others. He'd been found dead just downstairs, in the Oval Office, which gave the story an immediacy to her that it wouldn't otherwise have had. It was scary to think about, a man killing himself, or being killed, right here, where you worked every day. She was glad it had happened at night when she wasn't here. She began to read the article:

It has now been three days since anyone has seen or talked to Mrs. Amelia Colmer. Calls to her house and to her family home in Bethesda, Maryland, go unanswered. A call to the Colmer family home in Tuscaloosa, Alabama, was answered by the late congressman's mother, but when we asked if anyone there knew the whereabouts of Amelia Colmer, the lady hung up.

In the meantime, the inquiry drags on here in Washington. We are given to understand that the F.B.I.

Continued on page 6.

Page 6. Darlene turned to that page. Here were pictures of the Colmers—the late congressman, his wife, and—Darlene started. The third picture was of a man she recognized! He was . . . The caption said:

Attorney Lee Bob Colmer, elder brother of the late Congressman Winstead Colmer

Darlene frowned. Sure. She hadn't heard his name. The fat, sweaty man who talked like Li'l Abner.

He had appeared at the door of Peav's house one night, unannounced, not particularly welcome, she had guessed, but determined to engage Peav in conversation. Peav had let him sit down at the table where they had been dining. It had been embarrassing; she had been wearing a nightgown and peignoir at the table, and her hair had been loose; she had been without her glasses and had had to pick them up and put them on to see who was joining them.

And he'd sat there, rolling and smoking ragged cigarettes, drinking Peav's bourbon, and drawling with as much urgency as he could bring to that drawl—a cryptic conversation she had not been able to understand at all, not a meaningful word of which could she remember.

But why had he come to Peav's house? And why had Peav received him? The brother of a congressman mysteriously dead . . .

Maybe they had been trying to head off some kind of trouble.

Buzzers sounded in the offices of the West Wing. The President had reached the ground floor of the White House and was on his way through the colonnade. People who wanted to see Franklin D. Roosevelt, be the recipients maybe of a presidential wave and grin, stepped out of their offices and stood along the halls. No matter that the administration was sixteen months old; this President held his mystique, and long-time civil-service workers, who would not have risen from their desks to see Calvin Coolidge or Herbert Hoover come by, stood in their doorways and bade good morning to the President of the United States.

He reveled in it. The President—first cigarette of the morning, or maybe the second, burning at the end of its holder, which was firmly gripped in his teeth—smiled and nodded and waved as he propelled his light wooden wheelchair along the halls. Arthur Prettyman hurried along behind him, but the President liked to move himself, and he propelled himself at a fast pace with arms and shoulders necessarily grown strong.

He sped through the lobby, turned right, then left, into the secretaries' office. Missy held open the doors of the Oval Office, and the President passed through. "What's up?" he asked.

"Before your appointments schedule starts," said Missy, "there's a report here you ought to look at. From the Bureau of Labor Statistics. I underlined in red—"

"Read me what you've underlined," said the President as he lifted himself from his wheelchair to his armchair and Arthur Prettyman rolled the wheelchair into the adjacent study.

"All right," said Missy. She stood before his desk. "Average annual income for an American family— $1,348. That's an improvement."

The President nodded. "On our way back to 1929 levels," he said.

"Average weekly wage for a factory worker," she went on, "$19.91. For a white-collar office worker— $20.76. For a white-collar worker at the executive level—$49.16. Okay?"

"Looking up," said the President. "But what about spending figures? Is the cost of living—"

"Average annual expenditure for housing—$456," she said. "Including utilities. For food—$472. One family out of two owns its own automobile. How 'bout that? Three per cent of American families own their own homes. And so on. This report will be made public shortly. Okay?"

"Okay!" the President laughed. "So what next?"

"I'm sorry, Boss," said Missy. "I know you're trying to forget it, but you haven't really forgotten that you have to meet with Huey Long this morning."

"Lawd!" said the President. "No, I haven't forgotten. I've kept trying, the same way I used to try to forget Friday evenings when my mother was sure to force a tablespoon of castor oil down my gagging throat. I'm gagging, Missy . . . I don't suppose we could tell him I'm— No, we couldn't. Send in the Senator from Louisiana."

Senator Long's father once said, "My mother and my father favored the Union. Why not? They didn't have slaves. They didn't even have decent land. The rich folks had all the good land and the slaves—why, their women didn't even comb their own hair. They'd sooner speak to a nigger than a poor white. There wants to be a revolution, I tell you. Maybe you're surprised to hear me talk like that. Well, it was just such talk that my boy was raised under." Of Huey, his brother Earl said, "He's the yellowest coward that God ever let live." Of his conduct of the governor's office in Louisiana, his brother Julius said, "There has never been such an administration of ego and pomposity since the days of Nero. They beat a man almost to death, if he does not agree with them. A human life is not safe, and neither is his property. I don't know how they conduct elections in Mexico or Russia, but I don't think they could surpass what has been going on in Louisiana." When Franklin D. Roosevelt was elected President of the United States, Senator (since 1932) Huey Long said, "I never felt so tickled in my life. He told me, 'Huey, you're going to do just as I tell you,' and that is just what I'm agoin' to do."

This was the man, the Senator from Louisiana, who had asked to see the President this Thursday morning. The President supposed it was over the old question of patronage. He had refused to accept the senator's recommendations for a single political appointment in Louisiana. Senator Long had screamed. Again and again.

"Frank, I don't give a damn 'bout 'pointments," said he as he breezed into the Oval Office. "Didn't come to talk about 'em."

The President could not, of course, rise to shake anyone's hand, but the senator leaned over his desk, knocking over a glass donkey, and seized the President's hand. He was called The Kingfish, after the character on the Amos 'n' Andy radio show. He carried with him a boater straw, which he had tossed on a chair as he came across the room; and he was wearing a white linen double-breasted suit, with a wide green-and-yellow necktie. His grip was *too* hearty, his voice *too* friendly.

"I come t' tell you it ain't true, Frank—Mr. President. They won't be a Huey Long party in 1936. No, Sir. I ain't runnin' 'gainst my President."

"Pleased to hear it, Huey," said the President.

"No, sir. Why, if I was to turn 'gainst you in the Dem'crat convention, 1936, why, that sucker Al Smith might rear his ugly head ag'in. No way."

The President had long since learned not to believe a word The Kingfish spoke. But he smiled and said, "Well, good, Huey."

"Come t' see y' 'bout somethin' else," said Long conspiratorially.

The President nodded. Rarely did Long come to the point very quickly.

"Frank, I got a li'l project I dearly hope you'd see fit to support," said The Kingfish.

The President grinned. "What is it, Huey? Highway? Dam? Dredge a channel somewhere?"

"Frank, we got a problem, some parts o' th' *South*. Folks down there's in special need. I don't have t' tell ya. Special deep poverty in my part the country. And they's a *chanc't* o' heppin' some them folks. Make 'em firm Roosevelt Democrats. Make the same of a lot o' people. Little job. Little project. Hmm?"

"Called what, Huey?"

"Called the Sipsey Fork Reservoir. In Al'bama. Not even in my state. But big benefit to a lot o' people."

"Really, Huey? Real benefit?"

The Kingfish nodded soberly. "Really, Frank. *Really* big benefit." He shrugged. "'Course . . . 'Course we can prob'ly work some what y' call *mutuality* into it. You know what I mean."

"Like?"

"Well . . . You know. S'pose somebody was to deposit, say, a hundred thousand dollars in a bank somewheres, in the name of, say, Cadwallader P. McGillicuddy. And s'pose *somebody*, nameless now, was to *be* Cadwallader P. McGillicuddy. It c'd be *anybody*, Frank. Like, you got a son in business in California, I b'lieve. If he was to be Cadwallader—"

"I understand you, Huey," said the President.

"Well?"

"I believe the late Congressman Colmer, from Alabama, opposed this project."

Huey Long grinned and shrugged. "Oh, sho'," he laughed. "Winstead, he got to be a *Washin'ton* kind of fella, lost all *idee* what his constituents back home wanted, needed. He *dead*, though, Frank."

"So an obstacle to the Sipsey Fork dam project has been eliminated," said the President.

"Oh, le's don' use the word *'liminated*, Frank. Sounds like *ominous*."

The President of the United States swelled with indignity. "Who *murdered* Winstead Colmer, Huey? Do you have any idea?"

The Kingfish lifted his shoulders high and turned up his palms. "As God's my witness, Frank, I don't have the least idea."

"Who, besides you, is interested in the Sipsey Fork project?"

Huey Long shrugged again. "Thousan's of li'l people—"

"No, Huey, not thousands of little people. *Who?*"

The Kingfish ran his hand over his unruly dark hair, which had fallen over his forehead, as it did often. "Well . . . of course, they's *banks* interested, land developers, state legislators, county officers . . . why—"

"Jobbers," said the President.

"Why, *no*! Thousan's of *little* people."

"Tell your 'little people,'" said the President, "that any bill that contains an appropriation for a Sipsey Fork dam will be *vetoed*. Tell them also that any officer in the Army Corps of Engineers who ventures to recommend such a project will be cashiered from the service. Is that plain, Huey? Is that clear enough that even *you* can understand it?"

An hour later Huey Long sat in another office, talking to another man, in a building not far from the White House.

"Well, I thank y'," he said. "I give it my best shot." He shoved an envelope into an inside pocket of his suit jacket. "I tol' y' how he'd react. The man's got awful uppity since he got in the White House."

Otto D. Peavy the Third flexed his clasped hands and cracked his knuckles. "I'm afraid we're going to have to close our books on the whole Sipsey Fork deal," he said. "Fortunately, we didn't put much into it."

"You got somethin' in it more than money," said The Kingfish. "You got a big problem."

"What do you mean?"

Huey Long leaned back in his chair and grinned. "Some way, last week, *Congressman* Colmer chanced to get himself killed. Besides me, there's hardly a man in this town that will talk to you. I thought of keepin' away from you myself, except that"—He paused and grinned boyishly—"th' ol' Kingfish is invulnerable. If you arranged Congressman Colmer's li'l accident, it wasn't a smart move, Peavy."

"Senator, *as God is my witness*—"

The Kingfish interrupted him with a wave of his hand. "Don' use the name o' the Lawd like that there," he said. "Either you done it or you didn't, and swearin' in the name of the Lawd don' make no difference."

"We didn't kill him," said Peavy curtly, firmly. "We had nothing to do with it."

"Maybe Lee Bob, then," said The Kingfish. "For reasons you wouldn't want to get out. I don' know ex-

actly what them reasons are, but I can see you can't
let 'em get out."

"Lee Bob Colmer swears he didn't do it," said
Peavy, "and I don't think he's that stupid."

"Well, *somebody* did it," said The Kingfish, "and I
wouldn't want t' be in your shoes."

"Stebbins . . ." muttered Peavy. "Because of his
daughter."

The Kingfish shook his head. "If it was Les Stebbins, he'll get away with it. I wouldn't want to be
tryin' to hang a murder on a United States senator.
Not him in particular. He's got clout, Peavy."

Peavy blew a long, noisy sigh. "Somebody . . ." he
said.

"You'd growed up in Looziana, like what I did, you'd
know somethin', not only of th' French language but
also th' French *philosophy*," said The Kingfish.
"Mighty smart folks, the French. Mighty smart. What
they'd say in a situation like this here, is—*Cherchez
la femme*. That's what I'd do if I was you, Peavy.
Cherchez la femme. Find the wife. She ain't missin'
for just no reason at all. She hangs for the murder of
her husband, nothin' 'bout your business with Lee
Bob has to come out. It don't hafta, that is, unless you
fellows got her mixed up in it some way."

Peavy stood at his window and watched Senator
Huey Long walk up the street toward the Capitol.
People stopped him every few paces to shake his
hand. He would make political profit out of his walk.
"Every man a king" was his slogan. He talked about
sharing the wealth, and a great many people ate it
up. He was a charlatan, one of the most dangerous
men in America.

"Tebay! Where the hell's Tebay?"

Izzy Mullin, who had just come in and was about to
sit down, turned and went out the door, to find Walter
Tebay for the boss, before his mood got even worse.
Izzy did not like to see Peavy in a bad mood.

"Sorry," said Walter Tebay deferentially when he came in a moment later. "I was sending a wire to Chicago."

Peavy pointed to a chair, and Tebay sat down. Izzy closed the door, noted with a flicker of a frown that Tebay had taken the chair he had meant to take, and sat down faintly dissatisfied in another chair, to the side.

Tebay was a tall man, bald, with the most open face Peavy had ever seen. His eyebrows arched high, which made his eyes seem wide open. He looked sincere—*always* sincere, an unrelenting aspect of sincerity that masked devious dishonesty. He was an expert in his field. No, he was *the* expert in his field. If you wanted a man to cook the books, there was no better than Walter Tebay. He'd done it for Capone and Nitti in Chicago, and when he was released from Joliet, he was sent to Washington. He'd be working for the Enterprise Bank except that his name and face were too well known in Chicago. Here in Washington, bank examiners constantly overlooked his skillful tricks with the bank's ledgers. He was well paid and a man to be trusted.

"I've got a special assignment for you two," said Peavy. "It overrides everything else you're doing."

Tebay nodded solemnly.

"The business with Colmer and the Sipsey Fork dam is screwed up to a fare-thee-well. Our best chance of getting it unscrewed is some way to locate the late congressman's wife, then tip the cops about where she is. When that broad took a powder, she did us a big favor—maybe. So find her."

"How?" asked Izzy. He was a squashed-face, scarred little man, not the brightest fellow a man could have working for him but blessed with a sense of loyalty that was unexcelled. He would do anything he was told, and no one could force him to talk. "I mean, where do we start?"

"Walter will tell you," said Peavy.

"The dame couldn't just disappear," said Tebay. "She's somewhere, and somebody knows where."

"A brilliant observation, Walter," said Peavy. "So act on it. We don't have much time."

J. Edgar Hoover sat down in Mrs. Roosevelt's office. "It is very nice of you to give me some of your valuable time," he said.

She felt like telling him, yes, it was; but she smiled graciously and said, "Any time, Mr. Hoover. I know your time is valuable, too."

"Well, I shall be sparing of both of us," he said.

He was wearing a beautifully tailored light-blue suit, with black-and-white shoes, and when he tugged his pants up from his knees and crossed his legs, he showed light-blue silk socks that matched his suit. Someone had quipped that the Director of the F.B.I. dressed like a Milanese pimp. Mrs. Roosevelt thought the little joke uncharitable but had smiled over it, anyway.

"The President suggested that you know more about the Colmer case than he does," said Hoover.

"His responsibilities demand his attention to more important matters," she said.

"Ah. Yes, of course. And that is why he suggested I discuss it with you. May I hope you will share your insights with me?"

"I'm afraid I have no particular insights, Mr. Hoover," she said. "I've reviewed the information that has been developed. Frankly, the mystery constantly deepens. We had hoped your inquiry of Mr. Peavy would develop something—which apparently it didn't."

Hoover shook his head. "Mr. Peavy is a very solid American businessman," he said. "An enterpriser, the kind who built this country."

"I was under the impression he made his start by brewing and selling illegal beer," said Mrs. Roosevelt.

Hoover smiled. "Some of our greatest businessmen began small in enterprises of questionable character."

"Then the Peavys had nothing to do with the death of Mr. Colmer?"

"I can't believe so."

"Then I do have a bit of information that may interest you," she said. "The District police asked the Chicago police to watch for Mr. Lee Bob Colmer, the deceased congressman's brother, who left Washington for Chicago on Monday—leaving word here, incidentally, that he was returning directly to Alabama. Mr. Lee Bob Colmer arrived in Chicago yesterday, via the B & O and Pennsylvania railroads, and on arrival went immediately to the Enterprise Bank." She shrugged. "Which may be meaningless. Or it may be meaningful, indeed."

"You are suggesting, in other words," said Hoover, "that there may have been some kind of unholy alliance between Mr. Peavy and the congressman's brother?"

The First Lady smiled. "I had supposed, Mr. Hoover, that exposing unholy alliances is *your* business."

"Grapefruit," said Sally Rand. "I tell you, it's the greatest thing in the world, the greatest for your figure, the greatest for your complexion, and it's absolutely full of vitamins and all the good stuff like that."

"But it tastes rotten," grumbled Amelia.

Amelia sat at the window, looking down on the street while Sally ate the breakfast-lunch brought up by room service. Sally slept late, naturally. Then she ordered coffee and grapefruit and sat sometimes naked and sometimes nearly so and ate with relish. You'd have thought she was having steak with all the trimmings.

"You're getting a bit pudgy, kiddo," said Sally.

"Of *course* I am. I'm going to have a baby!"

"That's not what I'm talkin' about," said Sally. "Besides that . . ."

"My late husband liked it," muttered Amelia.

"How 'bout the guy who gave you the baby?"

Amelia sighed. *"He's* the one who liked it, really."

"How long had this been going on when— I mean, how long has it been going on?"

"A long time."

"Jeez, kiddo, how could you get away with it? For a long time? That husband of yours was no dummy."

"He played poker every Friday night," said Amelia. "With the boys. Some other congressmen, one or two lawyers from his staff. Every Friday night, until after midnight. That made it possible. Of course, there were other times." She swallowed and blinked. "He's a great guy, honey. My age. Win was . . . older. Win was in France in 1917–18."

"You going to marry this guy?"

"Oh, yes! He wants that. As soon as my name is cleared. As soon as—"

"And his name is cleared," said Sally. "Okay, kiddo. I have my big doubts, but I won't dump you. Sunday morning. Train for Buffalo. Shuffle off to Buffalo."

"I'm already packed," said Amelia.

"Think how much simpler life would have been if you'd taken up my offer," said Sally.

Amelia didn't respond. She and Sally had talked about that many times before, from time to time, over the years. She sighed and walked away from the window. Her mind was on something else.

"Sally . . . You don't suppose the cops have searched my house, do you?"

"I wouldn't be a bit surprised."

Amelia's face turned deep red, and tears filled her eyes. She shook her head. "No . . ." she whispered. "My *God!*"

11

It was a mistake to wait until after midnight. The worst time at all was the so-called wee hours, just before dawn. In a lifetime spent alternately earning a decent living as a burglar and suffering the brutalities of prisons, Isambard Mullin had learned a thing or two—one of them being the best ways to stay on the outside. Usually he entered a place not long after dark. Sometimes even before dark. Neighbors who happened to see you weren't alarmed by someone crawling in a window at eight or nine o'clock, the way they would be at three or four in the morning. Seeing you at three ay-em, they *always* called the cops. Seeing you at nine pee-em, like as not they laughed at their silly neighbor whose wife had locked him out again.

The house in Georgetown was easy. He walked around behind, quite casually, until he found a cellar window more shadowed than the rest; then he pushed the glass in with a hand wrapped in a couple of layers of burlap (so he wouldn't get cut). The glass fell on the cellar floor, but how much noise did that make? Not much, he could tell you. In fact, here it fell on a table piled with old clothes and made no noise at all. In a moment he was in—and no one the wiser. He pulled on his gloves, so as not to leave fingerprints, and climbed the cellar steps to the house proper.

He went around and unlocked doors—the front door, the back door, and the cellar door. He unlocked and tried windows. If the cops came, he would be out in a flash. Upstairs he found what he needed for a trick he liked. Just outside the bathroom window there was a big tree limb. He could go out the window, reach back and push the sash down, and climb on the roof. He could lie up there, quiet, for two or three hours, until the cops were gone and the neighborhood was dark and still again, and then he would come down and scoot off. One night he'd actually gone back inside the house and finished gathering up what he'd been collecting when the stupid cops interrupted his work.

Well. Okay. He opened the front door and stepped out on the porch. Tebay was waiting on the street a few doors away. Izzy figured Walt was more likely to be picked up for loitering than he, the best cat burglar in Washington, was for breaking into this little house. It was sort of silly, actually. What could a man get out of a dump like this? Besides, he was under strict orders not to take anything. Walt was to decide what they took, if anything. Employment had its rewards, but free-lancing was better. He—

"Okay! Back inside!"

"Don't be so nervous, Walt. We—"

"Get inside, before somebody sees us!"

"Nobody's gonna see us. Hey, this is nothin'! Piece of cake. The other one . . . now, that one was a piece of work worth taking pride in. In broad daylight, joint like that, hey—"

"Hey, never mind, Izzy! Let's get at it. I don't want to be in here all night."

Izzy sighed, shrugged. "You know what we're looking for?"

"Roughly," said Walter. "Let's start here, in the living room."

As your eyes got used to it, the house was dimly lit by full-moon moonlight, cold and gray, the stuff horror legends were full of. Izzy appraised the place. Congressmen didn't live as well as he had supposed. The furniture was very ordinary—a couch and chairs, a low table, a little desk and chair, an Atwater-Kent floor-model radio that was nice. Walt went directly to the desk, opened its one drawer, and started rummaging through. In a minute he was finished, muttering dissatisfaction.

They had a refrigerator in the kitchen. That was pretty good. Izzy opened it and found some Pabst beer. He opened a bottle and drank it while Walt went through the silverware and napkin drawers in the dining room. When he was finished he rinsed out the bottle so it wouldn't smell stale and left it in the kitchen sink.

Walt went upstairs. Izzy followed. Walt went through everything, including the pockets of the congressman's clothes that still hung in the bedroom closet. That gave Izzy the willies—going through a dead man's clothes.

"We'll take this," said Walt. He had found the checkbook in the nightstand drawer, and he handed it to Izzy to be dropped into the cloth bag Izzy was carrying.

Down on his knees then, Walt found a box under the bed. He pulled it out. It was the woman's keepsakes, an odd assortment of dried flowers, dance programs, little gloves, a lock of hair, a scrapbook.

"We'll take this," said Walt, handing up the scrapbook.

"Aw, gee, do we hafta?" Izzy complained. He was sentimental. "I never take—"

"The boss might need to know who her friends are, where she's been, what she's done," said Walt curtly.

Izzy shrugged and obediently dropped the scrapbook in the bag.

The police arrived five minutes after Izzy and Walt casually walked away from the Colmer house. They had walked around the corner to a car and had driven away, never realizing how close they had come to being caught. A neighbor three doors away had seen the police car on the street Tuesday morning, had seen it stop at the Colmer house and drop two men, obviously detectives, and pick them up later, and this morning she had read in the *Record* that Mrs. Colmer was missing. She had begun to keep an eye on the house, suspecting it could become a target for burglars, and when she saw two men leave the dark house and hurry away along the street, she had called the police.

Not long after the first prowl car arrived, another arrived with Lieutenant Kennelly and Gerald Baines.

"No, I'm sure it wasn't Mrs. Colmer," the neighbor woman insisted. "It was two men, one short, one tall."

"The short one could not have been Mrs. Colmer?" asked Kennelly.

"That would have made her the ugliest woman I ever saw—which she's not. Mrs. Colmer is a pretty girl. I've seen her often, spoken to her. This was not Mrs. Colmer."

Kennelly nodded thoughtfully. They were standing in the Colmer living room, now lit.

"Let me tell you how good a witness I am, Lieutenant," the neighbor said. "I've seen *you* before. And that gentleman—" She pointed at Baines. "You were in the Colmer house Tuesday morning. A police car dropped you off and picked you up."

Baines laughed. "She's got you there, Ed. Got us both."

Kennelly smiled as he nodded at the woman and thanked her; then he hurried upstairs.

"Got the checkbook, dammit," said Kennelly. "We should have taken it with us the other morning."

Baines nodded. "And Lord knows what else they got," he said. "We stubbed our toes here, Ed. We should have subjected this place to a thorough search."

"Two more burglars," mused Kennelly. "Making three. Maybe four."

"Right," said Baines. "Tonight's pair hadn't been here before. Whoever was here Monday or Tuesday got what he wanted—or didn't get it—and left. These are new ones."

"Exactly. If the Monday or Tuesday burglar had wanted the checkbook, he'd have taken it then. This pair was after something the first one didn't care about."

"Something else, let's not forget," said Kennelly. "These guys *broke* in, broke a window. The first guy *walked* in. Had a key, apparently."

"Suppose they all were looking for the same thing and couldn't find it?"

"If so, I'd sure as hell like to know what it is," said Baines.

"That seems to have been simple enough, and quick," said Peavy.

Tebay nodded. "Piece of cake."

"'Piece of cake,'" sneered Izzy Mullin. "If it was, it was because you were taken in through the front door by the best second-story man in Washington."

"Second-story man," said Tebay with a smile. "I thought you said you went in through the cellar window, Izzy."

Peavy patted Izzy on the shoulder. He knew what it took to please the little man and keep his loyalty—nothing more than an appreciative word, a slap on the back. "You did a good job, Izzy," he said. "As usual."

"It was the other one that was the good one," said Izzy.

"Yes, but damned dangerous," said Peavy. "And almost a disaster. Anyway, all's well that ends well. You go on and get yourself a nice dinner. Walt's got some work to do."

When Izzy had gone out, Peavy spoke to Tebay. "You could have some dinner yourself. Why don't you have the cook fix you up something? I've got the White House girl here, and I'll have to get her to bed before we . . . Okay?"

The tall, bald, taciturn Tebay nodded. Peavy returned to the dining room.

Darlene was at the dining table. She was wearing a sheer pink nightgown and was boldly exposed. Her blond hair was combed out. Her glasses lay aside on the table. Her left hand was curled languidly around the stem of a glass of red wine. She had learned some new mannerisms during her introduction to things like wine.

Peavy was pleased with her. Originally, of course, he had dated her as a matter of business, a matter of duty. But in truth she was not a bad-looking dame, and she was accommodating and undemanding and just dumb enough to be almost the perfect girl for a man who didn't want a broad sticking her nose in his business.

Except now— "Anyway," she said. "Like I was saying when you had to go out." Sometimes her voice was more adenoidal than at others. Sometimes it was downright whiny. "Anyway, I saw his picture in the paper, and I said to myself, 'Hey, that's the man that was at Peav's—'"

"Darlene . . . what if I told you he killed his brother? What if I told you he came here and asked me if he should kill his brother? What if—"

"That's not true! . . . Is it?"

"No, it's not true. And you wouldn't talk about it if
it was, right?"

"No, Peav."

"Okay. So if you wouldn't talk about it if that was
true, then I guess I can count on you not to talk about
his being here at all. Can't I?"

"Why, sure, Peav. You know I wouldn't—"

"Sometimes in business, embarrassing things happen. I wouldn't want people to know that man came to
see me. You can see why. He *didn't* kill his brother,
but he's a dummy, and he's made some people think
he did. So—"

"Mum's the word, honey," she said solemnly. "Don't
give it another thought."

"Awright," said Peavy to Tebay. "The broad's
asleep. Three glasses of wine, and . . . zonko! So what
we got?"

"I took their personal checkbook," said Tebay. "The
congressman was a sucker, let his wife sign checks on
a joint account."

Otto D. Peavy the Third had come down from his
bedroom in yellow silk pajamas under a maroon silk
robe. He adjusted his round, horn-rimmed glasses and
pursed his lips. Peering at the checkbook, he shook
his head and said, "This was a household account. He
wasn't sucker enough to keep *all* his money where his
wife could write checks against it."

"Pretty good balance for a household account," said
Tebay. "Over five hundred bucks. One check missing.
You can figure she wrote that one for the balance
when she blew."

Peavy flipped back through pages of neatly written
entries. "I don't see anything odd in here. Dull stuff.
Grocery bill, laundry bill, rent . . ."

"Well, I picked up this scrapbook," said Tebay. "Figured maybe we could find out something about who
her friends are, like that. Looka this."

Peavy began to flip through the scrapbook. "Odd,

one way," he said. "Here's a clipping, the announcement she's engaged to Colmer, and that's it. It stops
there. Not even her wedding in here."

"Probably they had a wedding book."

"Yeah, probably. Anyway, she . . . She had an active social life. Look at these dance programs. Love
notes, too. Looka these pictures. She was a cute kid!
White House . . . Here's an invitation to a reception
for staff . . . Hoover. Huh-oh! Hold it. Looka this!"

He pointed to a yellowed newspaper clipping from
the Youngstown *Vindicator,* August 3, 1927:

BURLESQUE TROUPE ALLOWED TO LEAVE
STRIP-TEASE GIRLS RELEASED

Six young ladies who imaginatively and fan-
cifully style themselves "ecdysiasts" were released from the Mahoning County jail this
morning and told that all was forgiven, provided
they never darken the doors of our fair city
again.

Prosecuting Attorney Chester Hummel ad-
vised the court that he was dropping charges of
indecent exposure and disorderly conduct against
the six girls, on their promise to catch the first
train out of Youngstown and never to return. To
be certain the promise was kept, sheriff's depu-
ties accompanied the girls to the station and saw
them aboard a train, which happened to be for
Pittsburgh.

The incident began last night at a "smoker"
held by the American Legion. Officers of the local
legion unit had rented the old Odeon Theater
and made it a burlesque theater for the night.
Only members of the Legion were supposed to attend, and the members were supposed to keep
the whole business very quiet. Unhappily for

them, the word got around quite widely, and among those protesting to Youngstown's mayor and police chief were the Reverend Father Lawrence O'Malley and the Reverend Mr. James Wiley. The performance had hardly begun when police officers rudely interrupted and carried the performers off to jail in a paddy wagon. Several officers were mauled by outraged Legionnaires, and several more arrests were made.

Assault on Church

Seeing that their show had been spoiled, two dozen furious Legionnaires then repaired to the Reverend Mr. Wiley's Church of the Nazarene and proceeded to knock the glass out of every last window in the building. *See the story in column 5.*

The young ladies—all sedately re-clothed—were by now guests of the community in the cells of the county bastille. By morning tempers had cooled. The young ladies were given a hearty breakfast and taken in the self-same paddy wagon to the station.

The entrepreneuse who brought the aborted show to Youngstown, and would have been its lead dancer, was the rising star of the burlesque circuit, Sally Rand. Girls of her troupe were Paula Jones, Sarah Irving, Patricia Horan, Amelia Rowlandson, and Judy Presser. We are truly sorry we missed their show.

Peavy grinned. "I wonder if the Congressman knew that—that his demure little wife was once a—what did they call it here?—ecdysiast."

"I bet he did," said Tebay. "The scrapbook was in a box under their bed."

"Yeah. And good work, too, Walt," said Peavy. "It just happens that Sally Rand is in town, performing at the Coconut Grove. You don't suppose the lovely Amelia has decided to rejoin the troupe?"

Izzy Mullin stood just outside the kitchen door at the Langford Hotel, speaking earnestly with a uniformed bellboy. He smoked his cigarettes down to the very edge of his lip, and the bellboy was at the moment so fascinated with the smoldering butt that he was not concentrating on what the little man was saying.

". . . so you see, my friend, you got nothin' to lose and a quick way to pick up a fin."

"Nothin' to lose but my job," said the bellboy.

He was a man of Izzy's age, similarly small, similarly scarred. Izzy had never met him, but he saw in him a kindred spirit. He thought he spotted in him the mark of a man who had done time. You could always spot them—including himself. Time in prison left an undefinable but unsubtle mark on a man.

"Tell ya what I'll do," said Izzy. "I'll make it a sawbuck. And if you lose the job, my boss'll get ya another one."

"You ain't gonna do nothin'—"

"Rough? No, buddy. All I wanta do is get a look at the guest. Just wanta see who she is."

"How 'bout me takin' a look and comin' back and tellin' ya what she looks like?"

Izzy shook his head. "Naw. Tell ya what. Instead of us changin' clothes like I want, suppose I just go up there *with* you. Suppose *you* knock on the door, get her to come to the door, and I can take a look. How's that for an idea? And you still get the sawbuck."

The bellboy nodded. "Deal," he said. "Trouble is, she hasn't called for no room service."

"So you got a telegram for her."

"I don't know her name."

"It's addressed to Sally Rand."

"Okay. The room is 804. You go up. Just hang around in the hall. I'll be up soon as I can."

Izzy had experience with this sort of thing. He did not hang around the eighth-floor hall. He strode briskly from the elevator to the door of room 804, then turned and strode just as briskly to the opposite end of the long hall. He made himself look as though he were on his way to a room, or from a room to the elevator. The last appearance in the world he wanted to give was that he was loitering.

The bellboy appeared. Izzy followed him four paces behind. At the door to 804 he caught up and stood behind him. The bellboy knocked.

"Who is it?"

"Bellboy. Telegram for Miss Rand."

"She's not here."

"Could you take it, please?"

"Push it under the door."

"Sorry, I can't do that. Somebody gotta sign for it."

Izzy heard a door chain rattle, then the snap of the lock. The door opened. And there she was. The boss had shown him the picture in this morning's paper, and this was the same broad, for sure. Pretty. Like the boss had said. Dark-haired and pretty.

"Well?"

Izzy knew what to do. He reached into his inside pocket, and he mimed dismay. "Jeez!" he whispered. He began to slap at his other pockets, turning his face into a mask of alarm. "Jeez, lady! I'll go back and get it."

She closed the door.

Izzy grinned and handed the bellboy his ten-dollar bill.

"Jerry? Ed Kennelly. Sorry to call you at home at this hour. But I got news for you."

Baines glanced at the bedside alarm clock, which was ticking away. It was after midnight. This had better be good. "What ya got, Ed?"

"Maybe nothing. But it's a telephone tip. Anonymous. Call came to me personally, at home. The guy

on the line says, 'I hear you're looking for Amelia Colmer. Try room 804 at the Langford Hotel.' I'm going
over there. Wanta come along?"

"Yes."

"I'll pick you up in fifteen minutes."

"Fifteen?"

"Don't worry. I got the place covered."

Two uniformed officers stood in the hall by the door
to room 804. The night manager of the hotel was with
them, half outraged, half apprehensive—also an
ashen-faced little old bellboy. No one had knocked on
the door yet, the officers told Kennelly.

"May I inquire—"

"I'm Lieutenant Edward Kennelly, District police.
This is Agent Gerald Baines, Secret Service. You
don't need to worry. We're not vice squad. We got a tip
that a witness we're looking for is in there. We have
to check that out."

"But that room belongs to Miss Sally Rand, the . . .
the fan dancer. It's true that one of the girls of her
troupe is in there, sick. But—"

"Nothing to worry about," said Kennelly. But he
turned to Baines, raised his eyebrows, and muttered,
Sally Rand?"

Kennelly knocked on the door.

"Who is it?"

"Lieutenant Kennelly, District police. Open the
door, please."

"Miss Rand isn't here."

"I want to talk to you, Mrs. Colmer," said Kennelly.
"Open the door."

Amelia recognized Baines immediately. Sobbing
softly, she led him and Kennelly into the suite. The
uniformed officers closed the door and remained outside.

"I'm very reluctant to place you under arrest, Mrs.
Colmer," said Kennelly gently. "But you are going to
have to answer some questions."

She shook her head. She was wearing a light-blue nightgown, covered with a white cotton robe.

"I go back," said Baines, "to the original question. Where were you the night when your husband was killed?"

Amelia looked up into his face. Her mouth stiffened, and she shook her head firmly. "I can't tell you, and I won't tell you. It has nothing to do with the death of my husband. I didn't kill him, and I don't know who did."

Baines sighed. "How are we going to believe that, Mrs. Colmer, when you refuse to answer that question and when you fled your home and your parents' home and have been living here secretly?"

"I wasn't under arrest," she said. "I had every right to go where I wanted."

"You knew we wanted the answers to some questions," said Baines. "You had to know, frankly, that you are a suspect. Still, you effected a sudden disappearance, first withdrawing almost the entire balance from your checking account. No one knew where you were. I think your father has known all along, but that's neither here nor there. It's not the typical conduct of an innocent person, Mrs. Colmer. I'm sure you can understand that."

She closed her eyes and sighed through the fingers she had pressed to her mouth. It was as if she had withdrawn from the conversation.

"Let me add something else," said Kennelly. "Since you left Bethesda on Monday, your house in Georgetown has been visited by burglars. Twice."

She looked up, stricken. "Oh . . . And ruined everything, I suppose."

"No. That's a point. Whoever they were, they were looking for something. We don't know if they found it or not. They took your checkbook. That's all we know is missing."

"Check— How do you know about my checkbook?"

"We, too, entered your house and searched, trying

to find a clue as to where you had gone. When we were in the house, which was on Tuesday morning, it was apparent that someone had been there before us. When we went back in connection with the investigation of the second burglary, which happened earlier tonight, we saw they had taken your checkbook, which we had looked at but left there."

"God, what else. . . ?" she sighed.

"What were they looking for, Mrs. Colmer?"

She shook her head. "I don't know."

"You put us in a difficult position," said Baines. "What choice do we have but to think you killed your husband or know who did?"

"I—"

The door burst open, and in charged Sally Rand, flushed, her eyes wide, her arms flung above her head. "What is this?" she shrieked. "What you doing in my hotel suite? Who let you in? *I'll sue!*"

"Sally . . ." said Amelia quietly. She shook her head. "Don't make trouble for yourself."

"Make trouble!" yelled Sally Rand. "I can make trouble." She swung toward Kennelly. "You wanta know somebody can make trouble? *I* can make trouble. I'm a businesswoman. I got lawyers. I—"

"You are interfering with a police investigation," said Kennelly calmly. "Uh . . ." He tipped his head to indicate she should step aside with him. He spoke quietly to her. "Lieutenant Edward Kennelly, District police. You haven't been hassled for an indecent performance at the Coconut Grove. But you're in no position to get crosswise with us. I suggest you calm down."

Sally had recognized Baines suddenly. "What's he doin' here? He's from the White House."

"Secret Service," said Kennelly. "Answer one question, Miss Rand. What's the connection between you and Mrs. Colmer?"

She shrugged. "We're old friends, that's all."

"So you gave her a place to hide from the police."

Sally frowned. "No. Hiding from reporters."

"Okay. So calm down. I wouldn't want to have to run you in, too."

"You gonna run her in?" Sally asked, dismayed.

"She won't cooperate," said Kennelly. "She won't answer the simplest questions." He shook his head. "I don't know what choice we have."

12

"Oh! this is *terrible!*"

"I knew you would want to be told as soon as possible," said Baines to Mrs. Roosevelt.

"Oh, you could have telephoned me last night! I don't care what hour. I don't blame you for not calling, Mr. Baines—I am sure you used your best judgment, in which I have every confidence—but I would have come instantly."

"No one had much choice, I'm afraid," said Baines.

"And the poor thing is in *jail?*"

Baines nodded. "There was no alternative. I agreed with Lieutenant Kennelly that we had to take her in and hold her. She absolutely refuses to cooperate. In any way."

Mrs. Roosevelt, sitting at her breakfront desk, slumped disconsolately. "I can't believe that poor, poor young woman killed her husband—or knows who did. I just can't believe it. And, Mr. Baines, she's *with child*. And in jail!"

Within half an hour Mrs. Roosevelt was at District

police headquarters. Warned that she was coming, Kennelly met her on the street before the building and hurried her in a side door to avoid the police reporters who lounged just inside the front entry, alert to any kind of story—and the arrival of the First Lady at District police headquarters would have been a sensational story.

"Mrs. Colmer's with another visitor," he said, once they were inside.

"Oh? Who?"

"Miss Sally Rand," said Kennelly, giving Baines a significant glance.

Baines had told Mrs. Roosevelt that Amelia Colmer had been staying in Sally Rand's hotel suite, so she was not surprised. "Perhaps we should meet with Mrs. Colmer together," she said with a smile.

They sat down in the office of the chief of police, the only office large enough to accommodate five people and out of sight of inquiring eyes. Kennelly insisted Mrs. Roosevelt should sit in the chief's leather-covered swivel chair, behind his desk. She faced the two other women across the desk—Sally Rand in a long, tight cream-colored linen skirt, with a dark-blue jacket, wearing also a jaunty white straw hat; Amelia Colmer in the drab, shapeless, ill-fitting gray uniform dress with the words DIST. JAIL stenciled in black paint across the back and DJ stenciled on the front. Baines took the remaining chair, and Kennelly leaned against a window sill.

"I've come," said Mrs. Roosevelt, "to see if there is not some way to secure Mrs. Colmer's release from jail. It is really cruel to keep her here, she being pregnant." She spoke directly to Amelia. "I'm sorry," she said. "I know you don't want it told that you are going to have a baby. But your health and the baby's health, both, could be severely damaged if you were to remain in jail, in the heat and—"

"I've made an offer," said Sally Rand. "She can come back to my suite until Sunday when I check out.

This is Friday. Maybe you can get this thing settled before Sunday when I have to leave. You can send along a woman cop to watch out she doesn't skip. After I go, I'll fund the suite for another week or so. In fact, I'll rent the second bedroom that goes with the suite. Surely you guys can solve your mystery in another whole week."

"Well . . . We'd like to accommodate you," said Kennelly.

"Mr. Baines," said Mrs. Roosevelt, "could the Secret Service spare an agent to stay in the suite, too? Surely you could. Certainly the man assigned to follow *me* around all day is wasting his time."

"I could make it a condition that she answer some questions," said Kennelly.

"Please, Lieutenant Kennelly," said Mrs. Roosevelt. "Why not be humane?"

Half an hour later Amelia Colmer and Sally Rand left the station in a police car, accompanied by two uniformed officers and a jail matron who would be stationed in the hotel suite. The chief of police had agreed to the arrangement Mrs. Roosevelt had urged on him, subject to the condition that Amelia wear the gray jail uniform and that all her other clothes be removed from the suite. He couldn't risk her being able simply to walk out when the matron wasn't looking, he said.

Mrs. Roosevelt remained in the chief's office with Baines while these arrangements were being made. Kennelly asked them to stay, if they had the time. Something interesting might come up, he said.

They watched from a window as the matron led Amelia to the car. Then Kennelly turned, smiled, and said, "Opportunity."

"I bet," said Baines with a grin. "I *know* what you did."

"Did. . . ?" inquired Mrs. Roosevelt.

"When Sally Rand showed up here, we really didn't

have to let her see Mrs. Colmer. But we did, and she was here almost an hour. Which gave us time to send two men into that hotel suite and have a look-see."

"You searched those rooms?"

"Yes, Ma'am. Our two men had instructions not to remove anything from the suite. They took a camera and lights and photographed anything they thought we ought to know about. They've been back fifteen minutes, and the lab is doing some quick developing and print-making. They say they found one or two interesting items, and they'll have pictures for us to look at very shortly."

"I see," she said. "Well, I suppose that's the kind of thing you have to do." She tipped her head and looked at him quizzically. "Incidentally, how did you learn where Mrs. Colmer was?"

"Anonymous tip," said Kennelly. "Someone called me and told me. I don't know who. I have no idea, in fact."

"Ah . . . So. Aren't you curious?"

"I am very curious," said Kennelly.

Mrs. Roosevelt rubbed her hands together. "You don't, I should think, suppose it was a public-spirited citizen anxious to help the police department with a difficult investigation."

"No."

"No. It was someone who wanted to focus the investigation on Mrs. Colmer."

"Certainly," Kennelly agreed.

"To shift the investigation away from himself," she suggested.

"Yes."

"And whoever had motive to do that is the real killer, which tends to prove Mrs. Colmer is not guilty."

Kennelly grinned. "Well, I can't follow your logic quite that far, Ma'am."

"I said *tends* to prove, not that it *does* prove."

Mrs. Roosevelt returned to the window and stared

out, sifting her thoughts. "Did she ask how you were able to find her?" she asked Kennelly.

"Oh, yes. I refused to tell her."

"Hoping she might feel betrayed by someone. Hmm?"

Kennelly nodded. "A possibility."

"In the thought that when she refuses to tell where she was when her husband was killed, she is trying to protect someone."

"Yes, exactly," said Kennelly. "And if it weren't for the fact that she's pregnant, I'd hold her in jail indefinitely, see how long she'd hold out."

"Can we withhold the news of her arrest from the newspapers?"

"I'm afraid that isn't possible. Too many people know."

"Besides," said Mrs. Roosevelt, "it may be advantageous for some people to learn of it. Someone may be moved to— Well, there are a number of things someone might be moved to do."

Two young detectives arrived shortly, gingerly carrying wet prints from the darkroom. Kennelly spread newspapers on the chief's desk, and the young men laid the photographs on the papers.

"Janson and Cooke," said Kennelly, by way of introduction. "You two fellows of course recognize Mrs. Roosevelt. Now forget you ever saw her. Nobody's to know she was here."

The two young men nodded soberly.

Janson spoke for the two. Although he looked not more than thirty years old, he was quite bald, with a gleaming sunburned pate. His eyes were pale blue. He was stocky, maybe a little overweight. "We did it the way you said, Lieutenant. I don't think the two women will notice that we'd been there. We identified the room Mrs. Colmer had been occupying, and we went through everything she had there, pretty carefully."

"Find anything especially interesting?" asked Kennelly.

"Well, first of all, she had a lot of cash. Hidden in her suitcase. Seven hundred seventy-five dollars."

"*Seven* hundred. . . ?"

Janson nodded. "Right. In her suitcase, under some clothes."

"Three hundred more than she withdrew from the bank," said Baines.

Janson did not know what that meant, so he continued. "The only other unusual thing we found is what we photographed. This—" He pointed to the wet photographs lying on the newspaper. "You see? It's a ring. But look how it's sewed to—" He stopped. His face reddened. He would not say what the ring was sewed to.

It was in fact sewed to a brassiere, securely attached to the inside of the white brassiere with white thread. It appeared clearly in four photographs, each one taken from a little closer range, until in the last one the camera had been too close for sharp focus and the image was fuzzy.

"We didn't touch it," said Janson. "If you decide to go get it, whatever fingerprints are on it are intact."

"It's a man's ring," said Mrs. Roosevelt, squinting at the photographs one by one.

"A Masonic ring," said Janson. "A very good one, too—very nice, expensive. Solid gold. Antique, too, I think."

Unlike the typical Masonic ring, square and compasses on black onyx, this ring was a simple circle, with Masonic symbols set in jewels and enamel, all the way around.

"There are letters engraved inside," said Janson. "The camera just couldn't get them, so I wrote them down."

He pulled a small sheet of notepaper from his pocket and put it on the desk. The lettering was:

#21 F & AM—'03—JBD

"No mystery in that," said Mrs. Roosevelt. "I would judge it means the original owner of this ring was a member of a Masonic lodge number twenty-one. Of course, that could be in any state. He joined the lodge in 1903, or was perhaps its master that year. And his initials are JBD."

"Worn next to her heart, as you might say," Baines remarked dryly. "Not her father's or her grand-father's, you would assume—worn that way."

"A thirty-second-degree Mason," said Mrs. Roosevelt, staring hard at one of the symbols. "More than thirty years ago."

"If the significance of her wearing that . . . where she was wearing it," said Kennelly, "is that it belongs to her lover, then Mrs. Colmer must have a sixty-year-old lover."

"Or it's an heirloom," said Mrs. Roosevelt. "Something treasured by someone and given to her as a token of a deep attachment. Worn hidden, where her husband wouldn't see it." She shook her head. "Or do we speculate too much?"

"Let's speculate a little further," said Baines. "The owner of the ring is who she's protecting, and it's who killed her husband." He shook his head at Mrs. Roosevelt. "I'm not sure we haven't treated her too leniently."

In suite 804 at the Langford Hotel, Amelia Colmer was not sure she was being treated leniently. She sat glumly in a chair in the sitting room, wearing the gray uniform of the jail, and watched the matron and an officer carry away her suitcase, in which they had crammed everything she had brought with her to the suite. Sally paced the room, muttering that she would sue everybody involved. And now, on top of all other indignities, a young Secret Service agent had arrived and announced he had been ordered to sit in the suite until another agent relieved him—which would not be until midnight.

"My name is Bill Epson," he said. "I, uh . . . I'll try not to invade your privacy any more than necessary."

"Privacy!" shrieked Sally Rand. "What privacy have we got left? Hey, where you takin' that suitcase?"

"No place, since it locks," said the matron. "It's locked shut, and it'll just sit here, where I can keep an eye on it."

"Paper, Mrs. Colmer?" asked Bill. "Like to look over the morning *Record*?"

"Why not?" she said dully.

Bill sat uneasily, not sure how he would spend long hours with these three women—the despondent Amelia Colmer, the seething Sally Rand, and the dour police matron. Amelia Colmer was exceptionally pretty. Except for what he knew about her, he could take a highly personal interest in her. And Sally Rand . . . Well, a lot of fellows would pay a price just to meet her. Even with her clothes on, she was fascinating. Her outrage was unskillfully mimed. He hoped she would give up that act after a while, so he could talk to her. It was going to be a long day if they could not talk.

Amelia Colmer was not a skillful mime either. Glancing at her, he could see she had turned pale. Her eyes were fastened on something in the paper. Her hands trembled. The paper rattled. Suddenly she jumped from the chair, ran into the bedroom, and closed the door.

The matron opened the door to see what she was doing, saw—as he, too, could see, through the open doorway—that the young woman was placing a telephone call. She turned and glared. The matron looked at him and shrugged. He shrugged back. There was nothing in his instructions that said she couldn't make phone calls. Apparently there was nothing in the matron's, and she closed the door.

Bill picked up the newspaper. He wondered what Mrs. Colmer had seen that upset her so. The page she had been looking at had only three stories, plus some advertisements. It was unlikely the ads had upset her. And the stories— One was about an earthquake in Yucatan. One was about shots fired at a British gunboat on the Yangtze River. One was about— He read the story carefully:

MYSTERY SHOOTING IN NORTHEAST NEIGHBORHOOD

Police acknowledge they have no clues to identify the lone gunman who came to a Vermont Street house about eight o'clock last evening, shot the occupant to death with a .38 revolver, and calmly walked away while terrified neighbors cowered and failed to pursue.

In a shooting reminiscent of Chicago gangland murders, 48-year-old Patrick McPherson was shot twice in the face and chest and died before assistance could reach him. Witnesses say he was not alone in the house, that besides the gunman at least two other people fled the house immediately after the shooting. They may be witnesses to the shooting and are being sought.

The pistol used in the shooting was found in a hedge not far from the scene of the crime. It was absolutely free of fingerprints, and police say it will probably prove impossible to trace.

Police who searched the house found a possible explanation for the execution-style killing. Although McPherson was not a physician, a room upstairs in the frame house was equipped with a small amount of surgical equipment laid out around a large wooden table. Also found in a cabinet in the house was nearly $3,000 in cash. Police suspect the man may have been an abortionist. Neighbors confirmed that many women did visit the house, some of them appearing ill when they left.

Amelia Colmer emerged from the bedroom before Bill Epson finished reading the story. Her call had been very brief. She sat down and appeared calm.

Bill went into Sally Rand's bedroom and placed a call to Baines. "Take a look at the story on page three of this morning's *Record*," he told him. "It put Mrs. Colmer into momentary hysterics and may have some relationship to something."

"Is there any reason I could not stop by and visit with Mrs. Colmer for a few minutes?" Doug McKinney asked Baines. "I was a friend of both of them, and she must feel she needs all the friends she can get right now."

Baines shrugged. "She's not being held incommunicado," he said.

"Even so. I don't want to stick my nose in where I'm not wanted. She may not want to see me. But unless you call Mr. Epson and say it's all right to let me in, I doubt they would—"

"I'll call him," said Baines.

"And would it be okay if I took her some flowers or something?"

Baines nodded and picked up the phone.

Doug left the White House at noon, picked up some flowers at a shop on E Street, and went to the Langford Hotel. Epson had received Baines's call and readily admitted Doug to the suite.

Amelia started when he walked into the room carrying his bunch of flowers. He smiled at her. She shook her head, and tears came to her eyes.

"I didn't get a chance to tell you how sorry I was about Win," he said to her. "Now, this . . . Anyway, I brought you a few flowers to brighten the place up a bit. And—"

Amelia shook her head again. "I'm so ashamed you should see me in . . ." She looked down and fluttered her hand over her gray uniform. "In this *awful* thing."

"It's only temporary, I'm sure," he said.

He glanced around the room, at Epson and the matron. Sally Rand was asleep in her bedroom now, behind a locked door. The matron and the Secret Service agent stared curiously at him, and he smiled weakly at them. He was wearing a light-blue double-breasted suit and looked cool and crisp.

"Uh . . . Would you mind if Mrs. Colmer and I spoke alone for a moment?" He gestured toward her bedroom. "With the door open, of course. I *am* a lawyer, you know."

Epson nodded. Doug gave Amelia his hand and helped her up from the chair. They walked inside the bedroom. She sat down. He remained standing.

Doug glanced at Epson and the matron, who continued to stare. He lowered his voice. "It had to have been his brother or Peavy," he said.

"They're not even checking them out," she said bitterly. "They've decided it was me."

"What was going on just before— I mean, did you overhear anything between the congressman and his brother?"

"Lee Bob didn't come to the house," she said. "He didn't want to see me."

Doug frowned. "And Peavy?"

"He talked about Peavy. He said he was going to get him for sure."

Doug nodded. "Where did you ever meet Sally Rand?" he asked.

Amelia sighed. "Win knew about this. My father invested heavily in Florida land. You know, in 1924, '25, when the boom was on. When it busted, he lost everything. All of a sudden we were *poor,* Doug. You wouldn't know. I'd met Sally. She was younger, just getting started. I needed money. *The family* needed money. I went to work for Sally. I toured with her, just one summer. Tent shows, mostly. Carnivals. Then I quit. It wasn't the thing for me. She wanted me to stay, said she'd make me a burlesque star."

Doug was grinning, shaking his head.

"Sure, you can't imagine," said Amelia. She smiled shyly. "Don't try. Forget it. Anyway, Sally has always been a friend. I came back to Bethesda, and my father helped me get a job as a typist at the White House."

"She's leaving town at the end of the week."

"I was going to go with her. I mean, not to go into her show or anything, but— Just to get away. For a while . . . You know . . ."

For a moment Doug faced her, frowning, his mouth open, unsure of what to say. "God, I'm so *sorry* for you, Amelia. To lose Win . . . Then to be accused. I'm doing what I can at the White House to turn the investigation toward Peavy, or maybe even toward Senator Stebbins. You know why."

She nodded. "Win didn't get Miss Stebbins pregnant."

"Uh . . . Where are your things?"

She nodded toward the sitting room. "In my suitcase. Locked. Watched. They took everything away from me. The idea, I guess, is that I gotta wear *this* and then I can't walk out the first time both those dummies fall asleep."

He smiled and touched the DJ stenciled on the front of her dress just below the yoke. "I guess nobody'd believe that stands for Dow Jones."

She looked down at the letters. "The back is worse," she said ruefully.

He returned the stares of the two outside. "One question," he said. "How did they find out you were here? Your friend Sally didn't—"

"No. A bellboy came to the door last night. He had a little man with him who said he was a telegraph boy. But he didn't have any telegram. Half an hour later the police came to the door."

"You have any idea who the fake telegraph boy was?"

"No."

"Can you tell me which bellboy it was?"

"I don't know them by name. But he's the only one like him. An older man. White. Short, wrinkled. He works the night shift, brings coffee and so on."

Doug nodded. "I'll do everything I can for you. Mrs. Roosevelt is sure you didn't do it, and so am I. Uh . . . So keep up your courage, Amelia. They really don't have a case against you."

She shook her head bitterly. "So they'll send me away for life anyway."

"Fill us in, Jerry. Have a martini with us, and fill us in," said the President jovially. "My wife is on her way to a do-good dinner, so I won't get a report from her this evening. You know everyone here, don't you? Missy. Louey the How. Harry the Hop. Sit down. Relax. If the President of the United States can take half an hour for an evening cocktail, so can you."

Baines smiled as he sat down. He was genuinely flattered to be asked to join the President for drinks. It was a new White House in which such informality prevailed.

The President's watch hung on a chain from his lapel and was in his breast pocket. He lifted it out and checked it. "Now is the time when all educated men are entitled to a sip of the juice of the grape—or the juice of the juniper berry, as the case may be."

"I wonder how you lived through Prohibition, Mr. President," said Baines as he accepted a slender stem glass filled with the ice-cold gin and vermouth, with the green olive lying at the bottom.

"The same way you did, Jerry," said the President. "The same way every civilized man did. Of course, I'd deny it if—" He chuckled. "Rum and Romanism," he said. "I've always been amply supplied with them. My rum . . . And—" He nodded fondly at Missy. "My Romanism, my Catholic conscience."

Howe dragged deeply on his cigarette. The thick smoke simply disappeared into him; very little of it ever trickled out. "Any developments in the big mystery?" he asked.

"Yes, as a matter of fact," said Baines. "Something that may be significant."

"Other than arresting Mrs. Colmer," said Howe, patting the newspaper that lay on the arm of his chair. "'Held for interrogation in the death of her husband; held not at the District jail but at some undisclosed place, for some undisclosed reason.' You've got the newspaper boys hot on that one. They've even called me, wanting to know where she is."

"Something other than that, Mr. Howe," said Baines.

"Let him tell us, Louey," said the President.

"Well," said Baines, "John Edgar Hoover went out to Chicago and came back with a laudatory headline. Lee Bob Colmer went out to Chicago and disappeared."

"Disappeared? How do you mean?"

"Lieutenant Kennelly of the D.C. police asked the Chicago police to put a tail on Colmer when he arrived by train from Washington. They did. They tailed him directly to the Enterprise Bank. When he left the bank he checked in at the Palmer House. That night he went out. He never returned to the Palmer House. Wednesday night. Thursday night. This morning the police entered his room and searched it. No sign of Lee Bob Colmer. Nothing to suggest where he might have gone. He left his bags, part of his money. He's missing."

The President pinched his nose and with his right index finger pushed his pince-nez into a more comfortable seat. "That gives me a funny feeling," he said. "An instinct. Call it second-sight. The Secret Service has authority to protect *any* officer of the federal government, I believe—not just the President. Put a watch over The Kingfish, Jerry. I could spare him, but I wouldn't want to lose him by murder."

Mrs. Roosevelt was in a happy mood when she returned to the White House a little before nine. She had attended a dinner of the Atlantic Union; and there, quite to her surprise, she had encountered an old friend from Allenswood School in England, where she had spent happy years just at the turn of the century. Horatia Fenster had married Percival Godolphin and remained in England. She was widowed now and was back in the States for a long visit. Mrs. Roosevelt brought her to the White House, insisting she must be her guest there for the night at least. They had picked up Horatia's bags at the Mayflower and brought them to the White House in one of the big black Packards.

Horatia was still the delicate beauty the young Eleanor had envied in 1900 and 1901—this in spite of years of childbearing, the rigors of the war years when her husband was wounded on the Somme, the difficulties of his five-years convalescence, and lately the complications of settling his affairs and arranging a new life for herself. She was the same age as the First Lady, forty-nine, but Mrs. Roosevelt thought Horatia looked ten years younger.

They walked through the White House, which was quiet now, in late evening. Their long skirts whispered on the floors. Horatia had been presented at Court, but still she pronounced the state rooms of the White House as impressive as those in Buckingham Palace.

"You were always the diplomat, Horatia," said Mrs. Roosevelt.

They arrived at last at the Lincoln bedroom where the First Lady kept her office. They sat down, and Mrs. Roosevelt called the night butler and ordered a tray of hors d'oeuvres and a bottle of the best chilled white wine the pantry could provide.

"I would waken Franklin, but—"

"Don't think of it," said Horatia Fenster Godolphin. "I shall perhaps see him at breakfast."

"Perhaps," said Mrs. Roosevelt, thinking of the way her husband took breakfast in bed, with his secretary sitting on his bed in her nightgown.

"Oh, I remember so many things, Eleanor," said Horatia Godolphin, happily reminiscent. "Weren't they *good* years?"

Mrs. Roosevelt remembered even better, perhaps. They had been good years, maybe the best of her life. She remembered herself arriving in England, a frightened girl dragged across the Atlantic in the custody of her Aunt Tissie. She had lost both her parents, and she had dreaded this school, where she expected the English girls to treat her like a poor orphan. In fact, the school had given her happy years. Mademoiselle Souvestre, the headmistress, had become her closest friend and confidante, the only person in the world who really cared about her, she had felt. She—

"Eleanor! Do you remember the time when we put black shoe polish in Pussie Sutcliffe's pomade?"

"I remember the poor thing crying for a week," said Mrs. Roosevelt. "Though I must say—"

"You must say she deserved it," Horatia Godolphin retorted. "She'd made other girls cry often enough."

Mrs. Roosevelt laughed. "I suppose so," she said.

"Oh, Eleanor . . . Do you remember how we locked Deaconess Trump out of her office?"

Mrs. Roosevelt's jaw dropped. *"Oh, my dear!"* she exclaimed. She clapped her hand to her mouth. Her eyes were wide.

"Have I said something wrong?"

"Not at all! *Au contraire,* my dearest Horatia! You have, I think, just solved a difficult problem. I hadn't thought of that for years, but somehow it was in the back of my mind, gnawing. I *knew*— Oh, Horatia! Oh, this is wonderful! It solves half of a very big problem!"

13

Sally Rand went out to do her show. At eight the matron was replaced by an older, fatter woman. She'd had her dinner, but Bill Epson had not, and he was grateful to Amelia Colmer when she suggested the room-service meal she was about to order could include a plate for him, too.

It was an odd meal. The matron took Mrs. Colmer into the bedroom and closed the door while the bell-boy wheeled in the table and set up dinner for two. He was not supposed to know Mrs. Colmer was being held prisoner in the suite. What he did think would have been hard to guess. Anyway, Bill sat with Mrs. Colmer at the little table spread with white linen and set with heavy hotel silver, and they ate salads, a veal entree, and a dessert and drank what must have been a gallon of coffee—she dressed in the uniform of the District jail, with DJ prominently stenciled across the fullness of her breasts. The police matron watched them eat for a minute or so, then absorbed herself in the newspapers she had brought when she came on duty.

Mrs. Colmer talked quietly with him. She told him to call her Amelia. She swore she had not killed her husband and was as mystified as anyone else about his death.

"I'm not surprised that they suspect me," she said. "I knew as soon as I heard of his death that they would."

"I don't know anything about it, Amelia," he said. "All I know is that they wouldn't suspect you nearly as much if you'd tell them where you were last Wednesday night."

She shook her head. "I can't," she said.

"What if they charge you with murder?" he asked. "What if they . . . convict you?"

She tossed her head, flipping her hair away from her cheek. "Well, sometime short of that—"

He wondered if she really took her situation seriously. She had been glum at first, and the newspaper story had disturbed her, but as afternoon wore into evening her mood had lightened. He could see no reason why it should, but somehow it had. She ate with apparent pleasure.

"Do you know New England, Bill?" she asked. "They say it's beautiful in the fall."

"Yes. I'm from New Hampshire."

"They say you should ride the train, all the way from Washington up to New York, then on to Montreal."

"Yes, on the Montrealer," he said.

"Someday I'm going to ride on all the great trains," she said. "The Empire State Limited. The National Limited. The Super Chief. That's the one. Someday I'm going to go to Los Angeles—"

She was interrupted by a peremptory rap on the door.

Bill pushed back his chair, rose, and went to the

door. "Who is it?" he asked, betraying a little impatience.

"Kennelly," said a voice muffled by the wood of the door.

Bill removed the chain, turned the knob on the night latch, turned the knob, and opened the door. "Lieutenant Kennelly? I—*Hey!*" The blackjack struck his forehead. He saw blood flying and knew it was his own. He staggered, then it hit him again, and he fell.

He remained conscious. Something roared inside his head, as if a big locomotive were bearing down on his eyes from the back of his skull, and the blood running into his eyes obscured his vision. He was too weak and unsteady even to think of rising. But he saw what happened.

The man who had hit him was masked with a silk stocking over his face, a gray hat on his head. The fat old matron faced him angrily, and the man hit her. He hit her in the face, and she fell back in her chair. Amelia was on her feet screaming. The man glanced around the room for a moment, then abruptly grabbed the suitcase that sat near the door. He went out into the hall, carrying the suitcase. For a moment he looked at Bill, then seemed to be satisfied he would not pursue. Bill saw that he was wearing rubber gloves, like a surgeon's. He walked down the hall, opened the door to the stairs, and disappeared.

The doctor shook his head. "That's a slight concussion, son," he said. "And a nasty cut. What the hell he hit you with, a cleaver? Anyway, you'll be okay in a day or two."

Mrs. Roosevelt had come with Baines. Bill had learned by now that the woman was irrepressible; probably Baines could not have left the White House without her once she learned what had happened. And there were police. God, it seemed like half the District force was in the hotel, under command of Kennelly.

Amelia was handcuffed to her chair and sat glumly staring at the wheeled table and their interrupted dinner. She had been crying, and Mrs. Roosevelt was trying to comfort her.

The fat old matron was gone. Her nose was broken, and an ambulance crew had led her out. It was she who had handcuffed Amelia to the chair, immediately, with the blood streaming from her nose—handcuffed her while Amelia shrieked that she'd had nothing to do with what had happened and was just as frightened as anyone else. The old woman had lost her temper and slapped her.

Bill had crawled into the room and to the telephone.

"Said he was me, huh?"

Bill looked past the doctor, at Kennelly. "That's what he said. Seemed reasonable, so I opened the door."

A uniformed officer came in. He was carrying the suitcase. "On the sixth floor," he said. "In the linen room. Looks like he went in there, cut it open, got what he wanted out of it, and left."

Kennelly took the suitcase from the officer and walked over to Amelia. "Let's see what's missing," he said to her.

Amelia stared open-mouthed at the suitcase. It had been neatly cut with a sharp knife and the leather peeled back like the top of a sardine can.

"Take the handcuffs off her, please, Lieutenant," said Mrs. Roosevelt with a smile, yet firmly.

Kennelly summoned a uniformed officer, who had a key. Amelia's right wrist was attached to the chair, and he quickly removed the cuff and freed her.

"Now, Mrs. Colmer," said Kennelly. "What could have been in here that the man could have wanted?"

Amelia shook her head warily.

Bill rose and came to stand beside her, where he could see and hear her.

"Would you like to look through what you had in

here, Mrs. Colmer?" Kennelly pressed. He pushed back the flap of cut leather, exposing a jumble of her clothes and cosmetics. "Hmm?"

She reached in cautiously and turned over a few pieces of clothing. She shook her head.

Kennelly turned over more clothes. He found and pulled out an envelope, a piece of the Langford Hotel stationery. The envelope wasn't sealed, and he pulled the flap away with his thumb, exposing fifty-dollar bills. "Ah. A strange burglar, hmm? Do you want to count it, Mrs. Colmer. I do."

She shook her head as he counted.

"Seven hundred seventy-five dollars, Mrs. Colmer. Is that right? Is that what should be there?"

She nodded.

"So he came here, knocked down a Secret Service agent, broke the nose of a police matron, and stole this suitcase—to get something out of it besides a handsome little stash of money. What was it, Mrs. Colmer? What's missing?"

Suddenly she reached into the case and began to pull things out. She pulled out everything, until the floor around her was littered with her clothes; and as she did it, she began to cry. When she was finished, she pushed the suitcase away from her, lowered her head, and began to heave with deep sobs.

"One Masonic ring, hmm?" asked Kennelly. "One solid-gold ring with Masonic symbols outside and the initials JBD inscribed inside. Right?"

Amelia began to shriek. In a moment she had dissolved into hysteria, throwing herself off the chair and onto the floor. Before anyone could restrain her, she rolled over and over, tearing at her face and hair, scratching herself, drawing blood. Mrs. Roosevelt dropped to her hands and knees beside her, to seize her hands and try to stop her. Kennelly and Baines grabbed Amelia. Then the doctor knelt over her. She continued to shriek, from so deep in her throat that part of her meal came up and was expelled from her mouth with her frightening, guttural cries.

The doctor took a syringe from his bag, and before anyone could argue against it, he injected Amelia with a powerful sedative. In a minute she relaxed. In two minutes she was groggy, half asleep, and shortly she lapsed entirely.

"You wouldn't have learned anything more from her tonight, in any event," said the doctor to Kennelly.

"We'll never know now," said Kennelly disgustedly.

"Should she be taken to a hospital?" asked Bill.

The doctor shook his head. "It's not necessary. Wherever you keep her, put a watch over her."

"You think she's suicidal?"

"Yes. She's suffered a damaging shock. I suppose you know what it is. I don't. Make sure that someone reasonably sympathetic stays with her."

Kennelly glanced around. "I suppose it would be wrong to put her back in a cell—though I tell you I feel like it. I suppose we could leave her here."

"I'll stay with her until you can get someone else," said Mrs. Roosevelt.

"I'd like to stay, too," said Bill Epson to Baines. He touched the bandage on his forehead. "I don't much feel like going home. Anyway—"

"Anyway, you've developed an overwhelming sympathy for her," said Kennelly sarcastically. "Maybe her jury will, too."

Returning to the White House at two-thirty in the morning, Mrs. Roosevelt had almost forgotten that Horatia was sleeping in the bedroom opposite the Lincoln bedroom and that she had sent a note to the President, asking him to join her and Horatia for breakfast. On her bed she found a note from him, saying breakfast would be served in the rose garden at nine.

She'd had a long day. Baines's call had come after eleven, when she and Horatia had been still chatting in her Lincoln-bedroom office. Horatia had of course been mystified—who wouldn't be?—by her insistence that she had to go out at such an hour because a burglary had happened in a hotel room. She set her alarm clock and went to sleep to the insistent rhythm of its ticking.

"Well, Eleanor," said Horatia as they walked toward the elevator at nine. "Your nocturnal excursion to the scene of a crime seems to have done you no harm. You were not gone long, I trust?"

"Actually," said Mrs. Roosevelt, "I was gone quite some time. The matter was most distressing. I told you that you have perhaps given me half the solution to a murder mystery. The second half remains elusive."

The President had preceded them. He was at the table already set up in the rose garden, his light wooden wheelchair pushed to his place, and he was scanning the morning papers as he waited for them.

"Horatia!" he said. "How very good to see you."

He and Horatia had not seen each other since 1905, the year when he had brought Eleanor to England as a part of the long wedding trip. Still, he recognized her, and he beamed and extended both his arms, so she could lean over him and kiss his cheek.

"Well, *do* sit down! I am surprised to see you but hope you will be our guest for a month at least."

Horatia was wearing white; and, though Mrs. Roosevelt was, too, she was conscious of the panache Horatia exhibited with everything she wore—a quality the young Franklin Roosevelt had noticed and appreciated twenty-nine years ago, which endured and captured his attention even now.

"I asked you to join me here at nine," said the President, "because, unfortunately, I have some people coming at half past." He swept his arm over the table obviously set for six. "As you can see. You will, though, find them people worth meeting, I think."

"I came very abruptly," said Horatia, "and without invitation. Perhaps—"

"If you are about to suggest you and Babs take your breakfast elsewhere, you risk offending me deeply," said the President.

The butler and ushers began to serve breakfast—melon, eggs, bacon, toast and marmalade, coffee.

"I wonder, Frank, Eleanor," said Horatia, "if you know the origin of the name Eleanor."

"In my family," ventured Mrs. Roosevelt uncertainly.

"But I mean the *origin*. The first Eleanor was Eleanor of Acquitaine, the mother of Richard the Lion-Hearted and so on. Her mother's name was Aenor. She died in childbirth, bearing Eleanor—and so the child was called 'Alia Aenor,' 'the other Aenor.' Isn't that a pretty little story?"

The President laughed. "'Alia Aenor,'" he said. "I like it."

"I should like to show you something, Franklin," said Mrs. Roosevelt. She reached for her big white straw handbag and withdrew one of the photographs taken of the Masonic ring that had been in Amelia Colmer's suitcase and was missing after the attack last night. "What is that, would you judge? Let me tell you also that it bears an inscription inside—#21 F & AM—'03—JBD."

"A Masonic ring," said the President. "Anything terribly significant?"

She nodded. "Maybe. It was photographed by the police yesterday morning, in Amelia Colmer's suitcase in a room at the Langford Hotel. Last night a burglar attacked the Secret Service agent and the police matron who were guarding her in that suite, and that ring was apparently the only item stolen."

"I can understand that," said the President. "The

identity of the owner of this ring shouldn't be too difficult to establish."

Horatia took the photograph and stared at it. "How
so?" she asked.

"Well, this type of Masonic ring is usually—not always—presented to the past master of a lodge. In
fact, see the little trowel here? That's the symbol of a
past master. Lodges are numbered state by state.
J.B.D. was probably master in 1903. The Masons keep
complete histories. An inquiry to the Grand Lodges in
as many states as necessary would probably turn up
the name of a man with those initials who served as a
master of a lodge numbered twenty-one in 1903."

"A man who committed a murder in 1934?" asked
Horatia.

"His father or grandfather," said the President.
"Not at all a difficult identification to make. I can understand why a man who had committed a crime and
might be identified by this would want it back. Of
course, if it's been photographed—"

"He'd have no way of knowing that," said Mrs. Roosevelt.

"Then there you have it," said the President. "An
important step on the way to solving your mystery.
Now if you can just figure out how he bolted the room
behind him when he left—"

"I *know* how he did that," said Mrs. Roosevelt. She
smiled. "I'll keep the information until I am sure. But
I know."

The President's guests arrived shortly. He had explained before they arrived that a number of entertainment personalities had agreed to make numerous
public appearances in support of the NRA. Some of
them were to be photographed with him in mid-morning. He had invited three, representatives of the film
industry, Broadway, and radio, to join him for breakfast.

The Hollywood delegate was Jean Harlow, the
vibrant young platinum-blonde who in a brief career

had made herself everyone's idea of a voluptuous, vaguely erotic temptress. The representative of Broadway theater was a handsome young actor who that summer was playing in the Jerome Kern musical *Roberta,* playing the crooner. His name was Bob Hope. The representative from the radio industry was a young singer who had made a nationwide name for himself—one Harry Crosby, known on radio as Bing Crosby.

"Oh, my!" giggled Jean Harlow. "My clothes! I do apologize, Mrs. Roosevelt, but we're being photographed."

Mrs. Roosevelt—to Horatia's great amusement—smiled at the girl and said, "Of course. It's an attractive outfit, in any event."

Jean Harlow was wearing her trademark—a white blouse of thin satin, obviously with nothing whatever under it, and grotesquely voluminous blue slacks, with legs a full twelve inches wide at the cuffs. The two young men were subdued by her.

All sat down around the table, where only the President was at ease. He was in fact hugely amused, as much probably by the awkwardness of the others as by the stilted conversation with which each of them tried to cope with the situation. Harlow grinned and drew in a deep breath—which threw out her breasts, thrust her hard nipples against the thin satin of her blouse, exhibited her most conspicuous claim to fame, and caused everyone else but the President to turn away or blush. Crosby had come prepared with a little speech, which now he could not quite get started. Hope was as amused as the President, likely, but was not quite sure he should be, and he lowered his chin and grinned behind his hand.

Then an usher appeared. "Uh . . . Ma'am," he said to Mrs. Roosevelt. "Do you wish to receive a telephone call?"

"From whom?"

"Well, Ma'am, it's . . . It's, uh . . ."

"Who, young man? *Who?*"

"Miss Sally Rand, Ma'am. She's the lady that dances—"

"Yes, I know!" the First Lady interrupted.

The President guffawed.

Gerald Baines appeared at the White House while the President was entertaining at breakfast and so was there to receive Mrs. Roosevelt's telephone call when she checked with his office after she spoke with Sally Rand.

"I don't know where you find the stamina, Mr. Baines," she said. "You were—"

"Mrs. Roosevelt, really!" he interrupted. "Where do *you* find it? *My* duties are only to—"

She laughed. "I shall very much enjoy sitting down and exchanging compliments with you sometime," she said. "This morning I have a somewhat different problem."

"Plus one more you may not know about," he said.

"Very well. Miss Sally Rand called me. She complains that the situation that developed last night is very dangerous and that the police protection for her suite is inadequate. I am inclined to wonder if she's not right."

"There is more than she knows about," said Baines.

"Even so. Mr. Epson is asleep, as is to be expected. The new police matron is— Well, let us just say that Miss Rand is not favorably impressed. Mrs. Colmer is about half awake and weeping."

"Well—"

"Mr. Baines, someone committed two violent assaults last night to steal that ring. Can we doubt he would have killed someone if that was what was required to accomplish what he was there to do? Now— the significance of that ring is a matter of speculation for us. But it is not for Mrs. Colmer. She *knows* its significance. That is why she was driven to hysterics last night. And if it can in fact be used to identify the

murderer of her husband, can we doubt someone will
kill her to prevent her telling?"

"He could have killed her last night," said Baines.
"What was to prevent him?"

"Perhaps he was an employee . . . a *henchman*. Perhaps he did what he was told to do. Perhaps someone
else will come—or he will return—to *harm* Mrs. Colmer."

"In any case, there are more policemen about the
place than Sally Rand guesses," said Baines. "No one
will enter that room again."

"We should call and tell her so."

"I'll call Epson. But I said I have a couple of new
problems. The first one may be minor, but if it's a co-
incidence it's an interesting one. A bellhop at the
Langford Hotel was beaten last night. An older man,
white. He was dragged out into the alley behind the
kitchen and worked over rather thoroughly. This was
just before the incident in the Sally Rand suite."

"Is there any relationship between the two inci-
dents, do you think?" asked Mrs. Roosevelt.

Baines shook his head. "I have no idea. Now. Let
me go on to something much more important. The
Chicago police department has found Lee Bob Colmer.
That is to say, they have found the *corpse* of Lee Bob
Colmer. In the lake. Shot in the head."

Mrs. Roosevelt closed her eyes. "All the more reason," she said in a strained voice, "to increase the police guard on Mrs. Colmer."

Horatia Godolphin saw and heard her friend's dis-
tress and stepped to her side to place a comforting
hand on her shoulder.

"At this point," said Baines, "the President needs to
get John Edgar Hoover in for a session. We'll get little
cooperation from the Chicago police from now on.
Would you ask the President to call a meeting with
the Director of the F.B.I.? Immediately."

"Who's in the West Wing?" Baines asked the duty
man at the desk between the colonnade and the executive offices.

"The President is in the Oval Office, Sir. With Director Hoover, Miss LeHand, and Arthur Prettyman. Mr. McKinney is in his office upstairs."

Mrs. Roosevelt glanced at Baines. "Let's ask Mr. McKinney to join us. He has been most perceptive. He might have something to contribute."

Baines could not say he liked Douglas McKinney, but he nodded. He told the duty man to call McKinney and tell him to come down to the Oval Office.

The President sat behind his desk. Missy had poured him a cup of coffee and was now pouring a cup for Hoover. She offered a cup to the First Lady, who shook her head. Everyone sat down. In a moment Douglas McKinney arrived, and he drew a chair toward the President's desk, from a row of them between the windows.

"I think Jerry has some information for you," said the President to Hoover. "I believe that's why we're together here."

J. Edgar Hoover could not suppress a scowl. He had been preparing for an afternoon at the track when the call came from the White House, summoning him for a meeting with the President. As if that were not bad enough, he had been told the President wanted to see him alone, without Clyde Tolson; and now he discovered he was compelled to confront Baines, who seemed to have some kind of inside track with the First Lady. He made a mental note to put tails on both of them. If Agent Baines and Mrs. Roosevelt— He had to put that thought back, to concentrate on the challenge they seemed to have for him.

"Yes, I do have something to tell you, John," said Baines, using the name he knew irritated a man who wanted to be called J. Edgar Hoover. "You went out to Chicago to see Otto D. Peavy. So I guess you know the man fairly well—"

"I do," said Hoover. "An impressive man. The only 'ism' he's for is *American*ism."

"Uh-huh," said Baines. "Well, since you know him,

maybe you can get him to tell you why the Chicago police pulled Lee Bob Colmer out of Lake Michigan yesterday afternoon. He had a bullet in his head."

"Why should Mr. Peavy know?"

"There was reason," Baines continued, "to suspect Lee Bob had something to do with the death of his brother Winstead Colmer. When Lee Bob left Washington, having lied to us about where he was going, we suspected he was going to Chicago and alerted the Chicago police to look for him. They followed him from the railroad station to the Enterprise Bank, then to the Palmer House, then out of the Palmer House. He left the hotel Wednesday evening and never returned."

"Well . . ." said Hoover. "That doesn't mean Mr. Peavy—"

"Lee Bob Colmer," Doug McKinney interrupted, "was involved in a consortium that borrowed money from the Peavy banks to develop a tract of land around a projected lake on Sipsey Fork, in Alabama. Winstead Colmer was blocking the Sipsey Fork project in Congress, and he was about to open an investigation into the Enterprise Bank of Chicago. That was motive enough to kill Winstead Colmer. Since Lee Bob's group was defaulting on a major loan, maybe that was motive to kill him."

"Speculation," said Hoover.

"I should like," said the President slowly, "the answers to some questions. I believe the F.B.I. can find the answers. First, I want to know how much money the Peavy banks loaned the Lee Bob Colmer group. Second, I want to know out of what funds that loan was made—meaning, out of ordinary bank funds or out of some other source. I want to know what the rate of interest was. I want to know what was done with the money from any such loan. I want to know how the whole transaction appears on the accounting records of whatever bank was involved. You may think of other questions as the investigation proceeds. I want the answers no later than noon on Monday."

"*Mr. President!*" Hoover protested. "Noon—"

"On Monday," said the President. "You may have to do some weekend work. There won't be time for you to fly out there. Put your Chicago agents on it. Immediately. There is good reason to think this Peavy gang killed Congressman Colmer—and now his brother. I want to *know*. By noon on Monday."

"But how—"

"You have in your possession a fact the Ottos Peavy don't know—that Lee Bob Colmer was traced to the Enterprise Bank. There's your wedge—now go pound it in."

When J. Edgar Hoover had left the Oval Office, Mrs. Roosevelt turned to Douglas McKinney. "Do you still regard Senator Stebbins as a suspect?" she asked him.

Doug glanced at the President, then at Baines, maybe flattered to be asked his opinion. "There are two items of evidence against him," he said soberly. "First, he threatened Representative Colmer. Second, we found the Marsh Wheeling stogie ash and wrapper in this office the afternoon I was struck on the head here."

"Negative evidence, isn't it, McKinney?" asked the President. "Would the man really come in here to commit a crime and leave his distinctive cigar ash and wrapper? Doesn't it look more likely that someone knew about the threat, knew that others had heard it, and tried to incriminate Stebbins?"

"I think that's much more likely the case, Mr. President," said Doug. "Rather crudely done, too."

"Unless," said Mrs. Roosevelt, "the intruder was here for another reason and left the cigar ash and wrapper as a sort of afterthought—a secondary reason."

Doug nodded. "That's possible," he said. "But obviously someone is trying to confuse the investigation. I visited Mrs. Colmer for a few minutes yesterday, and she told me someone had tipped off the police as to where she was. Who did that? And why?"

"Your answer, McKinney?" asked the President.

"The Peavys. They killed the congressman and now his brother. It was a professional job in each case, and they are probably not much afraid anyone will find the evidence to stick the killings on them. Even so, they want to send the investigators off in wrong directions."

"You are convinced, then, that Mrs. Colmer had nothing to do with the death of her husband?" asked Baines.

"Well, why would she want to do that, Mr. Baines?" asked Doug. "She and Mr. Colmer were a loving couple. She came from a somewhat difficult background, and being married to him gave her security and position she'd never known before." He shook his head. "I can't imagine why she would want to kill him. Particularly when she's carrying his baby."

14

Since he was already in the West Wing, the President decided to take an afternoon swim. Mrs. Roosevelt encouraged that, always, because the exercise was so important to him. Baines went off to try to initiate the check of Masonic lodges, even though it was Saturday and most offices would be closed. Doug McKinney returned to his second-floor office, saying he would be going home in a very short while. Missy slipped into the closet in the secretaries' room—the one where Warren Harding had made love to Nan Britton—and changed into her swimsuit. Arthur Prettyman helped the President change in his study, then wheeled him toward the colonnade and pool. Missy walked beside the wheelchair on one side. Mrs. Roosevelt walked on the other side.

"It's going to be very difficult to pin the murder on the Peavys," Missy remarked.

"On *anyone*," said the President.

"I'm not so sure," said Mrs. Roosevelt thoughtfully.

"I think I know who killed Representative Colmer, and how."

"We're going to need a lot more evidence," said Missy.

"No," said Mrs. Roosevelt. "We have all we need. At six this evening we can meet and resolve the mystery. Do you agree, Mr. Baines?"

"I'm not sure," said Baines, "but if you think so—"

"In the Oval Office, if you don't mind, Franklin. The place intimidates some people, and we may need to intimidate some."

"In the Oval Office," he agreed.

"And . . . You need not be present—unless you want to."

The President looked up, grinning. "My dear, I wouldn't miss it for anything!"

No one had made any effort to conceal from the newspapers the attack on the bellboy at the Langford Hotel. The Saturday morning *Record* carried a small inside story, telling that Burton Cadwallader, forty-nine, a night bellman at the Langford, had been assaulted and received injuries from an unknown attacker in the alley behind the hotel. It was a small story, but it did not escape notice.

"Uncle Burt!"

The little man, lying on a white-iron bed in a hospital ward, looked up at the stranger who approached him. He was still groggy from sedation, but he was sure he did not know the man who pulled up a chair and sat down by his bed. The man put a spray of gladiolas on his bed and reached for his hand. Cadwallader was groggy but not so groggy that he did not feel the texture on a folded bill in that handshake. He pulled his hand up to his face, opened it, and found a hundred-dollar bill.

"There's more where that came from, so just relax," the man said. "You haven't talked to the cops?"

Cadwallader shook his head.

"Good. Don't. My friend told you we'd take care of you if anything went bad. We didn't expect anybody to work you over, but the hundred will cover your hospital bills and more, and when we're sure you've been a good, quiet fellow there'll be another hundred. Maybe more."

Cadwallader glanced again at the hundred-dollar bill, as if he could not quite believe what it was, then folded it carefully and stuffed it into a pack of cigarettes from his bedside table.

"Two hundred," the man said. "Not a hell of a lot, either. You can make more if you tell us who worked you over."

"I'd tell you that for free, if I knew," Cadwallader muttered. His lips were swollen and cracked, his nose broken. "I'd 've told the cops, even—that is, until now that you tell me not to."

"What'd the guy look like?"

The little man shrugged. "Had a stocking over his head, under a gray hat."

"What'd he want?"

"Wanted to know who I'd taken up to 804. And why."

"So wha'd you say?"

"Said I didn' know. Which I didn't."

"So he banged you around."

Cadwallader nodded. "Hey, I was a *boxer*. Welterweight. Almost good enough for— Well . . . He was good! I couldn't lay a fist on him. But he could lay 'em on me. 'Course I'm forty-nine years old."

"Uncle Burt . . ." the man said in a low voice, leaning close over Cadwallader. "How did that guy *know* you took my friend up to 804?"

"Wish I knew, Mister. Wish I knew . . ."

The man rose. He gave Cadwallader a reassuring squeeze on the hand, then turned and strode out of the ward.

"H'lo, Walter."

The man was Walter Tebay, and he swung around to see who had used his name. "Who—"

Two men. A uniformed D.C. cop and a detective.

"Up against the wall, Walter," the detective said.

As Tebay leaned on the wall and submitted to a pat-down, the detective closed a handcuff around his left wrist, then the cop pulled his right hand down and locked his hands behind his back.

"Done any good embezzlements lately, Walter?" the detective asked. "Or are you into robbing hotel rooms? You and Burt Cadwallader? Or are you the guy that worked him over?"

"I don't know what you're talking about, you son of a—"

The cop pressed him under the chin with the tip of his billy. "Shut up, Tebay," he grunted.

In the ward, the man in the bed beside Cadwallader had rolled out from under the sheets. He was fully dressed. He grabbed Cadwallader's pack of cigarettes and tore it open. "My my, Uncle Burt!" he said. "You do have a nice nephew, to bring you a hundred bucks and a bunch of flowers."

Izzy sat in the car, down the street from the hospital, waiting for Walt to come back out. He was smoking a cigarette, and at the moment when he spotted Walt the butt had gotten hot; he was about to spit it into the street. Walt! My God, he was in handcuffs! Cops!

Izzy spat the cigarette and slipped down on the seat, then onto the floor of the car. A guy hopping out of his car just as the cops came out with his buddy might be a little too conspicuous. He pressed himself to the floor and waited. He stayed there until they had had plenty of time to go by. Only when he felt safe did he raise his head and look around. Gone. They'd got Walt!

No time to drive to Georgetown. He pulled the Packard away from the curb and drove five or six

blocks before he pulled into a gas station. He put a
nickel in the pay phone and rang the Georgetown
number.

No answer. But the boss had been there when—
The boss had been there, and here was his car. Somethin' wrong. He collected his nickel and tried the
number at the bank.

"Mechanics' and Husbandmen's Bank."

"Uh, I'm callin' for Mr. Peavy. Is he there?"

"No, he isn't. Can I take a message?"

Izzy frowned. "Who is this?"

"I'm a new employee."

"I'll try later," said Izzy, and he hung up.

He drove out New York Avenue. It was Route 50.
Somewhere between here and Baltimore he'd ditch
the Packard. He had— He had a couple hundred on
him. Hmm. Well, he'd pulled out of towns with less.
They wouldn't be looking for him much. He'd catch a
bus. Maybe make for New York.

"I'm entitled to talk to a lawyer. I'm *entitled*, by
God!"

Clyde Tolson looked to Hoover for consent to let
Otto D. Peavy the Third make a telephone call.
Hoover nodded. Tolson escorted Peavy to an adjacent
office, where he pointed at a telephone.

In his office, J. Edgar Hoover listened to Peavy's
call.

"Mort, what the hell's goin' on. I'm at F.B.I. headquarters. I can't tell if I'm under arrest, but it sure as
hell looks like it. I don't think I can walk out. I want
you in here. Fast!"

"You got trouble, Peav. You may not know if *you're*
arrested, but your father sure as hell is."

"For *what*, for God's sake?"

"Suspicion of murder. Lee Bob Colmer."

"They can't attach that—"

"Maybe they can. Colmer was being followed in
Chicago. They know he went to the bank out there."

"Even so, what have *I* got to do with it?"

"J. Edgar Hoover's puttin' the heat on, that's all. Can you take the heat?"

Hoover smiled as he listened through a long silence.

"Yeah," said Peavy. "Yeah, I can take the heat. Can the old man?"

Darlene Palmer's back was rigid as she stepped inside a tiny, wire-mesh holding pen in the basement of the F.B.I. building. She trembled as she heard the door clash shut. She spun around.

"I haven't done *anything*," she moaned tearfully. She grasped the wire mesh of the door with her fingers. "I haven't done anything at all."

Hoover shrugged. "Maybe not. Maybe we won't have to hold you long. Is there anything at all you'd like to tell us? It'll be a couple of hours before I can talk to you again. Maybe not till Monday, actually. Anything—"

"Call Mr. Tugwell," Darlene pleaded. "Call Mr. Peavy."

Hoover shook his head as he snapped the padlock on the pen. "Your friend Mr. Peavy is in custody, too, Miss Palmer. Well—"

"*Wait!* What is it you want to know?"

"What do you have to tell me?"

"If I tell you something helpful, will you let me out of here?"

He smiled. "Try me," he said. "What do you know that might be important?"

"Mr. Colmer . . ." she whispered, as if she feared Peavy would hear her. "I mean, Mr. Lee Bob Colmer . . . came to our house." She blushed. "To Mr. Peavy's house. He was quite agitated. Peav—that is, Mr. Peavy—told me it was important nobody know the man ever came there."

J. Edgar Hoover took a key from his pocket and

opened the padlock. "Miss Palmer," he chuckled, "you have just earned yourself a ticket of leave."

Kennelly believed in sweating crooks. He believed in the third-degree. In years past he had joined his fellow officers at District headquarters in beating them around the head with short lengths of rubber hose, which had been a damned effective way of making them talk, without putting any permanent marks on them. In years since he had welcomed the more subtle means of interrogation that had been developed in New York and other cities. They worked even better.

In any case, he was not going to take any guff from Walter Tebay. The guy was not a citizen; he was an ex-con, a Chicago hood come to Washington, and at the very least Kennelly would put the fear of God in him.

Tebay was mother-naked. He sat on a heavy wooden chair in a closed interrogation room, with his hands cuffed behind him and to the chair. His bald head and all the rest of him glistened from the stinking sweat that was pouring off him. Partly that was from the heat of the lights that shone on him, four big lights with big metal reflectors that focused all the light and heat from two-hundred-watt bulbs on him. Partly it was from fear, since two officers leaned against a table facing him and slapped their palms with one-foot lengths of heavy black rubber hose, as if they were eager to put some bruises on him.

"All I want to know at the moment, Walter," said Kennelly, "is where is Izzy?"

Tebay looked up into Kennelly's face. He was not miming fear; it was real. "I swear I don't know, Lieutenant. Honest to God!"

"Where's Peavy?"

"At the house. That's where he was when Izzy and I went to the hospital."

Kennelly shook his head. "He's not there. He's in

F.B.I. custody. His old man's in F.B.I. custody in Chicago. Does that give you some idea of how serious this is?"

"I got that idea," groaned Tebay, tugging on his handcuffs. "Believe me, I got that idea."

Baines accompanied Mrs. Roosevelt to the Langford Hotel. Wearing sunglasses and a scarf over her head, she entered through the front door without being recognized. Baines identified himself and her to police, and they took the elevator to the eighth floor.

Amelia sat slumped in a Morris chair, conspicuously despondent. Bill Epson sat opposite her, looking at her with unremitting sympathy. Two police matrons, who must have been the ugliest two women in the city of Washington, sat apart and glowered. Sally Rand was in her bedroom, with the door closed.

"It is possible," said Mrs. Roosevelt to Amelia, "that we shall have a little meeting later this afternoon at the White House. If so, I shall see to it that you are allowed to wear your own clothes, Mrs. Colmer."

Amelia shrugged.

"I believe I know who killed your husband. And why. I think the mystery will be solved today. I hope you have the courage to face it."

Amelia glanced at her for the briefest of instants, then looked away and withdrew from the conversation.

In the middle-to-late part of the afternoon, Mrs. Roosevelt met with Baines and Kennelly. They talked through everything they knew, put it all together in different ways, reached a conclusion, and decided to call the meeting she had suggested to the President.

By telephone calls from the White House, the summonses went out. At six o'clock everyone summoned assembled in the Oval Office. Besides the President and Mrs. Roosevelt, Missy LeHand, Gerald Baines, and half a dozen armed, alert Secret Service agents who stood around the room with their backs to the walls, watching everyone as if everyone were equally dangerous, the meeting included:

—J. Edgar Hoover, Director of the F.B.I., who had brought with him his favorite assistant, Clyde Tolson, and also Otto D. Peavy the Third and Darlene Palmer, both of them unsure whether they were or were not in custody;

—Lieutenant Edward Kennelly, with Mrs. Amelia Colmer, who was wearing a summery yellow dress but definitely in custody;

—Agent Bill Epson, Secret Service, his forehead covered with a thick bandage that did not entirely cover his angry red bruise;

—Douglas McKinney, legs crossed and comfortable in a light-gray double-breasted summer suit;

—Horatia Godolphin, sitting apart, a fascinated witness.

Chairs had been brought in to make room for so many people. The President sat at his desk, with Missy to one side where she could help him with anything he needed. Mrs. Roosevelt, Baines, and Kennelly sat in chairs in front of the President's desk and to his right. Douglas McKinney sat in a chair to the President's left. Hoover and Tolson sat on one of the two couches before the fireplace and would have been sitting with their backs to the President except that they sat turned, with their arms over the back of the couch—probably regretting they had chosen that couch. On the couch facing them sat Amelia, with Bill Epson beside her. Otto Peavy and Darlene Palmer sat on chairs facing Mrs. Roosevelt and the President.

"I must ask forgiveness of all of you," said Mrs. Roosevelt when everyone was settled and staring at her in quiet anticipation. "In the first place, I have meddled in matters that are strictly the responsibility of others, not myself, and perhaps I have impeded the—"

"Not in the slightest," said Baines. "To the contrary."

"I apologize, in any event, for this somewhat melodramatic confrontation," she said. She smiled. "I may make a complete fool of myself this evening and be cured forever of the proclivity to think of murder mysteries as intellectual problems to be solved, or as exercises in justice, where good will can contribute much toward a correct conclusion."

She paused, looked around the room, settling her eyes for an instant on everyone who faced her.

"The mystery of the death of Congressman Winstead Colmer has been solved," she said. "Mr. Baines, Lieutenant Kennelly, and I have reviewed the evidence and find the conclusion inescapable—though we are not terribly happy with it." Her glance swept around the room again. "It would be *so* much better if the guilty person would speak up now." She closed her eyes and lifted her head as though she were looking at the ceiling.

No one spoke. No one moved. The Oval Office was silent, as silent as it must have been that quarter hour when Winstead Colmer lay dead on the floor just inside the double doors that led to the secretaries' room.

"No? Very well," she said. She pointed to where the body had lain. "The body was found there, as some of us know, some don't. The room was locked. The doors were bolted. *All* the doors. And all the windows were securely latched. Still, Mr. Colmer did not kill himself, as we were supposed to believe. I won't review the evidence that eliminates suicide. It is more than convincing.

"So someone murdered him. Someone shot him with a pistol, in the head, from behind."

"There is a universe of suspects," said Otto Peavy grimly. He removed his glasses and began to wipe them with a handkerchief. "Are you limiting the field to someone here?"

"I will eliminate one right now," said the First Lady. "Mrs. Colmer. You didn't murder your husband, Amelia."

Amelia sobbed. She clapped her hands to her face and wept.

"But you know who did," said Mrs. Roosevelt gently. "You found out last night. Before that, you'd suspected. After last night, you *knew*."

Epson put his arm around Amelia and spoke quietly to her. She shook her head.

"I have here," said Mrs. Roosevelt, "a set of photographs. Anyone who wants to see them can look. These are pictures of a Masonic ring. It was almost certainly presented to the master of a lodge in 1903 and is a family heirloom. The man in whose family it is an heirloom gave it to Mrs. Colmer as a romantic gesture. Because she was married to someone else, she wore it sewn inside her clothes, where she could hope her husband would never discover it—and apparently he never did."

"May *we* see?" asked Hoover, and Tolson went to Mrs. Roosevelt's chair to take the prints.

"The man who gave Mrs. Colmer that ring is probably in love with her. Certainly she is in love with him. When her husband was murdered, the man I'm talking about suddenly realized that the ring, found among Mrs. Colmer's effects, would be evidence against him. He hoped that she would dispose of it or return it to him. But she didn't. And then, for reasons we have yet entirely to understand, she went into hiding. That made her a suspect in her husband's death, and the man who'd given her the ring was afraid the police would search the Colmer house and find it. So he went to the house before the police could get there and searched for it himself. He didn't—"

"How did he find out so quickly that she had disappeared?" asked Hoover.

"She decided to flee after Mr. Baines telephoned her at her parents' home in Bethesda to ask her why night personnel in the White House reported having seen her in the West Wing at night. She saw suspicion focusing on her, I suppose, and—"

"I was sure," Amelia sobbed, "you would find out who really did kill Win and then— I mean, I thought you'd find out and then you wouldn't think it was me anymore."

"What you didn't think, dear," said Mrs. Roosevelt, "was that suspicion would ultimately settle firmly on the man who gave you the ring. Do you want to tell us who it is?"

"Since you know, *you* say it," Amelia wept.

"To answer your question, Mr. Hoover," said Mrs. Roosevelt, "he knew she had gone into hiding because one of the first things she did was telephone him to tell him where she was. I surmise that. We don't know for sure. Amelia?"

Amelia nodded.

"Yes. The man didn't find the ring in Amelia's dresser because she had taken it with her. She cherished it."

Amelia bent over and sobbed pathetically.

"Then," Mrs. Roosevelt continued, "he discovered that she had been found and arrested. So last night, in a very desperate move, he went to the hotel suite where Mrs. Colmer was being held, attacked and injured Mr. Epson, attacked and injured a police matron, and recovered his ring at last."

"And you can identify him by the ring?" asked Hoover. "For sure?"

"That and other evidence identifies him. The ring is engraved inside with the number of a Masonic lodge, a year, and initials. The initials are not those of the man who killed Mr. Colmer but probably those of his father or grandfather. In any event, we will know within a few days what Masonic lodge had 'JBD' for its master in 1903. Then we will know who 'JBD' was, and from that point it is simple to identify his son or grandson."

Otto Peavy smiled. "I am relieved, Mrs. Roosevelt," he said. "No member of my family has ever been a member of a Masonic lodge."

"Don't be *too* relieved, Peavy," said Kennelly gruffly. "We have your boy Tebay in custody. He's been singing all afternoon. Like a canary. You sent your boy Izzy Mullin over here Sunday afternoon. Want to tell us why?"

Peavy shook his head. "I don't know—"

"You might as well. Tebay's spilled the whole deal—as much of it as he knows. A little cooperation might go a long way for you right now."

Darlene's mouth dropped open. "Oh, Peav!" she cried.

"You're sure—" Hoover began, raising a cautioning finger.

"Yes, I'm sure," said Kennelly. "Let him tell us, if he will."

"I had nothing to do with the murder of Winstead Colmer," said Peavy. "And neither did my father. On the other hand—" He shrugged. "On the other hand, we knew you'd try to hang it on us. Colmer had threatened to make trouble for us. His brother was into us for half a million dollars, which you'd find out sooner or later. So—"

"So you tried to shift suspicion to someone else," said Doug McKinney. "*You* got a man into the White House last Sunday afternoon. It was *your* man that hit me on the head!"

"Planting stogie ashes and a wrapper," said Baines dryly. "I thought your organization was smarter than that."

Peavy shook his head. "I didn't like the idea. I didn't like it at all. But Lee Bob Colmer was around every day, arguing, complaining, demanding— He figured he was a suspect, too, since it would come out sooner or later that his brother had killed the Sipsey

Fork dam project, leaving Lee Bob and his friends in debt to our bank for half a million. Besides, he'd had violent arguments with his brother, which he figured somebody had overheard and would report sooner or later. Senator Stebbins is an old loud-mouth dummy, and he'd talked about how he'd take a Mississippi gentleman's revenge on Winstead Colmer for making his daughter pregnant. So we—"

"So you sent Izzy Mullin," said Kennelly. "A professional burglar."

Peavy nodded. "A dumb idea. *Dumb!* Izzy went over that fence like a squirrel. He—"

"How'd he get in the Oval Office?" asked Baines.

Peavy glanced at Darlene Palmer. "I'm sorry," he said to her quietly. "He had a key. Darlene got it for me. She borrowed it for a minute one day—to get in the office to pick up a paper Rex Tugwell wanted, she said. A minute. Enough to make an impression, the way Izzy showed her."

Darlene Palmer began to cry. Peavy put his hand on hers.

"Then you found out where Amelia Colmer was hiding," said Kennelly. "You sent Izzy to the Colmer house and found something that made the connection for you. Right?"

Peavy nodded. "A scrapbook. A clipping. The Sally Rand connection."

"The fake telegraph boy!" said Doug McKinney.

"And you called me with the tip," said Kennelly.

"Walter Tebay called you," said Peavy. "Same reason. Give you another suspect. Because . . . Because, *I swear to you,* I had nothing to do with the murder of Winstead Colmer. And neither did my father."

"What about the murder of Lee Bob?" asked Hoover.

Peavy shook his head. "I don't know the first thing about that. The Chicago people don't call me and ask for permission to do anything."

"Is this man under arrest, Director?" Kennelly asked Hoover.

"Well, I— He's a businessman, and I—"

"Consider yourself under arrest, Peavy," said Kennelly. "You, too, Miss Palmer."

"On what charge?" Peavy asked quietly.

"Burglary," said Kennelly.

"Not murder?"

Mrs. Roosevelt shook her head. "Not murder, Mr. Peavy. Not, anyway, the murder of Representative Colmer."

Edgar Hoover frowned and sighed. He was uncomfortable sitting sideways on the couch where he had elected to sit, and he shifted. "Then who, Mrs. Roosevelt?" he asked. "Are you going to tell us?"

"I suppose I may as well," she said. She turned to her left. Her lips tightened, and she shook her head sadly. "Representative Colmer was murdered by Mr. McKinney."

15

The shocked silence in the room was broken only by Amelia's agonized deep sobs. Again, Bill Epson put his arm across her shoulder, bent near her, and spoke quietly to her; but she could not be consoled and wept pathetically.

Baines and Kennelly stared hard at Douglas McKinney. He had raised his chin, stiffened his body, and returned their stare with his own defiant scowl.

The moment of silence continued until finally it was broken by the President. "Well, McKinney," he said. "Do you deny it?"

McKinney raised his chin even more and regarded the President with a widening, derisive smile. "It is difficult to deny it when denial involves belittling Mrs. Roosevelt," he said. "But—" He shrugged. It was a shrug of contempt and dismissal. "—of course I deny it."

"My wife would not make such an accusation lightly," said the President.

"No," she said. "We can prove it."

"Please do," said Hoover skeptically.

"Well, to begin with there is the ring," she said.
"When tomorrow the F.B.I. joins the Secret Service in
telephoning as many state grand lodges as may be
necessary, we will learn the significance of the en-
graving in the ring. If necessary, members of Mr.
McKinney's family can be questioned about it."

"You have pictures," said Hoover. "But where is the
ring itself?"

Mrs. Roosevelt smiled. "It is between the arm and
the seat cushion of the chair where Mr. McKinney is
sitting," she said. "I kept an eye on him—out of the
corner of my eye—when the ring was first mentioned.
He took it from his pocket and pushed it down into
the crack between the cushion and—"

Kennelly was on his feet. "Get up, McKinney!" he
yelled.

"Please," said Mrs. Roosevelt. "You needn't precipi-
tate a struggle. It's there. Isn't it, Mr. McKinney?"

McKinney deflated. The color left his face. His jaw
went slack, and his mouth hung open. He nodded almost imperceptibly.

"You were carrying it *on your person?*" Missy asked.
She shook her head in disbelief.

"Hubris, McKinney," said the President. "Hubris.
It's been the downfall of many a fine, proud fellow."

"More hubris than you know," said Mrs. Roosevelt.
"In many ways. Am I right, Mr. McKinney?"

"The right doesn't prove your case," he muttered.

"That remains to be seen," she said. "Let me ask if
you can explain something else." She drew a deep
breath and glanced at Baines and Kennelly. "From
the beginning you were anxious that suspicion should
fall on someone other than Mrs. Colmer. Senator
Stebbins. Then Mr. Peavy. At first I thought it was
only because you were sympathetic toward a young
woman who had suffered a terrible loss. Then I began
to suspect it was more than that, that you were in
love with Amelia Colmer. Well . . . Why not? A young

man might well be, with such an attractive young woman."

Mrs. Roosevelt stopped and sighed. "But this morning," she went on, "in this office, you said that Mrs. Colmer had enjoyed a loving relationship with her husband, that in fact she was carrying a child." She shook her head. "But, Mr. McKinney, the fact that Mrs. Colmer is pregnant was a *secret!* How could you have known? Unless—"

He had begun to nod, and she stopped. Amelia cried even harder.

"Unless the child is yours, Mr. McKinney," Mrs. Roosevelt concluded. "And that is the case, isn't it?"

Amelia raised her face and looked at him, waiting for his answer.

McKinney turned toward Amelia. "The baby is mine," he said quietly. "And she had nothing to do with killing her husband. Nothing. Absolutely nothing."

"I was suspicious of you from the middle of the week," said Baines to McKinney. "Maybe even earlier. You were the only person in the West Wing the night of the murder. You kept odd hours around here. But on Wednesday you remarked to me that the locks on the West Wing offices are . . . I think the word you used was 'primitive.' Well, yes, they are primitive. But how many people who work here notice that? Then Mr. Howe said something about how you always seem to be on top of things, always anticipate what's coming up. He thought that's because you are smart, and maybe you are; but it suggested to me that you'd been entering other people's offices and reading their papers. That's how you knew so much."

The President listened with a grim, rigid face. He, too, had admired McKinney's apparent perspicacity.

Baines continued. "I put a tail on you, McKinney. Not the whole thing, just a little keeping track of you. You weren't home last night when the ring was stolen. My man lost you, but you weren't home. You went out and were gone plenty long enough to go to the Langford Hotel and do your dirty work."

"You were away from home Thursday evening, too," said Kennelly. "Want to tell us where you were?"

McKinney shook his head firmly.

"What happened Thursday night?" asked Hoover.

"Maybe nothing that involves him," said Kennelly. "But we are trying to find out who shot a man named McPherson. An abortionist."

Amelia bent double, slamming her forehead to her knees, and moaned and sobbed with new force. McKinney stared at her, his wan face filling with dark color. He shook his head violently.

"Mr. McKinney," said Mrs. Roosevelt. "The old cliché has it that confession is good for the soul."

He turned toward her. "That's about all that's left for me, isn't it?" he asked caustically. "The soul. Confession . . ."

"You're a lawyer," she said. "You know whether you should or shouldn't confess. You know what you face either way. You might be doing Amelia a service, anyway."

McKinney shrugged. "Why not?" He drew a breath and glanced at the distraught Amelia, still sobbing with her head down to her knees, being comforted awkwardly by Bill Epson. "Maybe you're right that it can help her, anyway."

"I should like to believe, Mr. McKinney, that she is entirely innocent."

He nodded. "She is," he said. He sighed. "So where do I start? The ring. Why not with the ring, since it probably did more than anything else to bring me down. It was of course my grandfather's—my mother's father. It was slipped off his finger after he died. It was given to me." He glanced again at Amelia. "She knows how much it means to me. She understood what it meant when I gave it to her to wear, as a token of something we couldn't publicly acknowledge." He reached down between the cushion and arm of the chair and pulled it out. He slipped it on his finger and stared at it pensively.

"I'm not sure it would have made any difference," said the President, "but why did you carry it on your person? Surely—"

"There have been some sneaky searches of people's quarters lately," said McKinney with a scornful glance at Baines. "My office, too. I did the old trick to folding a paper match into the crack between the door and frame, to see if it would have fallen down when I came back. It had. Anyway, I would have hidden the ring somewhere—where it would have been absolutely safe, until the heat was off. Meanwhile—" He shrugged.

"You've been in and out of every office in the Executive Wing, haven't you?" asked Baines.

McKinney nodded. "I lifted keys. Some I duplicated. Some I just kept. And I discovered there's not much difference between them, and if you study them you can see how to file one down to make it a master key that will open any door in the West Wing." He smiled gently, yet with total cynicism. "It gives a young man a competitive edge, to be able to explore offices, read files."

"Did you need that edge?" the President asked. "You have a fine education, a fine mind."

"Yes," said McKinney, lifting his chin. "I'm a Harvard man. I have a better education and a better mind than nearly anyone else in the West Wing. What I don't have, Mr. President, is impeccable political credentials. It's disgusting to see men with so-called degrees from so-called universities—"

"Like Winstead Colmer," the President interrupted.

"Yes," said McKinney contemptuously. "University of *Alabama*."

"A Harvard man," said Baines. "You were a boxer, I imagine."

"As a matter of fact, I was," said McKinney. "How did you know?"

"Another little clue you left, smart boy," said Baines. "The little old man you beat up at the Langford Hotel last night—the bellhop—was a semi-pro welterweight in his day. He told us you had to be a boxer from somewhere. He couldn't lay a fist on you. If you hadn't been a boxer, he'd have broken your nose. I would have called Harvard Monday morning to find out if you boxed in college."

"Did I leave any other clues?"

"Little ones," said Baines. "Enough to build a case. For example, when you went to the Colmer house to look for your ring, you should have acted like a burglar. You were too neat, too collegiate. It was obvious that you'd entered with a key, gone straight to the room where you thought you might find the ring, searched for it, and scrammed fast. If you hadn't been so nervous, you could have put things back where you found them, and maybe we wouldn't have known you were there."

"You *couldn't* have thought I'd go away and leave your ring in the house!" Amelia wept. She raised her head. "You thought I'd just—"

"I was afraid they'd taken it from you at the jail," said McKinney.

She shook her head. "I *was* wearing it when they came for me. In the usual place. But I was wearing a nightgown, and they had to let me dress before they took me to jail, so I put the ring in my suitcase . . . where you found it last night."

"It must have been quite a love affair, you two," said Baines.

"It was, Mr. Baines," said Amelia. "It *is*."

"Even though he killed your husband?" asked Baines coldly.

Amelia stared tearfully at McKinney. *"Oh, Doug!"* she sobbed.

"Mrs. Colmer," said Mrs. Roosevelt gently. "Maybe

you should tell us now where you were the night your husband was killed."

McKinney nodded. "You might as well, Amelia. It won't make any difference now."

She swallowed. "I went to see McPherson," she whispered. They had to strain to hear her. "I thought he was a doctor. He'd said he was. When I got to that awful house, I knew I couldn't do what I was there for. I left." She looked directly at Mrs. Roosevelt. "That's why I couldn't tell you where I was that night. I had gone to see an abortionist!"

"You didn't *have* an abortion?" asked Missy, horrified.

Amelia shook her head. "I suppose it was illegal even to *see* the man. I *couldn't* tell. Besides . . . Why would I have wanted an abortion if it had been my husband's baby? Everyone would've demanded to know who the father was, and it wouldn't have been too difficult to find out."

"You came to the West Wing, didn't you?" Baines asked.

Amelia smiled shyly. "Right here. In this office. On *this* couch."

"And your husband was killed here," said Baines. Her face clouded. "Doug . . ." she murmured.

"I think it's time you told us how you killed Representative Colmer," said Mrs. Roosevelt to McKinney.

"When I met Amelia," McKinney began, "something just *clicked* between us. I couldn't imagine her going on being married to that southern-fried idiot. He played poker every Friday night, no matter what was going on, and got sloshed on bourbon. So Friday nights were ours—Amelia's and mine. And other times. I—"

"Why didn't you urge her to get a divorce?" asked Mrs. Roosevelt. "Or— Or you could just have run away with her. You didn't have to kill the man!"

"Oh, yes, of course," said McKinney scornfully.

"What would happen to a new young lawyer whose affair with a congressman's wife became a public scandal?"

"Ambition," said the President. "Ambition and hubris."

"Her pregnancy was an accident," McKinney continued. "I told her to tell the congressman the child was his, but—"

"It couldn't have been," said Amelia disconsolately. "Not for the last two years."

"So, you see?" asked McKinney. "What would he have done to her when he found out? What would he have done to *me*?"

"What did you do to him?" Baines asked contemptuously.

"I planned it," said McKinney. "Actually, I had half a dozen plans, different ways of getting him into a situation where I could kill him. I liked the Oval Office plan best, because it gave me the best chance of making it look like suicide."

"You took the congressman's own pistol from his house," said Baines.

"I had a key," said McKinney. "I'd been in the house many times. I made a mistake with the pistol, though. I shouldn't have put new ammunition in it. I did that because I was afraid the cartridges were so old they might misfire. I couldn't risk that. I put in new ones, with rubber gloves of course. Since the cartridges had no fingerprints on them, I wiped the prints off the rest of the pistol. Why? Because Amelia had shown it to me one night in the bedroom, and I couldn't leave a pistol that had *her* fingerprints on it."

"You called the ushers' office," said Baines.

"Yes. I had the usher tell him Amelia was waiting in the Oval Office, that she had an emergency. I met him as he came into the West Wing, repeated that Amelia was in the Oval Office, and showed him through the halls. I'd left the pistol on the stand by the door—there. In the secretaries' room I pulled on my rubber gloves, which I'd been carrying in my pocket. He grabbed the knob and opened the door— And I stepped in behind him, picked up the pistol, and shot him."

"Then you knelt over him," said Baines, "and pressed his fingers on the trigger and grip of the pistol."

McKinney nodded. "I got up, switched out the lights, and left through the President's study. Upstairs, I tore the rubber gloves to bits and flushed them down the toilet."

"Which leaves us," said Baines, "with the question of how you bolted the door to the study."

McKinney grinned. "Leave me one element of mystery," he said. "I'll leave you all to figure that one out."

"It's not so difficult, Mr. McKinney," said Mrs. Roosevelt. "A child's trick, recalled to my mind by my friend Horatia Godolphin. Perhaps I should demonstrate."

She rose and went to the double doors between the Oval Office and the President's study. Digging deep in her purse, she pulled out a short length of twine, fishing line perhaps.

"It's really quite simple," she said. "Watch."

She made a loop around the knob on the bolt and pulled the two ends of the string toward the edge of the door. Then she stepped through into the study, pulling the ends through, and closed the door. Like this:

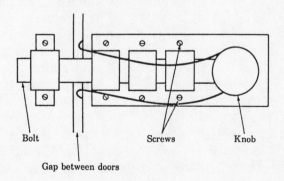

Bolt Screws Knob

Gap between doors

From outside, she pulled on the two ends of the string, and the bolt slid through its cylinder, across the gap between the doors, and into the short cylinder on the other door. Then she pulled on one end of the string, and it slipped through the crack between the doors and disappeared from the Oval Office.

McKinney watched, bemused. It was he who stepped over, slid the bolt back, and opened the doors. "Congratulations," he said. He sighed. "If not for you, I might have gotten away with it all."

"The abortionist?" asked Baines.

McKinney shrugged. "He tried to blackmail me. It was I who had found him and made the appointment for Amelia. She refused to keep it. She wouldn't think of having an abortion. I didn't know she was going to see him that Wednesday night." He paused and looked at Amelia. "If I'd known, I wouldn't have had to kill Colmer." He shrugged. "Of course . . . actually I would have, since she really didn't have the abortion. Anyway, McPherson called me. He knew who she was; he recognized her from her picture in the papers. He wanted to know what it was worth to me to keep him quiet. He was scum. I'm not ashamed of killing him."

"And of killing Representative Colmer?" asked Mrs. Roosevelt quietly.

McKinney shrugged. "I'm ashamed I wasn't more clever."

Epilogue

On Tuesday, October 2, 1934, Douglas McKinney came to trial on the charge of murdering Representative Winstead Colmer. On Thursday the jury returned a verdict of guilty of murder in the first degree, and he was sentenced to death. On Wednesday, December 5, he was electrocuted.

Amelia Colmer accompanied Sally Rand to Buffalo. For a few months she traveled with the Sally Rand troupe, helping to care for costumes, running errands for Sally, distancing herself from what was happening in Washington. In January she entered a home for unwed mothers in Columbus, Ohio. She never learned if the baby she bore was a boy or girl, since she had consented to its being placed for adoption immediately after birth.

She returned to her parents' home in Bethesda. By then her husband's estate had been settled, and she inherited a small fortune. She also was entitled to his congressional pension. She had let the lease run out on the Georgetown house, but she rented another. She enrolled for some university classes. In October 1935 she married Bill Epson.

He resigned from the Secret Service and with his family's help bought a partnership in a Chevrolet agency. Bill and Amelia had three children. He was a little too old for the draft in World War II, so stayed home and worked in Civil Defense. So did Amelia. In 1960 they retired to Fort Lauderdale, comfortably well off.

Otto D. Peavy the Third was sentenced to ten years in prison for having sent burglars into the White House and into the Colmer home. He was released on parole after forty-five months. Darlene Palmer was held in jail six weeks, testified against Peavy, then was released without having to stand trial on the charge of supplying Peavy with the key to the Oval Office. She waited for Peavy and married him when he was paroled. He could not return to the banking business, so became a clerk, later a manager, in a clothing store in downtown Washington. They had two children.

Otto D. Peavy, his father, was acquitted by a Chicago jury on the charge of having ordered the murder of Lee Bob Colmer. He was convicted, however, of tax evasion and a variety of violations of banking laws and spent two years in a federal penitentiary. He died soon after he was released.

Walter Tebay was sentenced to ten years for the burglary of the Colmer home. He served the entire ten years and became bookkeeper to an evangelist ministry after his release.

Izzy Mullin was never found.

The father of the baby being carried by Jane Stebbins was Captain Winston Hewlett, of the military attaché's staff at the British embassy. His divorce became final in September, and he married Jane immediately. They left for England shortly after the wedding, and the baby was born in London. Captain Hewlett rose to the rank of brigadier in World War II,

was wounded, decorated, and knighted. Lady Jane
Hewlett was an ornament of high British society for
twenty years.

In that context she often met Horatia Fenster Godolphin, who often sought her out to reminisce with
her about Horatia's 1934 visit to Washington and the
brief, tangential contact each of them had with the
horrible murder of Winstead Colmer.

Lieutenant Kennelly rose to the rank of captain. He
would work again with the First Lady, in 1939 when
she labored to clear the name of the lovely Pamela
Rush-Hodgeborne, again in 1941 when two corpses
were found in the White House pantry. Gerald Baines,
too, figured in the White House pantry murders.